Restore Me

Restore Me

Elyse Maupin-Thomas

RESOURCE *Publications* · Eugene, Oregon

RESTORE ME

Resource Publications
An Imprint of Wipf and Stock Publishers
199 W. 8th Ave., Suite 3
Eugene, OR 97401

www.wipfandstock.com

PAPERBACK ISBN: 978-1-6667-3044-9
HARDCOVER ISBN: 978-1-6667-2199-7
EBOOK ISBN: 978-1-6667-2200-0

SEPTEMBER 22, 2021

TABLE OF CONTENTS

Chapter 1 | 1

Chapter 2 | 6

Chapter 3 | 14

Chapter 4 | 20

Chapter 5 | 30

Chapter 6 | 40

Chapter 7 | 47

Chapter 8 | 53

Chapter 9 | 59

Chapter 10 | 65

Chapter 11 | 73

Chapter 12 | 80

Chapter 13 | 89

Chapter 14 | 97

Chapter 15 | 105

Chapter 16 | 113

Chapter 17 | 127

Chapter 18 | 138

Chapter 19 | 146

Chapter 20 | 158

Chapter 21 | 165

Chapter 22 | 171

Chapter 23 | 185

Chapter 24 | 196

Chapter 25 | 204

Chapter 26 | 209

Chapter 27 | 215

Chapter 28 | 222

CHAPTER 1

I T WOULD SEEM I'M wired to have an existential crisis roughly every twelve years.

I was in an accelerated social studies class the first time, flourishing under the attention and tutelage of one of the more gung-ho teachers in the school. Mr. Elliot was not my favorite teacher—by no fault of his own, I'm just hard to impress—but he knew how to assign projects that would lead you into deep water, if you let it. It didn't really line up with any curriculum we were studying, to my memory, but he asked us to explore our family history, and I dove in without even taking a breath.

My family tree is tangled and heavy with intrigue like Spanish moss. There were points in my research where it seemed to me that there were as many felons as judges, which piqued my curiosity just fine, and I found more than enough information in the attic to write my report on Waylon McCabe, a paternal uncle two greats deep who, after his arrest for bank robbery, managed to hijack the train that was supposed to be his ride to prison. He was caught eventually and served out the rest of his days under lock and key in Huntsville, but he managed to get some more admirable escape attempts under his belt during his time, as well as somehow become a father *several* times over, and a bit of a star in the prison rodeo while he was at it.

Towards the end of his life, he straightened himself out and became a born-again Christian. He tattooed himself extensively with Bible verses and preached to his fellow inmates behind bars until his last day. That's the part of the story my parents liked. We're a church-going people. To me, it was a pale ending to a vibrant existence. That's what I thought then, at least.

I got an A on my project, which, embarrassingly, hangs on my parent's refrigerator to this day, as well as considerable renown in respect to my peers after a possibly ill-advised prison break demonstration. What really stuck with me most, though, was not the story behind Waylon's name on my family tree. Instead, it was the other names, the ones with no stories at all. The myriad of family members who lived, breathed, loved, and died—and whose death blew all those experiences, the very imprint of their lives, away. Waylon McCabe lived on, a tenacious bloom on an otherwise dead tree. It occurred to me that I would be in its branches one day, with possibly nothing to show for my long and storied existence but my name. Perhaps one of my descendants would blow past me in pursuit of a relative with a more lively legacy, just like I did with so many others.

I could fathom my own mortality, but the finality of being long-gone and forgotten, a more profound kind of death, terrified something deep and primal in me and, much like I handled everything else, I reached for a pen.

I'm a bit of a compulsive writer, as I should have probably mentioned earlier. Almost from the moment I could write, there was hardly a time I wasn't scribbling something down. Words and phrases that struck my fancy would be penned to paper with a vengeance. Once they were there, I never forgot them, no matter what happened to the paper itself. I drove my mother just about wild with all the ink-stained notes I would run through the wash in my jean pockets. Maybe if my pockets had been bigger I might have carried a notepad, but Levi's weren't designed for my particular brand of person.

For all the writing, I had never much seen the point of keeping a journal. The day I returned Waylon's box of history to the attic, however, it struck me that a life carefully chronicled to be read by future generations might render the subject and author virtually immortal. Thus, the orange notebook with the soft, jelly cover became my companion, giving way to a bright leather-bound diary and, later, a succession of studiously college-ruled spirals.

I wrote long and I wrote short; I waxed poetic and clipped dime-a-dozen sentiments like coupons, and, occasionally, I would represent my mood throughout the day with a line like a rollercoaster that would dip and rise in time to my small triumphs and losses. Often, I would write out my prayers like a letter to God. Sometimes I would recount my day in detail, relishing the moments as if determined to press the texture of the experience into the hands of the reader.

A few entries refused to talk about the day at all, noting that no one would benefit from cementing its memory, and assuring the reader that my future self would be thankful to forget. I delighted in this especially, feeling the power of editing my life after the fact. I wrote devotedly to an invisible audience, to my future descendants, and to my future self. My handwriting changed deliberately twice: the summer before freshman year and halfway through senior year of high school. Becoming a new and better version of myself took purposeful and diligent changes.

Yes, as you've doubtlessly noted by now, I certainly took myself quite seriously. This, as will become apparent, wasn't liable to change.

◄○►

Now, over a decade later, and a much different person than originally intended, I reached for a heavy box at the top of my bedroom closet. The box creaked perilously, the cardboard starting to give way, and I not so much hefted the thing to the ground as I did facilitate a controlled fall. The condition of the box gave me momentary concern as to its contents, but that, at least, was an unnecessary worry. My journals, like an old teddy bear, waited patiently and intact inside, just as they had through tenures in attics, basements and harrowing rides in moving vans all the years previous.

I could not claim the same solidity of condition. My hands were trembling and bleeding. A laptop computer sat at my feet, winking the dazed, spider-webbed pattern of a savagely cracked screen. It was destroyed, that screen, but the contents of what had been plastered across it shortly prior was not. It was still there, menacing me in the invisible eternity of cyberspace. Even worse, it was printed behind my eyelids, vivid and technicolored whenever I closed my eyes. I blinked, and both fury and bile rose, the need to break, to burst out of my very skin. I prayed, desperate, through chapped lips that hurt and cracked and my wrent heart tore further to find God silent and myself alone. My fingers, frantic to save me, it seemed, extracted the first volume from the box.

It was my notebook, the juvenile orange number mentioned previously, and it fell open like a butterfly and spoke with a voice conjured by a blue metallic gel pen, leaving a silvery sheen on my fingers where I smeared the letters. I stared at the pigment, entranced, wishing to be enveloped and taken back.

2/26/2006
> *Today is Sunday, and it is the last day of winter vacation. Yesterday we got back from New Hampshire, where we had decided to*

go, I think, on the idea that we would suddenly like cold weather. Daddy, John, and I signed up for snowboarding lessons at a ski resort not far from our hotel. John is nine, so he had to go with a different group than Daddy and I. I have to admit, I felt a little nervous watching him walk off without us, but John didn't even look back, so I guess he was fine with it.

Snowboarding was hard and so was the ground. Time after time I fell down on my tailbone and knees. I could snowboard by the end, but stopping was a different story.

With shaky breaths, I closed my eyes momentarily, summoning the memory of that trip. I wrapped my raw senses with it like a blanket until I was there.

I felt the frigid cold numb my cheeks, the anticipation and rush of the slide down icy slopes. It hadn't snowed as much that year, so the ski resort had layered the slopes with man-made snow, which was hard as ice to land on. To my memory, we had sat on soft cushions the rest of the trip to ease our bruised tailbones and watched the Winter Olympics on the small hotel television screen. Apparently there was more to it.

On Wednesday, we drove to Mount Washington, home of "the old man in the mountain," a rock formation that looked like an old man's face if you squinted just right. Thing was, the rocks that made up the old man fell off years previously, which was a bummer since they already had him on all their street signs. But, as the brochure said, it is still an area of "great, natural beauty!" So we went to find all the hiking trails closed until summer. Beautiful.

My cynicism was unparalleled.

I think that hurt more than all the falling. Disappointment is a stillborn adventure. We pretty much turned around and went home, and here I am! About to get back to the ol' grind of middle school, even though it's left me pretty much pulverized already.

Oh, the unearned angst.

I think I'd like to have a job where I can travel when I grow up. No grind, all adventure, all the time. If a trail is closed, I hop in a car and drive until I find one that's open. Future-Me: you're welcome. I just figured everything out for you.

It was in the middle of this sentence that a searing pain in my left calf alerted me to the uncomfortable position I had been reading in, spellbound, on the dirty shag carpet in front of the open closet door. I stood up and shifted my weight to ease the cramp, looking at the dim room around me, as shocked as if I had actually time-traveled thirteen years.

The dresser mirror, like the laptop, was also shattered, freckled with dots of the blood that was still running from my hand and arm, which had begun to sting. The bed was in the gloomy disheveled state that indicated it had not been made for several days, lumpy with layers of unsmoothed and untucked sheets. The one working light bulb was beginning to blink in the ceiling fan, reminding me that I had still not found where the box of replacements was kept. It was one of a million small and currently insurmountable tasks I would have to complete simply to appear functional. The thought filled me with, if possible, a deeper feeling of hopelessness.

People whose entire lives had caved in moments before could not be expected to change light bulbs, could they? Anything else was preferable. The aforementioned journal entry nudged at my mind, and something ignited.

"Dare I?" I thought, sardonic in a knee-jerk sort of way.

I surveyed everything the remaining light touched like a glum lion king. It was not as if any good could come from remaining where I was now. Maybe there was something to the naive and tempting advice of my former self.

A carpenter bee bumped the bedroom window drunkenly, making me jump at the sharp, hard sound. At once, I was certain that another hour in this place would drive me irretrievably insane. I turned back to the closet and snatched up a duffel bag.

I packed wildly and blindly, for no particular weather, and an extended amount of time. Anything out of immediate reach was disregarded entirely, and fabric was wadded and stuffed unceremoniously and disrespectfully wherever there was room. The bag zipped with some difficulty and swung from my shoulder as I strode from the bedroom, through the front door and into the sweet summer air.

Dust motes glimmered in my wake and the sun warmed my face like an invitation, tightening the tracks that tears had left on my cheeks. The big blue truck started impatiently from its slumber and grumbled down the long, gravel driveway. In the rearview mirror, the once-dear little home grew smaller, and a sob threatened at the back of my throat.

I swallowed. I drove.

CHAPTER 2

I SHOULD NOTE, IN case you're dismissing me as crazy right now, that I would never have walked out on my life if it hadn't been early June. There's something about that particular month, and the smell of baked pine needles in the air, that loosens limbs calcified by months of tension. School was also out, and the impatience nurtured by long days locked inside teaching sixth grade infants spurred me onward as I roared down the street. The radio was off, the windows were down, and my spirits rose in a feeling that more closely resembled happiness than I would have thought possible in that moment. The only lingering worry at present was that I had no idea where I was going.

East was out of the question, obviously, as any further that way from my coastal home would empty me into the ocean. Unfortunately that left a combination of five cardinal and ordinal directions to choose from without any real preference.

At the four-way intersection not far from the house, my decision was mercifully made for me in the form of excessive roadwork and traffic in two directions. I maneuvered carefully through the light and kept going. West it was.

The landscape had bubbled into mountains by the time the sun grew too hot in the sky to keep the windows down. I rolled them up and flipped on the AC, scanning the local radio stations for anything tolerable. Sweet notes quickly fuzzed with static like a lollipop dropped on carpet, but I eventually found a country music station that seemed to stand the test of time and mileage.

When my stomach's growls eclipsed the chorus of "Jackson," I started scanning exit signs for somewhere to eat. Nothing in me felt the desire to stop, but reason compelled me anyway. I put on my blinker. If I were to continue on at any length, waffles would be wise.

—◄o►—

The Waffle House in question was right at the border between North Carolina and Tennessee, and its occupants were solidly crossing the border onto my last nerve. My appearance was, doubtlessly, disheveled, but the youth who gaped so openly at me were pushing the meaning of the word hipster to new heights of weirdness, which I found ironic. True, my mascara was probably more than a little smeared, but surely the neon green handlebar mustache of the man across the aisle was a bit more eye-catching.

Yet here he was, he and his friend, tattooed all over with variously stylized illustrations of the Grinch, staring at *me*.

I did my best to ignore them in favor of filling my squares of waffle evenly with butter pecan syrup. I would soon be far away. I smiled at the thought. There had been few opportunities to leave the state of North Carolina since my family had moved there ten years previous. I had not relished the relocation then.

Pushing a bite of waffle home, I thumbed to the back of the first journal, which I had carried into the diner like a shield. I eventually found what I was looking for.

> *6/20/2006*
>
> *We've arrived, and existence has started in Topsail, North Carolina. It's an odd place, and I'm not sure if I like it. It's hard to put my finger on what bothers me—you know, besides the traumatic upheaval of my social life—but I think it has to do with how space is used here. I'm aware that sounds high-maintenance and picky, but bear with me.*
>
> *Back home, the view from above was thick treetops. Every evidence of civilization—buildings, roads, etc—was sheltered by forest, cradled in valleys. Everything nestled in a way that was comforting, like it had grown there by itself.*
>
> *It's flat here, and empty, except for occasional clusters of tall, skinny pine trees. Journey outside and you feel exposed, uncovered. Our new house casts an unbroken shadow, which is unnerving. Everything becomes its own sundial.*
>
> *Which is another thing: time. How am I already about to start high school?*

At this, I glanced at my watch, realizing it was time to push on.

"How is everything?" My waitress had returned, an older woman with a bright apron and a wide smile. Her lipstick was red, and so was her hair.

"Great, thank you. Could I have the check, please?" I stacked my plates and pushed them neatly to the edge of the table, wiping up any rogue spots of syrup with a damp napkin.

"Thank you, Sweet Pea," she said, gathering up the dishes and handing me the check book. She paused, letting her eyes settle on my shredded hand. I tucked it quickly beneath the table and fished out a twenty dollar bill.

"Keep the change," I said brightly, sliding out of the booth and making briskly for the door.

"Have a good day," she called. I let the door swing shut.

Back on the road, I set my speed at ten miles above the limit and left North Carolina in the dust. The mountains were tough on gas usage, but I managed to put ninety-nine percent of Tennessee behind me before having to stop to refill my tank. It was growing late, but I wouldn't feel really accomplished until I was on the other side of the Mississippi River. The bridge was long, but I held my breath the whole way, nervous at the metallic creaking and the menacing water below.

I've fished in the Mississippi on family trips. The creatures pulled out of that brown water would make any reasonable person scramble for higher ground. There's no good earthly reason for a garfish to grow eight feet long. They're said not to be a threat to humans, but anything with a snaggletooth to that degree can keep far away from me in the water *and* on land. We found a small one beached on a rock a few years back that the birds had evidently picked at for a while. The bones were green as mouthwash, and it smiled at us until John poked it back into the water with a stick.

Exhaustion descended suddenly as my tires reached the other side of the river, and I decided to stop in West Memphis. I chose the motel with the best-lit parking lot and rented a room for the night from a weary-looking woman with an infant tucked into her shoulder.

"You just passing through?" she asked me, making polite conversation while remaining slightly wary. She eyed me for a moment and I wondered again just how wild I looked in my thrown-on clothes. My hand bore stinging cuts of bright red, and I could feel my shredded arm glued to the inside of my long-sleeved shirt with blood. My index finger throbbed, the tip mostly sliced off and hanging from a glass that had broken within my grip. I tucked it in my pocket where it protested loudly against the rough denim of my shorts.

"Yes, ma'am," I replied meekly. I lowered my eyes to the grey-flecked carpet, and ran my uninjured fingers through my hair self-consciously, hopefully sending the message that I was too fragile to be questioned further. It was closer to the truth than I wanted to admit. Her eyes softened.

"Room's on the second floor," she said, pushing the keys across the counter gently, so as not to jostle the baby. "Let me know if you need any basic toiletries, otherwise there's a Walmart down the road a ways." I nodded, offering a slight smile. She was humming a lullaby and lighting a cigarette as the door swung shut. I climbed concrete steps and fumbled to open the door with my left hand.

The door of the room closed audibly behind me, which made the imperceptible change in the noise level from outside a little incredible. Evidently, the walls were made of tissue. The lights blinked on, revealing a bed that actually looked diseased, stained and cigarette-burned as it was. I considered the woman's mention of the nearby Walmart. A sleeping bag might be procured there at a reasonable price and, if this room was any indication of lodging options along the highway, I'd be doing a lot of camping in the future.

A quick comb through my bag revealed no unconscious genius in my packing skills. I would never run out of shirts, but I had neglected to pack much else. As the Winnie-the-Pooh style was not in season nor legal in public, I would need to supplement this. Placing my bag gingerly on the chipped bureau, I slipped the key card into my pocket and backed out into the warm, moist night.

I am, as a rule, not a retail snob. Growing up I was more familiar with generic brands than the names they imitated and I frequented the Walmart at home more religiously than an actual church. After the dim light of the motel, the establishment glowed like a jewel upon its generous ocean of parking spaces, and my spirits lifted at the feeling of anonymity as I walked in the door. It looked exactly like the one at home, *but I wasn't home.*

Oddly enough, the closing of the automatic doors and the hollow sound of damp air conditioning was what it took to finally get into the adventure of my situation. If I had escaped hell, heaven looked like the entrance to the Walmart produce section, and St. Peter was a tired-looking man whose name tag read "Earl."

"Good evening," he intoned wearily, eyes staring at me, through me, past me, and seeing nothing. I flashed a bright smile that he missed entirely and found delightedly that my shopping cart only squeaked a little bit, and pulled to the right, which was the direction I wanted to go anyhow.

Spending far too much time in apparel, I stocked up on nondescript bottoms of various warmth as well as a few jackets. I had no idea where I was going, but those would tide me over until I did. At camping supplies I found my sleeping bag, a squashy purple thing refreshingly devoid of mysterious stains, and a cooler for road snacks. That was what I was most excited about.

I filled the remainder of my basket with all the sodium, sugar, and saturated fat it could hold. Half of my loot had a shelf life of over six months, most was a color not found in nature—and in fact, might have been just recently discovered—and one's label boasted, "now with MORE real cheese!" and neglected to mention what the rest consisted of. What a world.

I was hauling my trove towards the bank of cash registers when the hair care aisle caught my eye. Rows of unnecessarily sultry faces smirked from home dye boxes. The model on the box of "peacock black" fairly snarled at me. I imagined her modelling inspiration being a siren from the Odyssey, ready to sink a ship of self-proclaimed heroes to the bottom of the sea *for fun*. I added that box to the pile and headed to self-checkout, a triumphant warrior with her spoils.

Had it not been near midnight, I would doubtlessly have made quite the spectacle of myself hauling the seven brimming plastic bags up the outside concrete stairs to my room, fingers gone white with the grip of it all. I somehow managed to insert the key card and bully the door open without dropping a single package of Oreos, and kicked it closed behind me. A large moth fluttered to the ceiling light and promptly fried itself on the exposed bulb, falling with a feathery thump to the worn bedspread, an entomological Icarus.

Before I lost my nerve, I pushed open the bathroom door, tore open the box of dye and shook out my sweaty hair. It fell to my shoulders in a thick, red-brown curtain, ends still fresh from a chop just a few days prior. I winced, not yet used to the length. I always wanted my hair long, but never would commit to the regular trims the process would require. The end of the school year would inevitably find me at the hairdresser's, getting rid of ten month's worth of split ends. The damage was always extensive, and therefore so was the cut.

I paused, my eyes meeting my reflection in the mirror, clouded, questioning, tired. A small cockroach dared to peek out from a crack in the wall and scuttle lazily across the counter.

Bam! As if of its own volition, my hand slammed the bottle of dye on top of the little beast, the impact thankfully eclipsing the gruesome sound of a crushing exoskeleton. I rinsed off the resulting goo, mixed the shimmery powder into the dye, as directed, and the process began.

An hour later found me cocooned in the violet folds of my sleeping bag, swaddled against the damp chill of the robust air conditioner that roared near the window. My hair, still too wet to really judge the result, smelled faintly and not unpleasantly of mint. I silenced my phone and turned on airplane mode, having left my charger in the truck. With that, sleep took hold suddenly, and I let it carry me away.

◄◦►

I dreamed of infestations. In my exhausted mind, I sat up to find myself at home, in bed, the left side still warm. Pushing back the covers, I gasped, finding my legs covered in thousands of tiny, writhing centipedes. They bit at me, tiny pinpricks of pain like stars as I scrambled away, falling out of bed, scattering the ants that had established camp in the carpet.

Legs itching with venom and adrenaline, I leapt from the room, slammed the door behind me and found myself in the living room. Its name had taken on new and revolting significance.

Cockroaches.

The room fairly shimmered with them, small and large and in every conceivable species and color. They clung to the walls, nestled between the couch cushions, and piled companionably in every corner, filling the air with rustles and skitters and faint chirps. Flakes of skin and wing drifted in the slight breeze of a nearby vent, and I reflexively held my breath to avoid inhaling any of it.

I could not scream, sure that doing so would launch the flying ones at me, at my open mouth and I would die because I could not possibly live beyond that. I edged into the kitchen, where giant rainforest cockroaches hissed at me from beneath the table, and I wrenched open the door to escape into the backyard. There I knelt and put my face in the earth, filling my nose with the clean smell of dirt and grass, and I knew suddenly that I could never go back inside.

◄o►

I woke as if surfacing from a deep pool and lay gasping for a moment in the darkness. The dream was fresh in my mind, and I fancied the edges of my vision crawled with bugs, just out of sight. It was dark and still, though the traffic roared outside as clearly as if I were camped in the parking lot. A glance at the alarm clock told me it was barely past three o'clock. I had been asleep for maybe an hour, but I could not imagine closing my eyes again.

I rose cautiously, shucked off the sleeping bag that had sealed to me with night sweat and packed swiftly. A brief checkout encounter with the night clerk and I was back on the road, my cellphone feeding greedily at the charger. I lost the interstate somewhere and felt panicked at the very idea of doubling back, and so continued in a vaguely Northwest direction on a small state highway. The world very dark still, I perceived that there was not terribly much to see anyway, seeming to only pass huge pastures with small farmhouses in the middle, like buoys on an open and lonely sea.

About an hour on, my heart rate had slowed enough to feel my weariness again, and I pulled into what appeared to be a park. The truck purred to a stop in a spacious lot beside a playground. I noted the charming lack of troublesome teenagers, a scourge on the local play spaces at home. The world was a dove-grey, and I spotted a lightly-sloshing lake in the distance. I grabbed a snack box at random from the backseat and walked out on a smooth dock, settling on the porch swing-style chair at the end.

I swung gently and watched as the sky blushed with the dawn. A slight breeze stirred and dried my still-damp hair. I slapped a mosquito or two, but the rest of the insect kingdom stayed away, perhaps culled by the choir of frogs that had begun to greet the day.

I remained that way a long time, swinging and breathing and savoring Cheez-its. Almost a full day had passed since I had winged that broken-hearted prayer upwards at the mouth of my despair. The response then was silence. It was silent now, but of a different sort. I tried again.

"I need help."

Nothing. I swallowed my heart, which had welled up into my throat with disappointment. Yes, I was lonely enough that I hoped for a disembodied voice to come from the sky. I was desperate enough that I would have welcomed being struck down by a lightning bolt. I was crazy enough that the absence of both of these shows of a greater power disappointed me deeply.

"Are you even there?" I croaked, sure now that I was insane. Real crickets underlined the lack of divine rejoinder. I could laugh, if it weren't all so sad.

I waited, listening, swinging. At long last, I drifted to sleep. This time, at least, I didn't dream at all.

CHAPTER 3

"M AMA! SOMEBODY'S HERE!"

My eyelids, sandy, grated open over dry contacts. A young boy armed with a fishing pole was peering at me shyly, leaning over with caution, as if afraid to wake me, though his words were effectively being shouted in my face. The sun, similarly, looked down directly above me. I was curled in a ball, the swing rocking me like a cradle. The box of Cheez-its had fallen from my orange fingers and were tipped over on the floor of the dock.

"Daniel, get back!"

A woman's voice, savage and angry, came over my shoulder from behind the swing. I looked up from my catlike pose and met light brown eyes, startled and fearful. I wondered, a bit frustrated, just how disheveled I could possibly be, to deserve such a look. The shower earlier had worked wonders, but I suppose there's little defending spending the night on this dock as particularly well-adjusted.

"I'm sorry," I straightened up, a bit painfully, and launched out of the swing, sending its chains clanking in protest. "I fell asleep by accident. I didn't mean to take your spot." This last I addressed to the boy, who grinned, undaunted, revealing an impressive number of missing teeth. He couldn't have been more than eight years old, but couldn't have had a single baby tooth left in his head, and what he did have were in various stages of regrowth.

"That's okay," he said, settling on the edge of the dock, dipping both toes and bated hook into the water, "I don't mind sharing."

His hair was curly and dark and his skin already held a deep tan for early summer. His knees were more scab than skin. This kid didn't do anything halfway.

"Danny, let's find someplace else and let this lady alone," said his mom, a trifle more calmly. She still eyed me doubtfully, taking in hair that was probably more than a little crumpled, dark shadows under the eyes from lack of sleep, and day-old mascara. "Lady" was probably a generous moniker, but she had seemed to conclude that I wasn't zonked-out on crystal meth. Not currently, at least.

"But Mom, all the fish are here!" protested Danny, pointing out the sizeable perch just distinguishable through the thin layer of algae on the lake. My Cheez-its box, toppled over on its side, had chummed the water quite effectively. Fishy mouths, wide open, pierced the surface and created tiny vortexes, themselves fishing for crumbs. The boy would have no trouble catching something today. It was best to leave them to it.

"Please don't leave on my account," I said, embarrassed. "I have to go anyway."

I made to stride around the two and the world rocked momentarily, as if the dock were floating instead of fixed. I was, for a precarious moment, secured to dry land by just the outer edge of my foot and my arms went wide in a pathetically futile attempt to save myself. At the last possible moment, a clawed hand shot out and steadied me.

"Hold on there," the woman said sternly, "you don't need to be running off if you're not up for it." She kept hold of my arm as I sat down unsteadily at her feet. It was far from dignified and certainly did not help along her first impression of me, but I feared I would topple into the water otherwise. "Bless your heart," the woman huffed, a phrase always heaped with more judgement than the blessing it claimed. With her help, I maneuvered back into the porch swing. She then sat beside me and pulled a bottle of sport drink from her considerable purse. "Drink this. Don't you move or speak until it's empty."

I drank the vibrant liquid obediently and studied her out of the corner of my eye. She could have been anywhere between thirty-five and fifty. Dark-haired and tan, similar to her son, she moved and spoke with an effortless air of authority that seemed at once both tough and nurturing. Her fingers were sharp with press-on nails and bright with bedazzled rhinestone stars. Her oversized bag had the potential to store any number of useful things, and the edge of a badge peeked out of the pocket.

"Are you a nurse?" I asked, forgetting her prior instructions.

"What are you, deaf? Every last drop," came the stern reminder.

I complied and set the empty bottle meekly beside me. She was fussing with her son, smearing his face and arms with sunscreen until he appeared layered with glue. He took the treatment dutifully, but his eyes were fixed on his pole, the end of which had begun to twitch with underwater activity. The perch were beginning to test him, it seemed. I rose carefully, began to thank her for the drink and edge away.

"Why don't you sit a minute," she replied, tucking away the sunscreen. It was phrased as a suggestion, but did not sound like one. I sat.

I should interject and say that I don't generally take directions from strangers. I understand that it's not an advisable course of action in general. Being treated like a child would have rankled my spirits ordinarily, and, as a teacher ten months out of the year, I was not used to being the one taking orders. Then again, this woman had found me passed out next to a lake somewhere in Arkansas on a Thursday morning, hands bearing undeniable cuts and slices, braless, and in Walmart sweatpants that, I noticed suddenly, still had the small size sticker on them, running down my left leg in a red hiss.

So it was possible that I needed some direction.

The woman had pulled out a first aid kit and was saturating a cotton ball with rubbing alcohol. I realized her intention too late when she grabbed my shredded left hand and pulled back, but she held firm and steady.

"Be brave," she said, and presently the wounds began to sting as she dabbed at the dried blood and cuts. "There's glass in here!" she exclaimed disapprovingly, producing some tweezers and pulling a translucent shard from my nearly-amputated fingertip. That finger was numb as she examined it, and peering into the depth of the cut I felt once again a little faint. I leaned back and looked out at the lake. Danny had lost his bait already and was doggedly trying to spear another worm from the yogurt cup of dirt that rested beside him. They were good worms, the fat, red ones, but spirited, and getting one on the hook was a challenge.

"You need to hook them lengthwise," I told him. The advice cost me another moment of dizziness. I closed my eyes, trying to think of anything but sliced or impaled flesh for a moment.

"Length-wise?" He sounded dubious.

"Trust me," I assured him, after a moment of mouth breathing. "Perch are experts at getting things off hooks. You have to fix it so that they can't bite at the worm without getting the barb too."

"Okay," he shrugged.

The woman, the complete stranger, had bandaged my finger and now pulled my sleeve up to reveal other wounds. These had hardly been washed in my hurried shower and were black with blood that had dried and crusted. She paused only a moment before blessing my heart again and slathering my arm in ointment up to the elbow. I examined it when she was done and thanked her meekly.

"I guess you are a nurse, then." I said. She looked at me a little sharply.

"I am," she replied, "And, as such, I can see right off that you should have gone to get stitches for that finger probably two days ago. The edges of the wound are already dead, and a needle and thread would just tear through by now. You'll have a scar and probably some loss of feeling in that fingertip." Her words were blunt. "Your arms are definitely going to scar. But you know that."

I nodded, felt awkward, and tried not to appear like it. Danny reeled in a sizable fish with a whoop and holler, promptly let it go and dropped the hook back in.

"It didn't even get my worm," he said gleefully. He turned and looked me in the eye. "Thank you." I smiled in spite of myself at the combination of bright eyes, gapped smile, and obvious sincerity.

"Do you belong to that North Carolina license plate up in the parking lot?" The woman was still studying me as she tidied away her supplies.

"Yes ma'am." I was still meek and awkward.

"That's a fair drive."

"It is."

There was a pause. For the life of me, I could not think of something to say that would not say too much. Her eyes went over my face, and softened. She held out her right hand.

"My name is Ruth, by the way. I think I've forgotten to introduce myself." She chuckled and smiled for the first time, her teeth bright against her tan and far more consistently present than her son's. "Whenever I'm needed as a nurse or mama, my manners go out the window."

I smiled, took her hand, shook it warmly. "My name's Vera."

"Hey Vera, have a sandwich." She pulled her bag back onto her lap and reached inside almost up to her armpit.

The purse held a variety of lunch items, and I shared what was left of my Cheez-its as we dined on PB and J. The apricot preserves were slathered on the bread thick, and generous with lumps of golden fruit. It was the best meal I could remember, and I licked the sticky crumbs off of my new bandages the best I could.

As we ate, we chatted lightly about normal things. Ruth had scraped the day off of work because Danny had been begging to go fishing since school let out the week previous. His grandmother would have taken him, but had been busy planning vacation bible school for that summer.

"And you'd think she expected these children to come out with a bachelors in theology," she laughed, shaking her head.

I told Ruth that I had taken an impromptu excursion and was unsure of where I was really going, which was true. I told her my husband was away and being on my own in the house had become unbearable, which was also true. I told her the cuts in my hand were from a glass accidentally shattering. This was not exactly true, and the deepened crease between her eyebrows indicated that she knew this. I hastily launched into the other mundane details of my life, to deter any specific questioning. When I mentioned that I taught middle school back home, Ruth whistled low and long.

"No wonder you look so beat," she said. I laughed.

A fish flopped towards the center of the lake and Danny let out a long whistle at its size. I taught him how to smack horse flies out of the air into the water, to draw the fish back in. Not long after, a frog foolishly jumped onto the dock from the water, and I caught it up for Danny to look at. He forgot his fish for a solid hour as he fascinated over the exasperated amphibian, trying to feed him equally surly worms, which he refused. The afternoon had soon grown late, the light of the sun maturing towards orange as it began the early stages of its descent.

"I think it's about that time, Danny-boy," said Ruth, ruffling his hair. "We've got a picnic to go to."

"Can we stay here, please?" He turned luminous eyes to his mother, who, apparently made of stone, was unmoved.

"No, sir," she replied, "You've got responsibilities tonight, remember?" He scowled.

"I don't want to do that old play," he said darkly. "Aren't I too old for it yet?"

"It's tradition," said his mother. "You've got a real talent for acting, and those other kids really look up to you. No sense in hiding it under a bushel, honey."

"I know," he grouched, reeling in his line as if it pained him. He glanced at me, "Can Vera come?" I heard the pause that followed, felt Ruth look over her shoulder to examine me again. I felt like a test being graded, and realized with some surprise the score mattered to me.

She had softened towards me considerably after hearing I was an educator, but a few hours acquaintance did not merit any sort of invitation.

In the same way, an injured stranger in a park was not entitled to any sort of kindness and attention. Ruth was obviously a different sort of person, though, a conclusion that was strengthened by her response.

"She certainly can, if she wants to," came the reply. "Why don't you ask her and find out?"

I said nothing, and tucked the hook under the guides of the rod and pulled it tight, for safety. The way he was waving the pole around, Danny would catch every piece of exposed fabric and skin he passed on the way back to the car if it wasn't reeled in correctly. I turned to hand it back to him and fell directly over into the large eyes I found staring up at me.

"Can you please come to the picnic with us?" Danny asked, obviously aware and in full control of his sweet and innocent face. "Please? It'll be more fun with you around."

No, right? No was the only reasonable answer. The kindness was too much and my knowledge of where I was and who they were was far too little. Surely my answer needed no consideration.

But, apparently, it did.

I gave it some thought, and then some more. I allowed that it was crazy and I didn't really know these people. I realized I also didn't know what sort of church this would be, and could be something weird. The North Carolina mountains held little congregations that liked to handle snakes; Arkansas could have just as dubious a denomination. Also, wasn't I itching for solitude and travel not long ago?

Then again, I had no idea where I would be going next. Still spooked by my dream, and with my heart raw and aching, I had leaned into the kindness of the little family like a flower to the warmth of the sun. Reason be damned; I had no desire to leave yet.

I caught up my keys, decided, and made a concerted effort to rekindle the spirit of adventure from the night before. It should've been dimmed somewhat, seeing as I was now following a child, but whatever.

"Lead the way."

Chapter 4

Jonesboro, Arkansas, which was where I had apparently ended up, was known to some as the "City of Churches." This was a fact blithely recited to me by its youngest resident historian, the wise Mr. Danny Price, who had done a project on it the previous school year. Jonesboro certainly did have a lot of churches, though not by any means the most, nor was it even a city by the standards of anyone who had traveled outside the county. It was neat and well-kept, however, and boasted a behemoth of a building that turned out to be the church in question.

If the Parthenon had been renovated by wildly wealthy euro-centric Evangelicals, the result would have been close enough to the building that was First Jonesboro Baptist. Creamy, towering pillars held aloft a soaring steeple edged in bright gold. The peak was high enough to not be fully visible from our vantage point on the ground, but the gleam of it hinted at a gilded cross at its point. I was impressed, but also relieved. It seemed unlikely such a prestigious building would hold snakes.

"It's pretty, huh?" said Danny, taking pride in my awed reaction. "Pastor Mark said when I'm big enough I can climb to the top."

"Well, I'm going to be making Pastor Mark a liar, because you're never doing that," said Ruth grimly. She grabbed my elbow and steered us to one of the doors at the side. "Go and rehearse your lines," she called to her son, "We'll see you at dinner."

Danny reluctantly scampered away, joining a rambunctious group of children already digging into a chest of costumes. The kids looked up excitedly as Danny approached and surrounded him, chattering at full force. Ruth chuckled.

"The kid's got so many admirers he doesn't know what to do with them," she said, proudly. "I just need to keep him out of politics."

"Do they need help with the play?" I asked eagerly.

I was alone with Ruth, and suddenly aware that I would need to play the part of a functioning adult somewhat convincingly. And I have to say, I was kind of doubtful of my ability to fulfill that role. Sweatpants suddenly didn't seem appropriate in the face of so much decorum, nor was I eager to stumble through introductions to a congregation of grown people who had their own lives together.

"You've been real patient with him all day. I think you've earned some time with grown people," Ruth said firmly, as if able to read my thoughts. "Let's get you cleaned up, and then we can help Mama with the food. She's probably started bossing the whole kitchen around by now."

I was led into a cavernous gym locker room and fairly pushed into the shower. Ruth left me with the toiletry bag I had snagged from my truck, and I worked hard to cleanse myself of the combined slime of fish, frog, and worm. When I emerged and wrapped myself in a towel, she tossed a light green dress and sandals at me.

"They were in the lost and found," she said in answer to my questioning brow. "They'd be delivered to Goodwill tomorrow anyway. It might be a little less conspicuous than your sweats."

"It's certainly cleaner," I said, inspecting the cool fabric. Tiny leaves were embroidered along the sleeves and the hem in silvery thread. It was not an inexpensive dress. What sort of person would leave it and not come back for it, I wondered. I slipped it over my head and smoothed it. The dress was a size too large, but I didn't mind that in the least, appreciating the fit that grazed instead of clung.

Approaching the mirror to inspect the damage of fatigue, I was surprised to find myself appreciating what I saw. The dark hair color actually suited me, and blued up my grey eyes considerably. After a swipe of mascara, I emerged from the bathroom, feeling queenly, only to be handed an apron.

"All right, hot stuff," Ruth said, "I sure hope you don't have any qualms about working with garlic." She steered me through the swinging doors and I found myself awestruck once again.

The kitchen rivalled the gym. Let me expand on that for emphasis: the kitchen was roughly the size of a regulation basketball court. Everywhere were counters and utensils and cookware. The walls were lined with refrigerators and dishwashers, gleaming with chrome. There was an actual pizza oven, along with several enormous regular ones, all with more buttons than a spaceship. The far half of the room was devoted to a pantry of standing shelves that essentially resembled a small supermarket.

Men and women darted about with full loaves of bread, boxes of pasta, and bulk-size cans of crushed tomato. One counter held a cluster of teen-age girls busily icing what appeared to be seven or eight dozen cupcakes. The abundance combined with the smell of already phenomenal cooking was overwhelming. I was suddenly feeling dizzy again.

"We use this as a soup kitchen Monday, Wednesday, and Fridays," explained Ruth, correctly interpreting my facial expressions. "We get a lot of customers, so the size is warranted. There's no such thing as too many cooks around here." She hurried me towards one of the stoves. "Come and meet Mama."

The woman stirring a pot of sauce was thin as a rail, her hair in an iron-gray bun, and her eyebrows thick, dark, and arched boldly. She seemed frighteningly resolute, the way her daughter did at times, but she smiled her welcome upon our approach and offered the spoon for me to taste. I did so obediently and commented pleasantly on how good it was. She scoffed. It was the wrong answer.

"Your friend doesn't know anything," she said, waving her spoon at Ruth. She reached to the counter beside her and, to my dismay, threw an entire chocolate bar into the pot. "My mother came here from Italy as a young woman, and one thing she always told me is that American tomatoes are bitter." She arched her eyebrow further at me, as if daring me to disagree. I, not having much of an opinion one way or the other, and admittedly intimidated, responded politely.

"Oh?" I said, like an idiot. She seemed to take it as a challenge.

"The earth here is wrong for flesh fruits," she exclaimed, tossing in an additional chocolate bar. The sauce was darkening quickly with the added cocoa. "The natural sweetness is ruined by weak soil. Go to Italy and you'll see that I'm right. You'll taste the difference." She sampled the sauce, and found it more to her satisfaction. Her eyebrows relaxed from severe to simply critical. "Anyway, she taught me to compensate for it with chocolate. And so now I teach it to you." She offered the spoon again, and I complied.

"You can't taste the chocolate," I noted, surprised. They had been very big bars. "But the flavor is . . . "

"Richer, eh?" she nodded, smiling. "Now you know the secret for your own kitchen. Come stir while I check on some of the others. *Do not let it burn*," she cautioned. I nodded as firmly as I could to show my seriousness. I knew that my arm would fall off before I ruined that woman's sauce. "And you," she said, taking her daughter by the arm, "I hope you can still make garlic bread with those tacky nails."

Ruth, making a face at the proclamation, let herself be led away like a little girl and worked alongside her mother at the bread station, the two slicing and buttering in unison. I could see Ruth talking animatedly, at one point gesturing towards me. I realized she was explaining to her mother, with what little information I had divulged, why I was here, where I came from, and where I was going next. The lively old woman was about to learn that the stranger in her kitchen was, at worst, crazy and, at best, an aimless drifter.

My cheeks warmed and I turned to the stove, trying not to let the new-to-me dress be flecked with tomato juice. The mammoth kitchen was bustling with production, but it was evident that no one was above having a good time in the process. A teenage boy snatched a cupcake with quick fingers, darting away to the sound of the squeals of the girls icing them. A young husband and wife pair prepping vegetables for salad playfully snapped dish towels at one another and roared with laughter. Old ladies folded napkins and gossiped. Cheerful chatter and merriment echoed around me as I stirred and stirred.

It was easy to feel a bit out of place and foolish, tied as I was to this enormous pot in a borrowed dress far away from home, surrounded by happy, well-adjusted people enjoying their healthy lives and fruit tasting of soil better than what they walked on.

The cuts on my hand seemed to throb in that moment, and the bandages so carefully and kindly applied to them hung heavily on my arm. Though grateful for the dress I wore, I thought longingly of a lumpy sweatshirt I had bought the night before. It was not fashionable, but it had sleeves and was big enough to swallow me whole.

Minutes passed, and as the wholesome noise swelled in my ears, I turned, putting the spoon down carefully on its rest to look about for an exit. Spotting a door, I took two quick steps and found my path blocked by a figure whose hand extended towards me suddenly. I cringed back in surprise before realizing the hand intended to greet me, and shook it sheepishly, hoping my reaction had gone unnoticed.

It was a man, and his hand was warm and dry. Dressed casually in simple slacks and a black T-shirt, his smile was open and easy, and his eyes, light and blue, were direct. I averted my gaze, a bit startled, more than a bit embarrassed. He was tall, towering over my not-insignificant stature, and his voice was as warm and strong as the hand that held mine as he welcomed me, inquiring my name in syllables like honey.

"Vera," I answered softly, hating how unsure I sounded. I cleared my throat, and tucked some hair behind my ear, giving me a reason to let go of his hand and hide it casually in the folds of my dress. "Ruth invited me. Or, actually, Danny did."

"A born evangelist, that one," he replied, grinning broadly. "As long as we keep him away from politics, right?" He peeked over my shoulder. "So they have you on sauce ministry today?"

"I suppose you could say that," I laughed a little, regaining my balance and my spoon. "I was actually just wondering how much longer I need to stir it for."

"Until it is done, of course." Ruth's mother was back, and she shooed me out of the way to turn off the stove with a snap of the dial. "The salad is being finished now, so we are about ready to serve." She pointed me to the serving window, which opened to a large dining area teeming with people. I could see Danny on the stage beyond the tables.

"It smells wonderful in here, Julia," said the man earnestly, stopping to embrace her warmly. "Thank you for using your gifts of hospitality for our gathering tonight." She swatted him impatiently away with the dish towel, but looked pleased.

"Enough of that," she said, her smile undermining her business-like tone, "We need a clear kitchen, now, please. You should be focusing on your prayers, Father, not your stomach. Or flirtations," she added shrewdly. She glanced at me without subtlety and, horrifyingly, I felt a blush start behind my ears. He put his hands up in surrender.

"With you praying for me, what could go wrong?" he teased, and exited the kitchen, still smiling broadly as she threatened him with another flap of the towel. I could see him checking the sound system and rifling through papers at the podium on stage as I took my place at the window, but soon became immersed in my task. I ladled Julia's creation generously into bowl after bowl of spaghetti, greeting each guest with a smile that felt less forced over time. When the spoon touched the bottom of the pot, I felt a tap at my shoulder and turned to find Ruth balancing three bowls, all steaming enticingly. She handed me one and I received it with something like breathless gratitude.

"It's time to take our seats," she said, and led me to a round table where I sat gratefully between her and Julia.

Dipping garlic bread into the sauce, I felt that nothing had ever tasted quite so good. An elbow to the ribs bumped me effectively from my euphoria. Ruth jerked her head towards the stage and pointedly folded her hands in front of her, closing her eyes and bowing her head. I saw at once that the young priest from before was behind the podium, arms outstretched in welcome. I folded my hands obediently and closed my eyes.

"God, we thank you so much for days like these." The rich voice permeated the room graciously alongside the scent of garlic. "Surrounded by friends, anticipating warm conversation and incredible food, we see what we look forward to when we finally gather around *your* table!" His volume had climbed significantly, joyfully. I opened my eyes and fastened them on him as he continued his prayer with all the force, and some of the rhythm, of a slam poet. "Like David, I feel I could sing your praises before this amazing example of your creation forever." He paused and looked around impressively, a bit dramatically, even. I was reminded of an actor in a play, waiting for the music to start for a big number. My eyebrow rose as if of its own volition. Surely he wasn't going to sing? "But, instead, I'll demonstrate your mercy, and bless the food quickly, so we can dig in," he looked heavenwards, "Thanks, God." He finished the unusual prayer and the congregation spoke their "Amens" with a hearty chuckle.

I met Julia's eyes across the table. She smiled wryly. "Father Andrew is very modern." It didn't sound like a compliment.

"*Pastor* Andrew, Ma, and he's the youth minister. Of course he's informal," Ruth said, looking at me apologetically. "My mother was born and raised Roman Catholic, and sometimes struggles with the transition." I smiled.

"My grandmother is Roman Catholic. She would take me to Wednesday Mass all the time when I was little." It seemed I had finally said the right thing.

"Wonderful!" Julia clasped her hands, looking more delighted than I had yet seen her, "Someone who knows the Church! Tell me, what does your grandmother think of our new Pope?"

"She's holding out judgement, I think," I replied, grinning. "She's kept up her portrait of Pope John Paul in her living room, though. He'll be hard to beat."

"My thoughts exactly!" Julia exclaimed. She launched into a bit of a diatribe on Church politics and tradition. It was clear that, though a current member of the Baptist denomination, she missed the services of her youth dearly. "It's for the best, though," she concluded. "The community is good for Ruthie and her boy, and the Church doesn't think much of having children out of wedlock anyway."

"*Mama*," Ruth hissed. Pastor Andrew, settling into the seat across the table, caught the comment and looked up, eyes a bit mischievous.

"Ah, but the Church wouldn't be here if it weren't for a child consummated out of wedlock." He had wrapped his fork into a massive globe of spaghetti, which he drove into his mouth with only a little difficulty.

"A man of the cloth shouldn't speak so lightly," replied Julia with a tinge of contempt, "And not even the Holy Spirit will be able to save you if you choke on my good food and disgrace my name, Father."

Pastor Andrew swallowed and nodded penitently, though his eyes still danced. He looked at me, and made as if to speak, but was interrupted by a sudden circus of activity on the stage. We turned in our seats to take in the show.

Out leapt five plump toddlers dressed as little golden lions. They toddled back and forth, roaring in a brave attempt at being menacing, but only succeeding in being cute. A few young parents ran forward and crouched near the stage, taking quick pictures with their cameras. The lions waved and giggled, and the audience cooed their approval.

A gaggle of young kids in richly colored robes came forward with a scroll, almost unnoticed, until they shouted their declaration with all the authority of kingdom administrators.

"May King Darius live forever! Please issue an edict ordering anyone who prays to any god but you will be thrown into a den of lions!"

The baby lions roared their approval, clapping before falling back to all fours. On his throne, a gilded folding chair, the elegant, bejeweled and distinctly preadolescent King Darius settled back, and pondered, an exaggeratedly pleased look on his freckled face.

"Very well," he said, "The decree stands."

The young satraps, lions, and king faded into the background as the stage lights swiveled to the very front, where a lone figure paced, agitated, before falling to his knees.

"My God, You are great! I can serve no one but You!" cried the little figure, who I recognized as Danny by the dark curls and earnesty. His voice, small and high, somehow carried the timor of a conflicted but God-fearing soul. Every eye in the room was his.

He was tugged from the ground suddenly by the satraps and dragged before the king. I winced inwardly as his knees—which I knew already to be scraped and scabbed—slid roughly across the floor. To his credit, Danny held his composure. The king, however, was visibly distressed.

"Not Daniel, not one so favored!" he cried.

His tone startled one of the baby lions, who burst into tears. Some hurried hushing from the foot of the stage by his young parents placated him and he went quiet again, blinking away his tears and hiccuping slightly. The king covered for the interruption by striding about the stage, wringing his hands in a grand gesture of dismay.

"No edict by the king can be changed," reminded one satrap helpfully, face cracking wide into a wicked grin.

"May your God, who you serve, rescue you!" the king exclaimed to Daniel. Danny was brought to his feet and pushed, stumbling, into the golden mass of lions who roared playfully at him as the stage went dark.

When the lights came back on, signaling the new day, it was to behold a king fairly crying from relief and Danny, upright and proud, training the baby lions to sit and fetch. The audience chuckled at this. Many more cameras flashed.

"My God sent his angel and shut the mouths of these lions," Danny declared proudly, lifting his face to the light as if beaming up at his God from the pit. "They have not hurt me because I was found innocent in His sight."

"May you prosper greatly!" rejoiced the king, "I issue a decree that my whole kingdom must revere the God of Daniel!"

The curtains closed and the audience roared like so many lions. The young thespians stumbled out and took bows to thunderous applause, and then joined their families back at the dinner tables, preening in their elaborate costumes. More pictures were taken, and much laughter was heard. Danny, who had run backstage after his bow, approached the table in his own clothes, barely acknowledging the attention as he pulled the basket of bread towards him.

"You did good, Danny Boy!" Ruth ruffled his hair and handed him a napkin.

"It was fun, but I still think the lions shoulda been scarier," he said, mouth bulging. His grandmother admonished him about his manners and he chewed savagely for the next few moments to be able to speak with a clear mouth.

"The lions were supposed to eat the satraps," he continued sagely, sipping in a dignified fashion from his cup of lemonade. "Their wives and kids too. It's in the Bible."

"Well," said his mother, a bit aghast, "I can see why that part might have been left out of the play."

The evening continued pleasantly enough until the conversation turned to me. I omitted the complicated parts and made it seem as if I were simply on a road trip for my summer vacation.

"I like to travel," I said, as if this were a good enough reason for a young woman to end up at a random church function across the country. "I'm busy teaching during the year, so summer is kind of the only time I have for adventure."

"A teacher, how perfect!" Julia exclaimed. She had warmed to me considerably. "How would you like to help with Vacation Bible School?"

"Mama, don't try to rope her into anything," Ruth protested, with another conciliatory glance towards me. "She just said she teaches all year; I'm sure she's not looking to be stuck in Jonesboro for a week doing more of the same."

"Well, why on earth not?" countered Julia vehemently. "God gave her a gift, and He brought her here, didn't He?"

"And what's more of an adventure than wrangling our youth?" added Pastor Andrew helpfully. Julia pointed at him victoriously, as if that settled things.

"I think Vera was planning to get back on the road," said Ruth. They all turned to look at me. I scrambled to find a reply that didn't sound as pathetic as the truth.

"I was, actually," I said. "I think I'll be heading Northwest tonight."

"Where to?" asked Pastor Andrew, interested.

His blue eyes met mine simultaneously with this question, and I found that I could not have named a Northwestern American state if life itself depended on it. My mind was a vacuum, and I panicked, feeling the moment grow long.

"You will stay here." Julia ended the silence and reached out a wrinkled hand, covering mine. "If you don't have a set plan for where to go, I want you to stay with me and keep my old bones company for a while." Ruth frowned. I caught her meaning and agreed entirely. This was too much hospitality.

"But you don't know anything about me!" I exclaimed, a little surprised at the force of my own reaction. I drew a breath and willed myself to be composed for once. "I'm grateful, really. You've been so kind, but I never intended to hang around. I'm just seizing opportunities as they come. I hadn't even planned to pass through here this morning."

"But you did," said Julia. Her hands had recaptured mine and her dark eyes peered into mine severely. "I prayed for a teacher, and—look!—one was provided. Stop!" She put up an uncompromising hand as I opened my mouth to protest. "You have no plans and you're boney enough to be no danger to me. You can at least stay the week and help us with VBS."

I would have been furious at anyone else for assuming so deeply and invasively, but Julia was so sincere that I smiled before I remembered myself.

"It's settled!" Julia clapped her hands once and rose from the table. The kitchen was once again bustling with people helping to clean up, and she was, of course, supervising.

I looked around at the others at the table, a bit dazed by this turn of events. Ruth's face was inscrutable. Danny appeared to not have been paying attention and was braiding together strands of spaghetti. Pastor Andrew, however, was smiling broadly once again. He leaned back and took a deep draw from his cup of lemonade, the lights of the room catching in his bronze hair like a halo.

"Looks like you've been adopted," he said. "Welcome."

CHAPTER 5

J ULIA'S PLACE WAS HUMBLE, though it would have been hard not to appear so after the dazzling abundance of the church hall. A squat, tan little ranch-style house, it sat well off the road on a long and winding driveway, peeking out from behind numerous tall shrubs. The interior was less shy. Julia had painted the walls bold and serious: maroons and emeralds, even deep pacific blues. These walls groaned beneath the weight of a thousand family pictures in heavy-looking frames and decorative crosses. Pope John Paul, I noted, held a place of honor in the aggressively tidy kitchen, and Danny's art pieces throughout the years papered the refrigerator, the mantle, and several cabinet doors. The coffee table in the living room held several textbooks and bible guides, open and highlighted for quick reference. Every corner was swept and a small mat waited beside each door for Julia's little shoes to rest on. It was the small and efficient space of an involved and well-loved woman. I asked myself, again, what I was doing there.

"Take the guest room, through there," Julia indicated, more than a tinge of authority to her voice. "I imagine you'll want to wash up—there's a bathroom to the right. I'm an early bird and like to keep an early bedtime around here."

I nodded, understanding that I was being told to go to bed. I didn't mind as much as I would have otherwise. I supposed that enough had happened that I was more than happy to be told what to do.

"I will be up at six for morning prayers and breakfast. Join me, please."

I nodded, again, and drifted into the saffron guest room with my bag. I closed the door tight behind me, feeling that I had not been alone for about a hundred years. I made good use of the bathroom facilities, showering quickly so as not to use up the hot water, and slid into the bed. It felt fresh, as did I, and together we smelled soft and cared for, like lavender and Dove soap.

I reached into my bag and pulled out another journal, fighting weariness for one last bout of reflection. This one was bound in soft leather, a gift from my parents for my fourteenth birthday. It fell open in my lap, and I read on.

> *9/20/2007*
>
> *The sky was pearly gray as I trudged home, discouraged. Nothing very terrible happened, I guess, my spirits just plummeted severely as the day went on. I spent most of lunch studying for my AP European History quiz, but it was still hard. The vocabulary was easy, but the short answer was near impossible. There's just so much to remember!*
>
> *I almost envy those who lived in the 1500s. There was much less history to study then, if you even had to study at all. I'd have to get used to chamber pots, of course, but the knights! The art and architecture! The petty warring between noble families! Sure, life was hard, but at the very least it seemed to have more potential to be romantic and thrilling.*
>
> *I cannot stress how devoid of this my own life is. I'm currently in possession of a cold and have to blow my nose constantly as I pore over textbooks and try to understand how the Thirty Years War had anything to do with religion. Not very romantic. Not even a little thrilling.*

Years later, huddled in a strange bed in the midst of my own adventure, I rolled my eyes hard enough to catalyze a headache. If my young self could see me now, I could only imagine what her opinions would be.

Little Vera would want all the details that are too hard to speak about, and judge me mercilessly for my lack of planning, gumption, and tact. She would close her eyes in horror to the days prior to my road trip, and probably begin to feel quite happy with her box of tissues and history book.

There's a remarkable amount of romance in self-destruction, but not much dignity.

◄◦►

The next day dawned early and went so quickly I questioned my watch more than once, incredulous at the hours that dripped away so smoothly and easily. Julia roused me at six for prayers, which I, out of practice with

Catholic liturgy, stumbled through, and the aforementioned breakfast, which she had cooked with great gusto. I, a poptart-if-I-have-a-minute sort of breakfaster, felt a bit nauseous eating bacon, eggs, and cinnamon rolls so early. The meal was not a suggestion, however, and I managed a second helping so as not to harm Julia's feelings. This was good, because, as it turned out, I would need every last calorie.

I had been under the impression that the church had purchased a Vacation Bible School program like the one I had growing up. If I really strain to recollect, I could remember songs with cheesy dances, crafts made with paper plates, and some generally tropical theme that made wearing plastic leis somewhat appropriate. The whole experience was silly, only a little fun, and was not something anyone looked overly forward to. With the exception, perhaps, of parents who received those childless days like a gift.

Not so for First Baptist, which created a rigorous curriculum based on the perceived needs of the young members of their congregation. The whole church seemed to come together to create a meaningful program for their young ones. It was sweet in an it-takes-a-village kind of way. It was intimidating in about every other way.

This year, the focus was on peer pressure. This was decided after several emotional testaments by parents that their adolescent children were growing away from their families and were gravitating towards friends of different ideals.

"You mean, as pre-teen children generally do?" I commented to Julia. I received a swat from whatever text Julia was poring over in response.

It was a busy, bustling process that involved a concerning number of textbooks, several workbooks and a constant schlepping of supplies up from the bowels of the church hall's basement. I had worked up a sweat by noon, and after the break for sandwiches I was finally promised a more active role in developing the theme of the week.

Outed by Julia as a middle grades teacher, I was delegated the older children as a focus and was directed to the youth room for planning. It wasn't until I walked into the brightly-painted den that I realized my assignment had paired me with Pastor Andrew, who appeared far too delighted to see me.

"Youth team!" he exclaimed, holding up a hand for a high five.

I offered him a weak smack across his palm. Mouth twisting in a comic show of disapproval, he kept his hand raised and insisted we retry, claiming the high five wasn't "crisp" enough. It took two additional attempts before he was satisfied. I foresaw a long week ahead.

By the end of that day, along with the two that followed, all I wanted was to collapse into the deep and welcoming couch that sat beckoning in Julia's living room. Unfortunately, there seemed to be an unofficial rule that no one ever used that room. The couch served as mere decoration, it's open arms sitting empty as Julia taught me to make dish after dish in her small-but-efficient kitchen. She talked very little during these times, and fell into a certain rhythm that, with time, I could imitate. Often she just made small disapproving noises when I burned something, or, less frequently, nodded when I had stumbled into doing something right. I had never asked for these lessons, and knew how to cook well enough in my own right, but Julia set about teaching me "correctly" anyway. I found, after a while, that I didn't mind being taught.

Danny also came around often, dropped off by a hurried but slightly disapproving Ruth who was forever on her way to work. I ached with the thought that she considered me to be mooching off her mother, and caught her sleeve on Saturday as she was running out the door in her lavender scrubs. She attempted to brush me off until I, with a stubbornness worthy of Julia, followed her to her car.

"I don't mind you being here," she sighed at last, in answer to my blunt inquiry. "And Mama is grateful for the help, but, honey, you're not hiding from someone, are you?"

"What?" was my perplexed reply.

"C'mon." She lifted an eyebrow, pushed back a strand of hair with a flick of her press-ons. "You remember how I found you."

"Ruth," I started, then quickly became stuck on my own words. She put a hand on my arm and pushed up my sleeve, turning my forearm by the wrist to inspect the healing process. The bandages were gone, but the scabbing was deep and ugly, and my finger was still deeply sliced and white at the tip. It was generally numb, but I would sometimes wake in the night to a sharp prickling beneath the nail, like an ongoing static shock.

"I don't need all the details," she said, "Mama is adamant that we don't bother you about it. But I do need to know that she is safe taking you in. " Her voice shook with uncharacteristic vulnerability. "If you're running from someone, I'm sorry, I don't want my family in the crosshairs." I was aghast. Her assumption had never even occurred to me.

"No one's coming after me," I said quickly. "It's nothing like that, I promise."

She nodded slowly, mouth still tight.

"And, for what it's worth," I added, "I wouldn't have let y'all take me in if it was." There was a long silence as she eyed me critically, seemingly scanning for dishonesty.

"Then we don't have a problem," Ruth said finally. She opened the door to her car and hauled her purse into the passenger's seat, turning back to me with a softer expression. "You're welcome here," she said, conclusively.

And, as she waved and drove off, I finally felt as if I was.

—◦—

12/14/2007

    Well, I'm here.

    Our new church seems to do a lot of outreach weekends, and our youth minister, Marsha, has been hounding me to participate in one. Hounding is probably not the most generous word I could use, but she's definitely noticed that I've been trying to hang back. It's a really nice church, and I like Marsha and the other youth, but being new can be awkward.

    Anyway . . .

    I signed up for this weekend and so I'm writing from the floor of a church a few counties over. My group met our tenant, Joan, and I can say reluctantly that I think I'll be glad I came. We're going to be building a ramp in front of Joan's house, since she's confined to her wheelchair now, but I think we'll be doing her more good just by being around this weekend. She spent five minutes with Megan, Amber, and I, and said, "I always wanted a granddaughter, and now I have three!" Which was sweet, obviously.

    The group is good, too. They've all done this before, and have been really nice about explaining things to me. There's a big emphasis on serving others and "walking the talk."

    It's good, I think, but we'll see.

—◦—

"Don't you think that would cloud the message?" protested Pastor Andrew.

"What, you mean facts?" I snapped back.

We were arguing. We had been for the past few hours and his refusal to concede on principle was maddening in a way my scholarly heart could not abide.

The middle and high schoolers would be participating in a serious Bible study centered around overcoming obstacles in the face of fire. Pastor Andrew, however, was proving to be an obstacle to a genuine and open text-based discussion. My teacher-brain growled.

"Family trees are an enormous part of understanding the Bible in context," I said hotly. "Look," I stabbed at the borrowed Bible on the table with my finger in reference. "Goliath was the son of Orpah, who was the sister-in-law of Ruth that went back to Moab instead of staying with Naomi and honoring God." I paused for a moment and reran that sentence through my brain, to make sure I had it straight. I did. "Ruth stayed and was blessed for it, and so was her lineage. David was her great-grandson, and he would go on to triumph over Goliath all those years later. Making that connection is important, and I doubt they would put it together themselves."

"They probably wouldn't," Pastor Andrew conceded, "but what does it add to our discussion, other than being only *sort of* interesting?" Pastor Andrew's eyes sparked a bit as he leaned back and examined me with an irritating air of patience.

"Because choices matter, and it shows that even seemingly small ones can echo through time." I stood up. It looked ridiculous, and I knew it, but I had to pace to keep my thoughts straight. "We lecture these kids for years about how their grades and academic choices will affect their eligibility for college and beyond, but no one really emphasizes how their actions outside of school matter in the same way. They're kids, yes, but their choices form the type of people they'll be as adults. Don't you think that's worth illustrating?"

Pastor Andrew opened his mouth to reply, seemed to think better of it, and closed it again. He was thinking, and as I dropped back into my seat, he nodded thoughtfully. He finally leaned back in his chair and sighed.

"I can see the point you're trying to make, even if I think you're off the mark," he said. I glowered and his mouth twisted in a half-smile. He gave a casual shrug. "If it matters that much to you, we can add it in."

It was apparent he had no real argument to match me with, but wouldn't give me the satisfaction of a win. It was also apparent that he was laughing at me. This wouldn't do. After an hour of arguing brilliantly, I wanted a clear and decisive victory. The table we sat at was piled in books, but I moved them to the side and stood up again, leaning to close the smug distance his laid-back posture created.

"No," I insisted, hoping my tone would be the needle that finally got under his skin, "We'll add it in because I'm *right*."

To my chagrin, he grinned widely and leaned back towards me, filling my vision with dancing blue eyes and stubbled terrain across a strong jaw. He was tall enough that, even standing as I was, we were face-to-face. His breath smelled of peppermint and I suddenly found that I was afraid to move.

"Fine. You win, okay?" he said. "But only because I admire that warrior spirit of yours." His half-smile still in place, he got up to go refresh the coffee pot. "I look forward to fighting with you more, Vera." His phone rang, and he left the room to answer it, leaving me alone with my books and angry words.

I was still simmering well into Sunday's family dinner around Julia's square butcher-block table. She had prepared a pot roast which, while not Italian, also had chocolate amongst its major ingredients and the taste was like medicine to the soul.

"You and Pastor Andrew seem to make a good team," noted Ruth dryly over a glass of iced tea. "Mama said she could hear you yelling all day."

"He's not the easiest person I've ever worked with," I said stiffly, trying not to feel embarrassed.

"That man!" Julia spouted, "I don't know how he can be so flippant! I'm glad you're with us this year, Vera. He needs a challenge."

"Well, that's me," I grimaced, someone else's words spilling from my lips, "I'm certainly difficult."

"Oh, honey, you can put that attitude away," protested Ruth. "I'm glad you've got some backbone. Besides," she shot a sly look at Julia, "Mama never said Pastor Andrew didn't enjoy it."

My face burned, and Danny, until this point wholly uninterested in the conversation, looked up from his peas.

"Are you married?" he asked suddenly.

"Danny!" exclaimed Ruth.

"What?" Danny said defensively. "I know *you're* not, and Gramma hasn't been for about a hundred years. Maybe Vera is."

"It's an intrusive question, young man," interjected Julia. "And if you think I haven't been married in about a hundred years, I haven't told you enough about your Grandfather. You met him, you know."

"I did?"

"Oh yes. Bring me the album on that shelf over there."

The plates and cups were pushed aside to make room for the ponderous volume. Julia thumbed through the pages gingerly until she found the pictures in question.

"There, you see?"

We gathered around to look closer. I recognized the couch in the living room, which had apparently been in use at least once, supporting a number of dark and silver-haired people who squinted at the camera as if unsure of where to look. The one smile flashed from the swarthy face of an elegant-looking older man in glasses and a checked shirt. His eyes were turned instead toward the pink baby swaddled in his arms. Realizing this was Danny, I found Ruth in the doorway off to the side, bringing in a fresh bottle, and Julia leaning over his shoulder, her hair a darker gray than of present.

"That's me?" asked Danny. He was a bit more fascinated than I thought he should be, given that the room I lived in currently had about eighty of his baby pictures on the wall.

"It is," said Julia, "and that's my Frank. We could hardly get him to give you up." She turned to Ruth, whose dark eyes were gathering mist. "Do you remember when we'd try to put him down for naps?"

"He would sit with Danny on the couch until they both fell asleep," Ruth sniffed, swiping at her eyes.

"And then he'd wake up and growl at us if we tried to move the baby to his crib," added Julia. "Never missed a trick, that man." She smiled fondly at the photo and gently closed the album, placing it back on its shelf.

"He sounds wonderful," I said, standing up to clear the table.

It felt like an intimate discussion for a family, and I hurried the plates into the kitchen as they talked. I took my time and rinsed everything carefully in the sink before loading the dishwasher. Finding the broom in its tidy corner, I swept the crumbs from the linoleum and then wiped down the counters with a damp cloth. The kitchen, as mentioned, was small, and the cleaning process was short. I ran out of things to do quickly, and this was a problem.

I had begun to feel things, and it did not feel good. It seemed that concentrating on mundane tasks would not lessen the ache that had begun to spread from the center of my chest. I placed a hand to it and pressed in, putting my forehead against the door of the freezer. Over the running dishwasher, I could still hear their voices.

"And that, little man, is a reason why we love you so much," Ruth was saying. She sounded congested, and I knew her tears had spilled after I left the room.

"I thought it was because I'm yours," said Danny, perplexed.

"That's one reason," confirmed Julia. She spoke slowly, seeming to pick her words carefully. "Your grandpa Frank loved you so much, and so we love you that little bit extra as a way to honor him."

"That's confusing," said Danny, unimpressed. Julia laughed her dry cackle.

"Hold onto it for now," she said, "It will make sense one day."

A few minutes later, there was the wooden sound of chairs scraping back from the table, and my head jerked back from its resting place on the freezer suddenly enough to dislodge a few photos from their magnets. Face wet, I retreated to my bedroom, and the door closed behind me before the photos had fluttered fully to the floor.

When had I last spoken to my parents? Or John? I couldn't remember. Life before my escape had taken on the haze of repressed memory. Turning to my phone, plugged into its charger, I scrolled quickly past the most recent messages from colleagues before reaching our family group chat and scanning the last few texts.

I had not contributed to the conversations or updates for over a month. May had dawned bright and rife with year-end tasks and testing, so I had warned them that I would be preoccupied for a while. They respectfully allowed me space to work my way out from under last-minute mountain, but when I had not surfaced, they appeared to grow worried.

I was aware of the phone calls I had sent to voicemail in the last few weeks, but I hadn't seen these messages.

"*Where's our Vera?*" Mom had texted at the end of the month. "*We need to get together to celebrate another school year down!*"

No reply had come, and John gamely tried next.

"*Text back, fool,*" he wrote, complete with clown emojis. "*I want to hear about what adventures you have planned for this summer.*" This was sent about a week ago, probably as I lay bleeding in the dark on my bedroom floor. I wouldn't have replied then even if I had seen it.

I ached to think that my family was feeling ignored, but replaced my phone on the bedside table anyway. I could not imagine a phone call that would not prompt questions I couldn't answer. I didn't want to lie, but being honest seemed an unkindness at this point. If they were worried currently, I shuddered to think how they would feel if they knew what had happened, and the sort of "adventure" I was stumbling through now. I would have to wait until I had something good to share.

CHAPTER 6

10/07/2008

I think church, when done right, can feel like a preview of heaven. Or, at the very least, not much like earth at all.

After we blessed the food this evening, Marsha asked me to help lead one of the mission trips this summer. I accepted, of course, but the anxiety! It's really humbling to be trusted with so much, but what if I can't make the experience as special as it needs to be? I remember being a wee lil middle schooler lost in a sea of youth and not being able to feel connected or loved at all. If my family weren't such "church people," maybe I wouldn't have continued to participate. There's bound to be at least one person there teetering on a similar fence, and if they fall on the wrong side, that's a soul lost! That's a soul I've lost, and how could I bear it?

Will every moment and decision in my life always seem this critical?

—◦—

THE NEXT MORNING DAWNED bright and anticipatory and, even with the abundance of planning done in the days prior, I was nervous enough to have extra difficulty stuffing down Julia's usual breakfast feast.

"Isn't gluttony a sin?" I moaned in protest, as Julia heaped more bacon on my plate. She ignored me, adding an extra biscuit to the pile for good measure.

The first week of school every year I would script every moment. That way, when my mind went blank, as it inevitably always did, I would have a hard copy of my entire day to glance at. As I entered the youth room, I found myself wishing I had done the same for this first day.

Pastor Andrew, on the other hand, was the picture of confident unconcern.

"Youth Team!" he said by way of greeting, arm up for his customary high five. I tried, as ever, to ignore the gesture, but he kept his hand raised long enough that I unwillingly reciprocated. To his credit, he did not insist on trying it again, though the half-hearted slap was decidedly uncrisp.

We were to spend the morning leading Youth Bible Study for grades eight through twelve, and the afternoon overseeing the group service projects taking place on and around the church campus. It seemed to me to be a way to justify child labor for the sake of free landscaping, but Pastor Andrew assured me that it was good training for the mission trips happening later in the summer.

We situated ourselves in the youth room, opened the doors and let the kids meander in, alternately yawning and looking terrified. I tried to arrange my face in a way that was less teacher-ish, but I already longed to tell one boy to pull up his pants. Pastor Andrew, thankfully, beat me to it.

"C'mon Sean, leave a little to the imagination." Pastor Andrew shielded his eyes and pretended to clutch pearls. "It's not a full moon for another two weeks at least."

Sean grunted and pulled up the aforementioned pants. He seemed less than thrilled to be involved, but was, at least, compliant.

The kids all seemed to know each other, but were unsure how to navigate their acquaintanceships in this particular setting. I was happy we had decided to provide a coffee urn for them. Some parents had been against it, but stirring their off-white, over-creamered creations at least gave them something to do with their hands as they sat uncomfortably on the liberally floralled donated couches. Something would need to be done if we were to have any real type of discussion.

Pastor Andrew was thinking along the same lines, as he popped into an adjacent closet and came out with piles of magazines, scissors, and glue sticks. He set them on the low table the couches were crowded around and handed each youth a sheet of sturdy cardstock. They took it reluctantly, holding back aggravated expressions with only some success.

"I know, I know," said Pastor Andrew, smiling. "We're all much too cool for ice breakers here, but we might as well make sure we all know each other. Vera doesn't know anyone, for example, so let's help her out. We're going to make collages that represent who we are as people. Think about your personality and your interests. Get creative." The kids cast dubious glances over at me, and began flipping through the magazines. A copy of *Horse and Hound* landed in my lap, and Pastor Andrew handed me a sheet also. "You too, new kid."

I scowled openly before remembering that I needed to set a good example.

The icebreaker process was more successful than I would have anticipated. As they selected their words and images, some of the kids started to haggle over each other's materials.

"You got a perfume insert? Lemme have that!"

"Beautiful by Estee Lauder doesn't exactly seem like your scent, Liam."

"Don't box me in, Jessica, I'm multifaceted."

"Has anyone found anything sports-related?"

"Seriously, who even subscribes to *Good Woodworking*?"

"Woodworkers, probably."

"If I were a woodworker, I'd want to be *great*, not just *good*."

"I can beat that. I found a copy of *Emu Today*."

"Well, there is that emu farm across from the fairgrounds."

The chatter was light and pleasant, and I knew they would all be much more comfortable participating with each other after poking fun at the magazine collection. I was gluing a label on my cardstock when the glue stick was whipped from my hand by a critical-looking youth pastor.

"*Toyota*?" He read my collage disdainfully. "What is that, a picture of a beagle? Do you even have a dog?"

"I might get one someday!" I said defensively, "And I *do* have a Toyota truck."

"Nice, Vera, very personal," he replied, with an obvious eye roll.

The kids, to their credit, actually took up for me.

"Leave her alone!" chided Jessica, a dark-skinned girl with striking gray eyes, "This isn't exactly easy to do at the spur of the moment."

"Yeah!" Liam added, "If you want soul-level stuff, you'll have to buy her dinner first, *Drew*."

Pastor Andrew threw a glue stick at him, which Liam batted away good naturedly and returned fire with a crumpled magazine page. War ensued for the next few minutes until I called it, feeling that someone ought to be the adult. We were gathering the shrapnel up off the floor when Sean approached me, pulling up his jeans self-consciously as he deposited a wad of paper into the garbage can I was holding.

"Toyota makes good trucks," he mumbled sheepishly. It took me a moment to place what he was talking about and then I smiled, appreciative.

"You think?" I said. "My brother drives a Ford and he says they're better."

"Toyota's foreign, but they're reliable. You can trust them for driving long distances," he replied. "You know what my grandpa says about Ford?"

"What's that?"

"He always says Ford stands for Fix Or Repair Daily." Sean grinned, and I marveled at how the expression completely transformed his face. A ragged-looking child with an earring and a wisp of strawberry-blonde mustache hair, he was shabby compared to his surrounding affluence at church. That smile, though, was bright, rare, and valuable.

"Thanks, Sean," I said. "Appreciate the support." He nodded and shuffled away.

The kids weren't yet done with their collages when it was time for them to rotate to a different station, and we conceded that the real bible study would begin the next day. It was a shame, but the bonding exercise seemed to be crucial, and had certainly fulfilled its purpose.

"Funny how you can just slap two pieces of paper together and become the crowd favorite," pouted Pastor Andrew.

"Some people appreciate a little restraint," I replied with a shrug.

"Can't say I've ever found that," he returned, winking, "but I'm willing to learn, Teach."

"Then start by listening for a change, *Drew*." I left at that and headed to my next assignment, the kitchen.

The snacks for the afternoon needed to be prepared, and I was soon to learn just how many of God's creatures could be made out of celery and peanut butter. According to the two teens running the show, the possibilities were endless. Recognizing them as the young ladies in charge of frosting cupcakes a few nights before, I asked the obvious question.

"Do you two *live* here?"

They twittered like birds at my question and flitted around adding raisins artistically to completed works.

"It feels like it, doesn't it, Lacey?" said one laughingly to the other.

They flew about the cavernous kitchen with the grace and efficiency of a synchronized dance, their aprons appallingly monogrammed in pink and green, their blonde hair pulled back into perfect matching ponytails.

They stopped only momentarily every few minutes to snap a flawlessly staged picture of their creations.

"These turned out just darling," Lacey stated approvingly, preparing her third photo. She had used a melted chocolate-caramel candy to cement together two pretzel "wings" to make a sweet and salty butterfly. She laid them on a gingham napkin and experimented with different filters on her phone. "Annabelle, did you find that little basket? I swear there was a sweet little Easter basket back in the pantry."

"Found it!" The other girl produced it, woven and roughly the size of her palm. "Let's melt one of them a bit more so it can perch on the handle."

"You read my mind!" replied Lacey, and set to the task with enthusiasm. "There—perfect!" The photo was taken and posted with a few taps of her French manicure. "This is good. Instagram could use a little class."

"Especially now that Jessica has an account," Annabelle said cattily. They looked at me quickly, evidently wondering if I might indulge in gossip myself.

"Maybe that's something you could discuss with her, instead of talking about it to others?" It was the right answer, the teacher answer. Their answer was a not-so-subtle roll of the eyes.

"What's cookin'? Anything good?" Pastor Andrew's long arm snaked around me and grabbed an apple slice from the counter. The girls giggled far harder than the comment merited.

"That's why we can't allow you in here, Pastor!" chided Lacey, batting heavily tarred eyelashes. "We wouldn't have anything left for the little ones."

"Ahh, they won't miss an apple slice," he took another bite, "maybe two," he added, reaching for another. He winked at me.

The adoration of the bystanding teenagers made the gesture less than charming. I was suddenly very aware of my close proximity to the pastor. It was familiar, but felt oddly intimate. Lacey nudged Annabelle and I felt certain that they had noticed the same. It was time to leave.

"Well, it looks like you two have it under control here," I said, hopping down from my stool and wiping some lingering peanut butter from my hands. "I'm going to see if anyone else can make use of me." The girls shot a sly glance my way.

"Certainly," smiled Annabelle, "I'm sure Pastor Andrew would appreciate some help."

"That's not a bad idea," he said. He mimed a jump shot. "I'm about to head over to the court to do some hoops ministry before yard work. You should join."

"That sounds fun, doesn't it, Vera?, " asked Lacey

"The Lord's work can be *so* rewarding!" added Annabelle. She smiled hugely.

I caught their drift, and made my excuses, much to their disappointment. My steps led me resolutely in the opposite direction of the gym. Those girls may have set their minds on being church busybodies, but I certainly wasn't going to provide them any more material to do so.

I spent the rest of the day in a blur of motion which ended with tending to an oasis of vegetation in the corner of the church grounds. Julia was overseeing this project, and had set her mind to supplying the kitchen with home-grown fruits and vegetables. She was already beginning to see success. A greenhouse already stood, steamed opaque in the late afternoon sun, and vines prowled along the ground, melons beginning to bloom from their tendrils. Okra grew in its weird and thorny way in a row by the gate, and I wondered, not for the first time, what emergency prompted the first person to attempt to eat them. I loved okra, cooked, pickled, and fried, but it was an undeniably unwelcoming-looking vegetable.

Our task was to plant an orchard, so we picked up the supplied post-hole diggers and got to work, finding that no sooner was one hole finished than Julia wanted it moved elsewhere.

"Not *there*," she would say impatiently, wiping her brow with floral gardening gloves, "Further out. The roots need room to *breathe*." It was a distinctly unfunny comment when the resultant redigging left us so breathless.

When the church bells sounded at five o'clock, the youth headed to the sanctuary for closing prayers, and I took advantage of the moment to steal some time for myself. After hauling the equipment back into the shed, I filled a watering can until it brimmed and set to watering the vegetable section of the garden. My nose filled with the spicy smell of tomato plants as I doused the slightly drooping stalks. The sun was beginning to descend, casting the world in a peachy-syrup hue that seemed impossible in its brilliance and made my eyes water. Crickets sprang from the path of my sneakers as I finished watering the herb garden and replaced the watering can back in its greenhouse nook. Then I sat, exhausted and hidden by countless fruitful stalks and leaves until Danny found me and dragged me back home to dinner.

We dined together family-style, Julia, Danny, Ruth, and I, and, with the passing of the bowls and the laughter and conversation, it had begun to actually feel like family. It was lovely, of course, but I was uneasy. It seemed disloyal to be sitting so familiarly with this family when I was ignoring my own. My mother had ventured another text sometime during the course of the day. I dared a peek at it as I readied myself for bed.

"*Earth to Vera! Give us a shout when you can!*"

I would have to answer for my extended silence soon. But not now. Tired though I was, I continued my nightly ritual and opened up an old journal. It was time to see what little Vera was getting up to.

> *1/1/2009 Happy New Year!*
>
>   *What a year it's been! Last year my one resolution was just to get through my first year at Topsail High; that turned out to be a low bar. I'm finding that I like change, that it challenges me, and that God's not going to let me get hurt. This year is a new chapter, and God is such a clever author.*

"Bless your heart," I said aloud, borrowing Ruth's condescending endearment.

> *I think my resolution this year needs to be to pray more. Marsha always asks me to lead prayer circles at Youth Group, but I think I need to aim higher. It's easy to say the right thing when you know all the Christian buzzwords, but that's pretty hollow. I'd like to have a real relationship with God, one where I'm really talking to Him, and I know He's listening.*

My lip curled and I tossed the notebook back onto the floor beside the bed. Switching off the light I settled into my pillow in a room that was dark and quiet.

CHAPTER 7

THE WEEK SEEMED TO fly by after that first arduous day. The youth dove deeply into stories of the Old Testament, and I was delighted they found my additional research far from, as Pastor Andrew claimed, "only *sort of* interesting."

"Wait, so Goliath was pretty much cursed from the start, then?" questioned Jessica. "Since Orpah wussed out as a daughter-in-law?"

"I'd say it was the men in Naomi's family who were cursed," said Liam. "They all kind of dropped dead all of a sudden. We need to be looking more closely into *that*. Cold cases: Old Testament Files." Jessica threw a couch pillow at him, and turned back to Pastor Andrew and I.

"I wouldn't say cursed," I replied carefully, "But it certainly affected how everything proceeded from there."

"You can definitely see how God takes notice of those whose choices reflect respect and honor," added Pastor Andrew.

"But why is Goliath held to that mistake?" Sean spoke up from his position deep inside the couch and all eyes swiveled to him. Even as the group grew more comfortable, he rarely uttered a word. As a result, or perhaps by design, everyone listened extra carefully when he had something to say. "He didn't ask to be born into the family he was. How is that fair?"

He was looking at me, and I weighed my words with caution.

"I don't think there's a good answer for that," I said finally. "All I can tell you is that there are choices and consequences." Pastor Andrew made a face; I knew it sounded like a brush off. I tried again. "Was Goliath born with obstacles in place to worship the correct God? Absolutely. But we're all human, and all uniquely flawed in ways that keep us from the right path. We are bound to fail at one point or another." The kids were silent and solemn. I understood how fatalistic it sounded, and cast about my empty brain for something redeeming to say.

"But," Pastor Andrew cut in smoothly, "Does God welcome all those who seek Him, flaws and all? *Without a doubt.*" I shot him a grateful look. He winked.

This time, I smiled back.

"Thanks for that," I commented later, pulling a barstool up to one of the kitchen's many gleaming counters. "It wouldn't have been too great to end on that particular note."

I took a bite of apple and chewed thoughtfully. Pastor Andrew drizzled a generous serving of honey over his own apple slice. Lacey and Annabelle, ever helpful, had prepared a large variety plate of toppings for the pastor's afternoon apple. I had not received the same treatment, but I was endeavoring not to take it personally.

"Just preaching the truth," he replied breezily. "God's there for all of us, as long as we keep seeking Him." I smiled, noncommittal.

"You dive pretty deep and conceptual sometimes," he went on. "You ever think that the kids might need something a little more topical at this age?" I frowned at him.

"Pastor, I am an educator. I'm entrusted with preparing young minds for the rest of their lives." I placed my hand over my heart sincerely. "I feel that responsibility deeply."

"Right, very admirable and all," he said, rolling his eyes, "But does that mean you're duty-bound to bombard them with every ugly truth at once?"

"I'm not *bombarding* anyone," I frowned.

"But consider that you might be discouraging them from the faith before they have a chance to try it for themselves."

"These kids are going to have to navigate life as adults one day," I said. "What good will their faith be if it can't stand up to harsher truths?" Warmth was creeping up into my hairline, and I grabbed the honey to drizzle on another piece of apple. I wasn't hungry anymore, but I was embarrassed and needed something to do with my hands. Why did I have to get so angry?

Pastor Andrew held up his hands in surrender.

"I get it; don't smite me," he was smiling, but kindly. "But God's love shouldn't be lost in the analysis either. We make mistakes and bad things happen, but we're still loved." He wiped his mouth with his napkin and got up, placing a hand on my shoulder as he walked out the door, "And one of these days you need to just start calling me Andrew."

Annabelle and Lacey were giggling as they cleared the counter of food.

The garden was coming along beautifully. The orchard had been planted with peach, apricot, and lemon trees and looked as healthy as could be hoped for as they waited to fully root into the deep soil. Julia worried the increasing temperatures would stunt them and spoiled them with water morning and evening. The watermelons had swelled up big and beautiful, and Julia had deemed them good enough to eat at the Vacation Bible School closing picnic on Saturday. Several youth, hearing this, had autographed their green rinds with their names in marker, staking claims to pieces of the biggest and ripest. A fair amount of tomatoes, also, had ripened, and Danny and I had a magical afternoon harvesting: I the tomatoes, he the fat green horned worms that hung sneakily from the plants.

"They're supposed to look scary, but they're not," he explained, showing how the "stinger" of the caterpillar was actually flexible and harmless. He conceded that they were pests and bad for the garden, but flatly refused to kill them, turning his nose up resolutely at the bucket of soapy water offered by his grandmother. Instead, to Ruth's dismay, he kept them in a terrarium to watch until they cocooned.

"Why don't we leave them somewhere in nature where they'll be happy?" she wheedled winningly, adding, under her breath, "Like anywhere but my house?"

"I'll let them go away from the garden when they're moths," he said stubbornly. "It won't take long. See how big and fat they are? They'll pupate any day now."

"Lovely," huffed Ruth. She turned to me with an exasperated look. "Of all God's creatures, why does he always choose the ones that *wriggle*?"

Vacation Bible School closed in a blaze of glory that Saturday with a late afternoon picnic. The kids performed the songs they had been practicing as well as a few original skits illustrating their favorite parts of the week. Lacey and Annabelle performed a coquettish duet about serving in the kitchen that raised eyebrows, but rewarded the audience afterwards with cake pops that earned a hearty round of applause.

When the sun had set, Pastor Andrew and I gathered one last time with our youth, around a fire instead of the well-used coffee table in the youth room. The kids spoke fondly of their time with us, with all the wistfulness of long-gone years instead of a handful of hours over the past week.

"What are your plans for the rest of the summer?" Jessica inquired brightly, as if determined to haul the sun up from its resting place beyond the horizon. "We go to our vacation house on Lake Texoma every year for the fourth of July. You should all come over and we can have a reunion!"

"I'll be working," replied Sean gloomily.

He had shared earlier in the week that his grandfather needed more help than ever in his advancing age. He owned and ran a sweet potato farm that, while successful, was certainly a lot of work. Sean had wished aloud that they could hire on some employees to alleviate the workload, but his grandfather was convinced they couldn't afford the extra expense.

"C'mon, Eeyore," said Liam, "Those potatoes can stay put for one weekend."

He elbowed Sean in the ribs. Sean grimaced, but seemed to lighten a little. I wondered if he secretly liked his nickname, glum implications and all. It was a sign of belonging, something Sean, and every one of them, needed.

I wondered suddenly if the little group would maintain their friendship into the school year. It hurt to think of them passing in the halls as strangers. I pulled out a bag of marshmallows and handed them around. We laughed and ate and talked until the fire burned low and the kids headed off to their respective homes, calling promises over their shoulders.

Waving and laughing as the last car pulled away, I turned and began cleaning up the fire pit, pouring sand over the last smoldering embers and clearing away chocolate bar wrappers. Delighted, I found that one wrapper still contained a good bit of chocolate, and popped it happily into my mouth as I worked. My favorite moments in Jonesboro so far were always tinged with cocoa.

Free of the fire's roar and raucous laughter, the silence seemed very sudden, though punctuated by a chorus of crickets and the occasional thrum of a bullfrog. I turned and found that the lightning bugs had come out, and now swirled around me like a galaxy of dizzy stars. In the distance, heat lightning pulsed in the darkened clouds. All felt very close, and warm, and wild. Released from whatever pressure lingered regarding bible school duties and, still, wonderfully and frighteningly far from home, I laughed and ran and cartwheeled through the fairy lights like a child, tumbling into soft grass dizzy and exhilarated.

"Well, that was positively undignified Ms. Vera." Pastor Andrew, back from locking up the youth room, laughed at me as he sauntered over, offering a firm grip to pull me to my feet. I should have been embarrassed, but my eyes were still only for the magic of the world around me.

"It's all so wonderful sometimes," I said, giddy. He nodded as if he understood.

"We've done a good thing this week."

"Do you think they'll remember anything we told them?" He laughed.

"You're a teacher, you should know the answer to that."

"I guess," I laughed too.

"Thank you, by the way," he added, turning a bit bashful, "for being here to help. It's hard to reach them sometimes, the older kids, and I think they only opened up because you were here."

"Why, Pastor, was that an actual compliment?" I teased.

"I mean it," he said. "You did good and you did it well."

I blushed hotly as his words sank in. It was a good compliment, and the most thorough bit of praise I think I had ever received. If I were still journaling, I knew I would write that down as a monument to a job well done, a testament to my possession of actual competence.

"Well, maybe it'll be enough to keep them coming back to church," I said. I was grateful for the dark in an entirely different way as he studied my face.

"So, we never discussed what you would be doing now," he remarked. "What are your plans?"

I had none. It was something I had somehow forgotten amidst all the activity, that now pinned my heart heavily into my ribcage and sent the warm feelings of a moment ago far away. A tear surprised me, coursing down my cheek. I realized Pastor Andrew had not set loose my hand from helping me to my feet, and I pulled from his grip. He let my hand go, but lifted his to capture the rogue tear along my jawline. For a breathless moment, he looked at me, solely me, with a warmth that was, like this place, foreign and wonderful.

"I haven't entirely figured it out yet," I replied. I moved back a step and cast my eyes down, hoping he would leave it be, but he didn't.

"Have you prayed about it?" He was serious, but I laughed anyway. It was a rough sound, choked with repressed emotions.

"Of course," I sighed quickly, uncomfortable.

"And what did God say?"

"Nothing." Not that he ever did.

Horrifyingly, more tears lined up and followed the first, feeling as if they had burst from the torn lining of my heart. The word had sharp edges. The life I thought I had was nothing. My plans for the future had resulted in nothing. And then there was God, who had watched it all happen and done nothing.

"Are you sure you're listening?"

Andrew's voice had grown soft, and his eyes searched mine in the dark. He reached for my hand again and held it, the useless fingertip still numb to his comfort. A lightning bug careened between us, dazzling and disorienting me before winging away into the darkness. I snatched my hand away, suddenly furious. It was such a ridiculous question to ask. As if anything could possibly be that simple!

"I'll be sure to consult scripture, Pastor," I said, spiking every word with venom. I turned and marched quickly towards the parking lot. Incredibly, he followed me.

"You could always stay here for a while," he said, undaunted. "There are positions available at the church, and I wouldn't mind recommending you for hire. We work well together."

"Is that right?" I replied drily. I fumbled at my keys, dropping them on the warm asphalt. My hands were shaking. He bent, picked them up, and offered them to me.

"Well, when you're not acting like you know everything." He smiled crookedly. When my scowl only darkened, he sobered. "In all seriousness, pray on it. Sometimes we can't hear God until we've really surrendered to Him."

Fighting words were ready to spill from my lips, but the buzzing of my phone mercifully interrupted. I bade him goodnight and climbed into the truck, pulling the phone from my pocket.

It was my dad. The single text was brief, measured, meaningful. *"Vera, call me. Now."*

CHAPTER 8

11/26/2009 Happy Thanksgiving!

Maybe it's maturity talking, or possibly all the tryptophan, but I'm more grateful for my family than anything. John and I get along better now than we did when we were younger, and I might even dare to call us friends now? Mom is a wealth of advice and love, and she works really hard for us. And then there's Daddy. Can I even write this without crying? Neither of us are overly demonstrative people, but his love for me, and mine for him, is one of the only things on Earth I think I can be sure of.

◄○►

I HAD DRIVEN BACK to Julia's in a daze, parking outside the little house, trying to calm myself down enough to have this conversation. Despite my feelings, the time had come. A text from my dad required immediate response, and I knew it. I took deep breaths and willed my shaking hands to hold my phone steady. Like the obedient and responsible daughter I hadn't been recently, I hit the phone icon next to his name, and leaned my head against the driver's seat window, cradling the phone to my ear. The phone rang twice, then connected.

"Vera?"

His voice was like sandpaper, and the sound smoothed my ruffled emotions down into one: sadness.

"Hi Daddy." It was all that I could vocalize before I choked on my feelings and dissolved into silent, warm tears. Really, it was annoying how much I was crying lately. I fished blindly in the glovebox, hoping a version of myself with more foresight had packed a packet of tissues. I hadn't, of course, and I eventually settled for a fast food napkin.

"Where are you, honey?" The question was a formality. The family locator app on his phone had no doubt already found me. It was an invitation to explain myself.

"I'm in Arkansas, actually," I attempted a breezy laugh while stopping the flow from my nose with the less-than-absorbent napkin. "I've, ah, I've been helping out with a church program here."

"A church program?" My mother's voice sounded excitedly in the background. Apparently, I was on speaker. I could imagine them both listening in the kitchen, my father seated at his place at the table, my mother dragging a chair alongside him and leaning in anxiously.

"Yeah," I said, "I kind of stumbled into it. They needed help teaching Vacation Bible School, and I said I would."

"That's wonderful!" My mother was gushing. It had been years since I had attended church with the family, and any evidence of a possible resurgence in faith was a great relief to her. I decided to play to this.

"It was a really good experience, and I've made some good friends within the church leadership. I think you would really like the way they plan everything, Mom. Maybe you could bring it up to the church board and they could do something like it next summer." My mother started in, eagerly asking questions, but my dad cut her off, not one to be distracted.

"Why are you there?" The impossible question, but one I had practice in answering by now. I decided on the fun version of the lie.

"I just felt like I needed a road trip," I said, tugging on a lock of hair anxiously. "School was so stressful this year, I needed to go somewhere I wouldn't run into a horde of familiar children." I tried the light laughter again. It rang false in my own ears, and did not seem to fool my dad either.

"Where is Austin? Is he with you?"

My throat locked up and for a moment I was actually unable to breathe at the sound of his name. My husband. Of course they would ask about him.

"No," the truthful answer burst forth seemingly on its own, "he had to go to California for a few weeks. Field training."

"Are you going to go meet him out there?" My dad clearly wasn't buying the spontaneous road trip story. "I'm assuming he knows where you are."

"Ah, I might," I said uncomfortably. "I'm not sure if it'd be possible yet. Playing it by ear." Silence on the line. Beyond the windshield, I saw Julia peek out her front door. Spotting me in the truck on the phone, she

waved and turned the porch light on. She would be going to bed, I imagined, but wanted to make sure to leave the door open for me. "I definitely
plan on heading to the West Coast, I'm just killing time and trying to see
the sights. I've never really gotten to travel by myself before." I was just
saying things now. I wasn't even sure if that made any sense.

"There's good reason for that," he replied, "It can go really wrong
if you get into trouble. Do you remember how to change a tire? Do you
have your emergency kit in the car?" I bit my lip.

"I'm fine, and I'm being careful."

This was also not true. I had been fortunate to run into the people
I had. Any number of horrific things could have happened while I was
in my rash, emotional state. I would need to be more level-headed in the
future.

"You need to keep us updated on your travels, Vera." He sounded
tired, and I knew he was fighting the urge to order me home. I was an
adult, and was able to make a mess of things if I wanted, but it wasn't
without emotional consequence for my family. "We were worried. We
need to know that you're safe. Please." My heart hurt, and I nodded, forgetting that he couldn't see me.

"I will, and I am. I'm sorry, Daddy." I meant it. He sighed.

"So where are you heading next?" That was the question of the
night, wasn't it?

"Truthfully, I have no clue. West, I guess."

"You know, I always wanted to take you all on a trip out west. There
are a lot of places you could hit while you're out there." And he was off,
regurgitating a list of names and places and backstory that overwhelmed
and motivated me. That was my dad, terribly knowledgeable, and cognizant of the potential for a good adventure. His mind fell along the same
lines as mine had: hiking and camping. "I'll send you the link, and you
can check it out," he said. "There are a ton of National Parks, and a lot of
ground to cover, but maybe you could see one or two before you head to
the coast."

"I'll check it out," I promised, relieved at the turn the conversation
had taken.

"Well, please let us know what you decide, and check in as much as
you can," he said. "I will buy a plane ticket out there if you run into any
trouble."

We spoke our I love yous and hung up. I breathed in and out deeply,
listening to the tap of a gentle rain shower that now sprinkled the truck

and Julia's little house. The porch light was warm as I shouldered through the front door and closed it securely behind me, locking it against intruders and the past few uncomfortable hours.

—◦—

8/14/2010 First day of classes/Happy Birthday to ME
 And, all at once I'm a college student and officially an adult. What a huge occasion that doesn't feel like anything yet. I'm nervous for my first day of school, but excited, and I know that's how it should be. I've prayed for this day and I know it'll be great.
 Another new chapter, right? Maybe even a new book? I think if I make my mind up to be the heroine of my own story, I'll feel much less used up and ragged about everything.

—◦—

Ruth and Danny were at the table when I emerged with my bags the next morning. I was bleary-eyed after a late night of packing, and hung over from all the emotion of the day before. An Irish goodbye and a quick getaway sounded appealing, so I was thrown off by the number of faces that greeted me in the cheerful breakfast room.

"Good morning!" Julia bustled from the kitchen with a basket of bagels in hand. "Come eat quickly." She eyed me, and seemed to take in the bags I was carrying for the first time. "You can put those down."

"I probably need to get on the road," I began, but Julia shook her head quickly and waved her arm.

"I don't want to hear it," she said firmly. "We observe the Sabbath in this house." I looked at Ruth, who shrugged.

"At least come to the morning service with us," she said, "I'm sure there are a few people that would want to say goodbye and thank you for all the work you've done." I opened my mouth to protest and was silenced by a severe shake of her head. "Be brave," she said curtly.

I couldn't think of anything less appealing if I tried. Danny made his position known by pulling out my chair, looking up with hopeful expectancy. I sighed, put my bags down, and slid into my seat. Julia pushed me the apricot preserves—my favorite—and that was that.

—◦—

"What are you doing here?" The now-familiar voice boomed through the cavernous worship space. I, not having paid much attention to the service in lieu of thinking about my travel route, winced noticeably. Pastor Andrew was at the pulpit, apparently giving the sermon that morning for Youth Sunday.

Of course he was; he was everywhere.

"Does no one else work here?" I hissed at Ruth, who shushed me. She was transfixed, much like the rest of the congregation. I settled back in the pew and tried to pay attention.

"I've asked that question a thousand times throughout my ministry and, I have to say, I've gotten some interesting answers," he continued. "Some are good, you know. Smart, even. You can tell who has been to church before, right? 'I'm here to worship,' that's pretty good. 'I felt called to hear His word in His house,' I mean, come on! Be still my liturgical heart!" He smirked.

"Mom, what's liturdgical?" asked Danny.

"Ask me after the service," Ruth whispered, flapping her hand at him.

"The youth have the best answers, if you ask me," continued Andrew. "How about 'my mom made me?'" The congregation chuckled as a few youth raised their hands in confession. Andrew waited for the noise to subside, and took a more serious tone. "If I were to divide these responses into two categories, each would fall easily under 'seeking'—those truly looking for God and truth—and 'hiding.'"

Of course, everyone feels the priest is looking directly at them during the sermon, but I had reason to believe Andrew found me specifically in the crowd for that last word.

"We know of Jonah. We know of the Prodigal Son. We know of Adam and Eve. We know of Peter and his denial of Christ. They hid themselves out of fear. They hid themselves out of guilt. They misunderstood entirely who God is and relied instead on their own understanding of the world which, inevitably, falls short. As, we know, we all do."

He glanced at his notes, and stepped away from the podium.

"There are people in this room who go through the motions of believing, but don't really. They disguise themselves with the right words, the right knowledge, with acts of generosity and kindness, but are not actively seeking a relationship with God. They are dead where they sit, infested with fear, and guilt, and doubt."

The congregation murmured, uncomfortable with the strong wording. I was riveted in my seat.

"To those, I have a message," Andrew's voice was forbidding. The people cringed, bracing. "He loves you," he said softly. "He loves you, and he wants to bring you home. He wants to clothe you, heal your wounds, make your heart whole again. He will separate your transgressions as far as the east is from the west; he will drive out the darkness and conquer death. He will never leave you; he is with you right now."

There was a lump in my throat, and I feared I would be unable to swallow my tears. Andrew had returned to the podium and gathered his notes.

"So what are you going to do?" he concluded, setting the microphone back in its holder. "Hide . . . or seek?"

CHAPTER 9

SAYING GOODBYE WAS ODD, tearful, and a far cry from the easy departure that I had originally intended.

Ruth had reached for me first. I embraced her carefully, narrowly avoiding scratching a cornea on her nails as she wrapped her arms tightly around my neck. She whispered that I was in her prayers and then fished in her purse for bandages and antibiotic ointment.

"Take it," she said firmly, disregarding my cries of protest. "You never know."

Danny had approached me without embarrassment, offering his hand for a firm shake, and wished me good travels. His conduct and manners at that age, as always, blew me away. I wished him luck on future fishing expeditions and promised I would send him a postcard from wherever I ended up. He brightened considerably at the prospect of a pen pal.

Julia offered a short hug and made me promise I would come back to stay if I needed to. She pressed a wrinkled ten dollar bill into my hand which, like her daughter, she refused to take back. I pocketed the money, reasoning that I could always mail it back to Ruth later. The little family had given me far more than I could repay already, and my gratitude increased even more now, at the warmth they were showing me at our parting.

Pastor Andrew was a bit less understanding.

"So you're leaving," he had said, unsmiling. It was a statement, not a question, and his sober air made me, incredibly, long for our juvenile bickering of days gone by.

"It's time," I said, avoiding his eyes.

Andrew nodded, not saying anything. I looked up briefly and wished I hadn't. His eyes were fixed on me, suddenly complex with a confusion of frown lines. He was dissatisfied with my answer, obviously, and waiting for me to go on with his now-familiar stubbornness.

"I'm being called elsewhere?" I smiled winningly, hoping to keep things light.

Stony silence was my response. I sighed.

"I've heard you," I said, finally meeting his gaze. "I have. And I have a lot to figure out, but I've always had to figure things out for myself."

He nodded and looked down, as if deep in thought.

"Wish me luck?" I reluctantly raised a hand in the air, poised for the high fives so dear to his youthful heart. He let me hang a moment, which I deserved, and then slapped me five so soundly everyone in a ten-foot radius turned at the noise.

"We've got a Youth Trip out to Ouachita in August," he said. "I wouldn't mind your help if you're in the area. And hey," he crunched into an apple slice from the coffee hour cart, "you're welcome here. Any time." He turned and made long-legged strides back to the church. "So hurry up and run away so you can come back again," he tossed a grin over his shoulder, "prodigal."

―◌►―

I was grinning despite myself as I pulled back onto the road. If there was one thing I now valued in a person, it was consistency. I wasn't likely to forget Pastor Andrew any time soon. That said, the safety of miles between us was about the best thing I could think of.

Entering into the spirit of what was once again a road trip, I rolled my windows down and set the music app on my phone to shuffle. Whole counties passed under my tires to the tunes of Hall & Oates, David Bowie, and Panic! At the Disco. At first I ignored the signs for roadside attractions in the interest of time, but when my lower back began to protest somewhere in Missouri, I reconsidered. I was, after all, on an adventure. I exited at the next sign I saw and headed into Springfield.

The sign was for—and I don't want a lot of judgement for this—The World's Largest Fork. How one can drive through the middle of America without seeing one of the world's largest anythings is my question. That said, there may have been a sense of letdown when I parked and actually walked up to the thing.

It was in an office park, and it really was just a big fork. Gleaming brilliantly in the noonday sun, the fork stood at a slight angle, digging into its small plot of earth with its partially submerged tines. There were a few people taking humorous perspective photos already, so I hung back to let them finish before approaching. The small sign at the base informed me that the utensil signified the home of the Food Channel and provided a hashtag for social media posters. The shining metal was flawless and unsmudged and, looking up from the plaque, I soon saw why. A security guard sat in a nearby van, apparently providing the eccentric monument protection from passing motorists. I had to think that it couldn't be the most rewarding job but I, a middle school teacher, certainly could not judge. I snapped a photo for posterity and sent it to the family group chat, attempting to be more forthcoming with them regarding my whereabouts. By the time I had hustled back to the truck, my phone had dinged with Daddy's response.

"*Reached a fork in the road? Any chance we'll see you spoon?*" I groaned, but couldn't resist a quick reply.

"*Knife one*," I typed, hating myself a little, but laughing anyway.

The irony of my little detour, and my father's pun, was that I truly found myself now at a fork in the road. I intended to reach my first National Park, Badlands, the next day, but I had the option now to either head to St. Louis for the night or continue further west to Kansas City.

I took my question to Google, which provided me with lists of attractions for both. It was a picture of a Kansas City barbeque platter that made my choice for me. After days of spoiling with Julia's good cooking, my stomach growled for more than the drive-through fare I would have otherwise provided. The GPS on my phone said I would be there in three hours and I pressed down on the accelerator. I planned to shave a significant amount of time off of that estimation.

◄○►

Tucked in a small booth two and half hours later, I sank my teeth into a heavily-sauced barbecue sandwich and sighed with contentment. It had been almost a full day since my bagel at Julia's, but a meal like this deserved to be eaten hungry.

The restaurant in question was the least-assuming place I had seen, with a short menu, paper plates, and a small dining room. There were only a few other patrons who were mostly congregated at the bar, sipping beer and watching one of the many games on the various monitors or scrolling on their phones. Uninterested in screen time, I dug in my bag for another journal, pulling out the same soft-covered one from before.

I read for quite a bit, juggling page turning and eating, and the pages proved to be absorbing, if not absorbent, as evidenced by my careless smears of barbeque sauce. Church activities had clearly taken up much of my time and mental space in high school. One entry bemoaned a fight I had had with my mother over classes or, rather, my lack of interest in them.

> *12/9/2010*
>
> *The mission trip the weekend before finals was amazing, and did so much good, but may have affected my scores a little bit. My parents are less than pleased with my exam grades. Granted, I didn't do perfectly, but my grades are high by anyone's standards! They pushed me to get involved in a church group , and now that I am, it's "interfering with my studies." I suppose I can empathize with their position. I'm supposed to be learning to be a productive member of society. Why should the little matter of my soul get in the way??*

I couldn't help cringing at that. The quotations! The emphasis! The overdone punctuation! What an unflattering snapshot of the workings of a teenage brain. Imagine using church attendance as a means of rebellion. I shook my head.

A few pages further revealed that my fervent concern wasn't entirely soul-based anyway. Oh, the memories came flooding back.

> *1/22/2011*
>
> *It would be nice if the boys in our small group were even the least bit appealing. One of the new members, Tanner, seemed promising at first. He's older, kind of quiet and mysterious, which is good. It sounds stupid, but I liked the way he listened to the reading. He seemed like a deep thinker and, every once in a while, I'd catch him looking at me. That's pretty good too, I thought. Note the ominous phrasing here.*
>
> *So, he asked me to sit with him at dinner tonight and proceeded to put his hand on my knee under the table. I didn't want to make a big deal out of it, so I didn't really do anything until his hand started moving higher—like, under my skirt. I pretty much jumped up and hid in the bathroom until he left. Can you believe that? I had literally just been asking him how his Christmas break had been.*

The kid had never talked to me again. I heard later that he was a major customer of his high school's dealers, and was pretty much always using and abusing some sort of narcotic. Sheltered as I was, I had mistaken him for being contemplative and mystifying, instead of simply high.

I guess it's a good thing that happened so quickly. I had been in a room with him, what, an hour? And I had all these ideas of who he was as a person. It took me about five minutes to get to know this idea of him and then I was captivated and done for. Why do I do that?

"Someone seems lonely." A tall man slid into my booth on the other side of the table. I had long since filled up on barbeque and pushed the rest of my basket away. The man grabbed one of the remaining fries and grinned as I looked up at him, startled. He was my age, maybe a bit older, in a baseball cap and flannel shirt that was fitted tightly to him. He had brought his drink from the bar and, from the smell of things, had already emptied quite a few there. "Smile, darlin'! I'll keep you company."

"Not lonely," I replied, "just reading."

I was flustered and, frustratingly, felt a nervous flush start at my ears and creep across my face. He smiled even wider and I closed my notebook, uncomfortable. I reached for the check and recoiled when he snatched it first.

"Why don't I get this for you?" He waved it between two fingers, just out of reach. I shook my head and glanced around, hoping a waitress might be nearby. "C'mon," he wheedled, "You're still not smiling! You've got a nice man right here paying for some good barbeque and a drink," he winked, "if you want." He was drunk enough that his face didn't quite recover from the wink, one eyelid sleepily refusing to open all the way.

He was grotesque, obviously, but despite this, or perhaps because of it, I found myself warming to the idea of a drink. It had been a long time, a self-imposed sobriety, really, based mostly on the feeling that I was using alcohol to ease anxiety more than anything. But didn't I deserve to not feel so terrible, to not feel *anything*? Even just for a while? It was stupid, to be sure, given where I was, and how I was, but the notion was oddly tempting.

And, really, I had been far more stupid just trying to do the right thing.

The man was waiting, lurched forward over the table and smiling emptily, a puppet with cut strings. He was obscene, and that was fortunate, because my repulsion jerked me to my senses.

"No thank you," I replied quietly. He looked at me, eyes blank.

"I still haven't seen that smile," he persisted stupidly. His head swiveled lazily to look back at the bar, where a few of his friends sat watching. "I bet it's real pretty. C'mon now!" He reached out with clumsy fingers to brush my hair behind my ear. I jerked away.

"No thank you," I repeated, "I need to go."

I tried to keep the snarl out of my voice. I was angry, but also uncomfortably aware now of the audience at the bar. I didn't want to humor him, but I was suddenly afraid of what he'd do to save face in front of the other men if I rejected him outright. I waited a long moment and glanced up. His smile had faded and was replaced by an ugly smirk.

"Oh, did you think I was hitting on you?" He said this loudly, hauling himself up from the table. "Just thought you oughta stop looking so goddamn miserable. I mean, c'mon," he reached for my notebook, snatching it with more dexterity than I was prepared for. "Put the book away. We can have a little fun here, right?"

"This isn't fun," I had to raise my voice to be heard above the laughter now coming from the bar. "Give it back and leave me alone."

There was a long, silent moment where he stared at me. I stared back with a fierceness I didn't really feel, and watched as my words seeped into his brain. He blinked first.

"Whatever, then," he sneered. "Have fun being frigid, bitch." He threw the notebook at my face and then the check, which fluttered into my lap. He turned and rejoined the group at the bar. "Let's go Royals!" he hooted.

I pulled some cash from my wallet with trembling fingers and dropped it on the table as I left. The parking lot was full of shadows and I sprinted to the truck, fumbling with the keys for a heart-stopping moment before I was in, door slammed shut, locked, the engine growling to life. I had planned to stop here for the night, but my tires squealed with reassuring power and soon Kansas City was safely behind me. I didn't stop shaking for fifteen miles.

Chapter 10

9/29/2012

> *This is the first time in forever that I have been able to write before midnight. My life is just so full right now!*
>
> *I think I've finally got my life in balance, and I can safely say that I really like college. My classes are really thought-provoking. I haven't watched one movie in class this year so far, can you believe that? Admittedly, that's setting the bar pretty low.*
>
> *I love all the friends I've made here. There's always something to do and someone to do it with. And I've joined a great bible study that I'm looking forward to every week.*
>
> *I'm doing so well! It feels like tempting fate to write that down, but I want to mark the occasion somehow. I'm happy.*

--◦--

I'M SURE OMAHA, NEBRASKA is a lovely city, but I was not destined to see it. I bypassed the luminous cityscape in favor of a truck stop with lots of lighting. I quickly used the facilities and returned to my truck's cab, pushing back and reclining the seat for comfort. Or, at least, the intention of it. I squirmed uncomfortably trying to find a position where I wasn't being jabbed by a seatbelt or canted in a way my neck would hate me for tomorrow. I finally gave up on the idea of comfort and stared out the windshield, tears prickling at the outer corners of my eyes.

I had never spent the night in a vehicle in this sort of sense. My parents, adventurous pioneers as they were at times, would occasionally drive through the wee hours in an attempt to get someplace in a hurry, but that was rare. In any case, it's a much different thing to drift off to the whirring of wheels, the metal contraption around you being steered by hands you know to be capable, the road and other cars mere abstract concepts outside the cocoon of safety. By contrast, my truck rocked a little when passed by some of the mammoth vehicles parking here for the night. I had parked beneath a streetlamp for safety, and now dirty yellow light streamed through my windshield with a brightness that would be hard to sleep through. Raucous laughter came from all directions, almost drowned out by the incredible noise of the nearby highway. Also, I was alone. Hard to forget that one.

I was very tired, but very awake. What's more, because I knew I needed rest, and would not do well without it, sleep became that much more elusive, chased away by the pressure of necessity. I would need to distract myself. I cracked open the next journal and read of a simpler time until, at long last, I managed to drift off.

◄○►

4/23/2013

I'm not sure exactly what I think about him, but I think it's good.

Is that believable? I, your Vera, may have found a man I can approve of.

I suppose we'll both stay tuned.

Whatever my former self expected of the future when she penned those words, it wasn't that I would be twenty-five and unsticking them from my face at a truck stop after unwittingly using my journal as a pillow. I yawned and felt briefly irritated that I could not stretch in the cramped truck cab. Kicking open the door, I dropped wearily to the pavement and reached heavenward, my bones creaking their protest.

It was very early, so much so that even the truckers were yawning. Drivers, armed with coffee, were scaling the stairs back up to the semi-trucks and getting back to their long journeys. I made my way inside where I found the women's bathroom mercifully empty. This truck stop, additionally, provided automated showers. Coin-operated and vaguely clean, they stood tantalizingly in the dim light of not-quite-warm over-head bulbs. I was achy and tired and fairly certain there was barbeque sauce in my hair. A quick glance in the mirror confirmed it: this was happening.

I paid the station attendant and indulged. The air conditioner was working at full capacity, but the water was wonderfully warm and worked miracles on my wrinkled spirit. Some of the greatest songs ever written have been about the love between two people. I decided then that it was a great injustice that no one had yet developed a serenade to the humble hot shower.

"Feeling better?"

The station attendant was a woman in her thirties with rhinestones winking at the corners of her eyes. Her makeup was bold and flawlessly contoured in a way that required a steady hand. She looked less like a gas station employee and more like a glamorous actress playing a gas station employee. I poured myself some coffee and decided the look suited her. I asked her if it took a lot of practice to do her makeup so expertly as I handed over my payment.

"Girl, yes," she replied, "But it's worth every minute. It's my craft." She handed me my change. I smiled my thanks and pushed through the doors into the new day.

I thought about that comment long after I had pulled back onto the road. A craft, now there was a concept. I had been teaching for several years already, constantly honing my skills and developing new strategies and ideas, but could that be considered a craft? My craft? I couldn't claim any real level of expertise. The past year had often felt more like staggering forward, never catching my balance fully, but propelling forward with enough force not to fall down completely. There certainly wasn't much joy in it.

Not to say that things were awful. Compared to my first year, teaching now was an absolute picnic. I shuddered, thinking of those first ten months.

I, like many young educators, went to work for the first time with an excitingly unblemished planner, idealistic rules and procedures, and boatloads of ideas and enthusiasm. Looking around at the seasoned veterans during the first teacher workday, I had been struck by how tired and jaded everyone had seemed already. It became irritating very quickly, as a lot of my suggestions had been met with scoffing during the language arts planning meeting.

"We're not allowed to teach novels," one teacher snapped at me, impatient to the point of rudeness. "Admin don't like them. They take too long and the kids don't get as much out of it as targeted skills practice."

"But can't what we're reading be used to deliver those lessons and practice?" I argued, incredulous. "Isn't that kind of the whole point?"

"We use short stories and passages mostly," chimed in another teacher. Her eyes were sympathetic, and she spoke softly, as one might speak to calm a wounded animal that had to be put down. "It's a more efficient use of class time."

"I suppose we're allowed to assign them independent reading, then?"

The first teacher snorted.

"Sure," she said, "but good luck enforcing it."

The stubborn spirit in me had rebelled against this information, and I had quickly drawn up my own lesson plans to submit, separate from the others in my hall. We were going to read a novel together, one of my favorites, and it would be great.

When school started, however, I was quickly consumed by learning lessons of my own. Student teaching had taught me nothing about classroom management and, in the low-income school where I was working, anticipating and handling behaviors was a major part of every class. It was difficult, I found, for any student to simply walk into the classroom and sit at their assigned desk without altercations. Opening their binders was another struggle, and many were unable to afford them in the first place. The disruptions were at such a level that I decided to introduce the novel study much sooner than I had planned. Other teachers were still drilling expectations and procedures, but I thought I might be able to captivate my students into good behavior with a story.

It was a historical fiction piece, which nicely lined up with what the students were going to learn in social studies, so I decided to start the class by playing a quick video on the time period, to establish context. This was the right move, I knew, classified as pre-reading by my well-worn teaching textbook, and I was confident. My students were ornery and distrustful of teachers, ill-prepared for school and behind in both academic and social-emotional skills. Regardless, I would be charming them into a love of reading in a single day; there was simply no other possible outcome.

It was with this level of naivety that I was setting up the projector when Mrs. Bigby, my administrator and supervisor, walked in. The children were filing through the door, bickering after being shunted in the crowded hall, and took little notice of the extra adult in the room. She waved at me and pointed silently at her notebook, letting me know that she was just here to observe. I felt a twinge of nerves as she settled into a chair at the back of the room.

Here's the thing about observations: formal or informal, they are terrible. Even now, I will tell whoever is listening that judging an educator's effectiveness based on a randomly selected class period once a quarter is a disservice. But I digress.

That day, if the students knew their vice principal was watching their every move, they gave no indication based on their behavior. I fielded a few off-topic questions and redirected a child who had wandered from his seat to stare out the window, where Canadian geese were feeding in the back field. He honked, goose-like, in response to my request for him to be seated, but eventually settled himself as the video came up on the screen. I clicked play and the video ran for five seconds before starting to buffer.

"It stopped!" yelled two students, helpfully.

I refreshed the page and found that the Wi-Fi was out.

"You can use my hotspot," offered a girl in the back row.

"Your phone is supposed to be in your locker, stupid," said the boy next to her. Her face grew dark and angry.

"Shut up," she swatted at him. He leaned back in his chair out of reach.

The hotspot became unnecessary, however, as the power suddenly cut out. The lights went off, as did the projector, and the classroom was enveloped in darkness. Several girls screamed. There was a commotion as the boy leaning back in the back row lost his balance in surprise and fell out of his chair. I hurried to help him up and glanced at Mrs. Bigby. She scrawled something down in her notebook and looked back up, unfazed, it seemed, by the unexpected circumstances. Clearly, the observation was to continue.

I need to think on my feet.

"Sorry about that, class, perhaps we can revisit the video some other time. Instead, let's see what you already know about the time period in our novel. Who can tell me something about Ancient Greece?"

"My mama's got a lot of it on her stove," came one voice out of the darkness.

"They were old," came another.

"They live on Mount Olympics," said a third. I grabbed onto that comment like a life raft.

"Mount *Olympus*," I corrected gently. "And the Ancient Greeks didn't live there, but they believed their gods did. Does anyone know anything about the Greek gods? Let's raise our hands, please!" I added hastily, glancing nervously at Mrs. Bigby.

Their memories jogged, a few students were able to offer some correct information about the Olympians, helped along significantly, I suspected, by having seen Disney's *Hercules*. The majority of the class, however, did not seem to have much prior knowledge at all. I decided to move on while I was ahead.

"The novel we are starting today has Ancient Greece as its setting. Do y'all remember what we learned a story's setting is?"

"Place and time," called out one girl promptly.

"That's exactly right," I said, a bit amazed.

"We learned that in fifth grade," she replied.

"Right," I said, "Well, let's acquaint ourselves with our novels."

Passing out the books became its own adventure, one that veered an already precarious situation into uproar. One student volunteer skipped kids he didn't like, garnering a very vocal protest that I had to diffuse. The other volunteer seemed to grow weary of walking the books to each desk, and elected instead to frisbee them directly to the students, with varying degrees of accuracy. In the five minutes this took, students had begun talking amongst themselves and the volume level of the room was increasing, along with, I noticed, the temperature. The lack of air conditioning was going to be a problem soon.

"All right," I said, once everyone finally had their book, "listen up!" I had to raise my voice to be heard above the din. The room eventually quieted. "Let's turn to the first page. Please follow along with me as I read."

I started the reading, making sure to infuse my voice with drama and emotion. As I read, I walked amongst the rows to ensure everyone was on the correct page. Walking and reading was an unexpected challenge, but my proximity to the students seemed to have a good effect. With the exception of one girl, who fell asleep immediately, the class seemed, for the first time, to grow focused. They laughed at the appropriate moments and shushed one another if someone happened to throw out an unhelpful comment. We were going to have great discussions about this; I could feel it.

When the lights came back on, I cursed myself for not having flipped the switch off while there wasn't power. The sudden contrast in brightness was dazzling and I could not blame the children for protesting and rubbing their eyes. I tried to carry on as if nothing had happened, and read a minute more before a boy at the center of the room caught my attention.

His head was tilted back and his brown eyes were huge, focused on the ceiling. I glanced up to behold a massive cockroach crawling upside down along the ceiling tiles. I looked back at the book and continued reading, praying none of the others noticed.

It was not to be. Curious as to what the boy was looking at, other pairs of eyes went upwards. A faint murmur could be heard throughout the room as the kids nudged each other, pointing to the large specimen making its way to the front of the room.

The roach eventually reached a light panel. It paused at the edge of the ceiling tile, as if sizing up the new landscape, and proceeded forward. There was a barely perceptible scrabbling sound as its legs lost purchase on the plastic, and the room gave an audible gasp. I looked up from my copy of the book to see every eye in the room on a cockroach hanging by two legs from the ceiling. Even Mrs. Bigby had put down her notebook at this point.

It made a valiant effort, but the weight of the insect worked against it, and it could not pull itself back up. It landed, with a brittle thump, on my desk at the front of the room. It scuttled quickly out of sight and the classroom erupted into madness.

I leaned my head back and cackled at the memory, easing into the fast lane to pass a dawdling RV. It felt good to laugh about it now. It had certainly not been funny then.

In the end, Mrs. Bigby had been kind but firm. Waving aside my apologies and excuses, she made it clear that technology issues and performing vermin sometimes came with the classroom. In time, she had assured me, I would know how to plan for the unexpected and adjust on a dime.

"What I'm concerned about," she said, "was your pacing, and your classroom environment." She went on to point out that, aside from starting the novel, very little skill work had happened. The activity had caught their attention, but done nothing to prepare them for the end-of-year test and the grades beyond. Moreover, I would need to get my management style together. "They're not taking you seriously," she said.

I was wounded and embarrassed. Instead of taking her advice and trying to reach out to my overworked and harried colleagues for help, I withdrew and tried to fix the problem myself. I pushed and planned and floundered. By the end of the year, things were only incrementally better. On the other hand, I had an extensive list of mistakes not to make for the next year, which proved helpful. Every year I grew more experienced and capable until I was the one leading the planning meetings. By then, however, I was also the one with an outlook every bit as cynical as my colleagues that first year.

It was well earned. That first year of teaching had been the worst of my life, and the stress carried into every moment. If I hadn't been too stubborn to ask for help, and if life at home hadn't been such an inferno in itself, perhaps it wouldn't have been so bad. But it was. It was, like everything else, so much worse than I had imagined.

"I wish everything were different." I surprised myself by speaking the words aloud. In my reverie, I had zoned out. The only response was the hum of my vehicle around me as we traveled onward.

Chapter 11

8/19/2013

This morning I may have bent time and space to my will. I awoke from a luxurious sleep to see that the time on my clock was a mere seven minutes before math started. Journal, I still had to get dressed, and the math building is a good fifteen minutes away, but I still made it to class on time. That's an actual miracle, right? Should I alert the Vatican?

Austin is in my math class this semester which, of course he is, since he's taking every math class the university offers. I can't imagine how boring it must be to be an engineering major, but he evidently likes it.

I like him.

(Oh, God, did I just write that in my journal like a nine year old?)

I had not managed to squeeze breakfast into my time warp this morning but, halfway through class, when I was just starting to starve, Austin turned around and put a green apple on my desk. It was significant, that green apple, a testament to our friendship, one might say, and a wink to a conversation we had the day we met. And, also, maybe he just knew somehow that I'd be hungry?

He's been thinking about me, right? That's what that means?

—◇—

As the landscape was becoming more and more sparse, I decided to stop to pick up some things for my national parks visits to break up the monotony of the drive. I made my way to a large outdoors store and, ever-conscious of my limited teacher savings, selected the cheapest camping supplies that were available. There was a lot to choose from, and

I spent more time talking myself out of getting items than anything else. In the end, I settled on some basic gear and dehydrated food and lugged my haul to the register. A perky man in a fleece vest was there to greet me.

"Are you part of the co-op?"

I, struggling to heave my items onto the counter, shook my head no.

"Would you like to be part of the co-op?" His teeth flashed unrelentingly. They were very white, and his hair was brushed just-so over his tanned brow. He was simultaneously so clean and outdoorsy that he could have been a catalogue model that had fallen off the page into real life.

"No, that's okay." His smile faded, which sounds negative, admittedly, but in reality just meant that he relaxed into a normal facial expression.

"We have to ask," he shrugged and began scanning my items. "Are you planning for any camping trip in particular?"

"I was thinking about visiting some national parks," I replied, a little wary of giving out too much information. His face brightened.

"Then you're going to want one of these." He reached over to the shelf next to the register and picked up a small, navy booklet. "It's a National Parks Passport. Every park or monument you visit, you can get a stamp at the ranger's station." I examined it dubiously. "It may seem a little lame, but there's a lot of information included." He showed me a page detailing sites in each region of the country.

"There are a lot more than I thought," I said in wonder. He nodded.

"It surprised me too, the first time I saw it," he said. "I've actually made it my goal to get every single stamp in my passport before I turn forty."

"Why forty?" He shrugged again.

"Seemed far enough away to be reasonable, but close enough to be motivating."

"Well, good luck," I said, handing him the passport to be scanned. He was no more than twenty years old, from what I could tell, but it was still a lofty goal. I couldn't help but be a bit inspired, however, and when I left the store I altered my route on the GPS to take me directly to the Badlands ranger station.

◄○►

9/12/2013

> *I may have just gotten back from a date.*
>
> *Austin asked if I wanted to get dinner, and, journal, he took me out to an actual restaurant. We're talking off-campus. We're talking food priced in double-digits. We're talking cloth napkins and candles on the table. Candles!*
>
> *He opened the car door for me and pulled out my chair when I went to sit down. We sat and talked and laughed for hours. He told me about how he plans to commission in the military as an officer after he graduates next year. I told him about my church group and how I was applying to the education school this semester. Afterwards, we ordered coffees and talked some more until the candles burned out.*
>
> *I know this makes me sound like a dweeb, but it all felt so adult.*
>
> *Oh my god, he's texting me now. He's asking when he can see me again. I'm guessing he's not talking about class on Wednesday morning.*
>
> *Are we dating?*

◄○►

The landscape of South Dakota was beautiful, but endless. Time passed oddly and I began to feel a bit flattened, the landscape so wide that the sky appeared to rest heavily on top of my truck as I drove. I was beginning to count bison when, mercifully, my phone rang. I didn't waste the second it would have taken to check who was calling; I was more than ready to chat with a telemarketer at this point. I answered eagerly.

"How's it going, Scrub?" My brother's voice answered and the corners of my mouth, while not actually curving up to a complete smile, did twitch in that direction.

I had been expecting to hear from John, but hadn't quite figured out what I would say to him. I had contemplated telling him everything, a sort of knee-jerk guilt reaction after holding so much back from my parents, but now I shied from the prospect. I loved my brother, but I wasn't sure I was quite ready for him to see the mess my life had become. I was the older sibling, and it was embarrassing.

We chatted lightly for a bit about friends, family, and general goings-on. He was currently preoccupied with a small group he had formed at his church for young adults. It was rewarding, but a huge time commitment given everything else he had going on.

John was going into his senior year at Duke University and currently in the middle of some summer courses that would allow him to graduate with a double major in biology and philosophy. What he would do with the two was anyone's guess, but no one's worry. John had boundless potential, with a quick intellect, well-developed social skills, seemingly endless energy, and, appropriately, a lot of confidence. I was massively proud, if minimally and perpetually annoyed by it all.

"So where are you now?" he asked, having worn out the conversation on his fabulous life. "Is Austin with you?"

"Ah, no," I said, biting my lip. "He's in California right now. Doing Officer stuff. You know how it is." I had tried to keep my voice breezy, but it sounded forced to me. There was a slight pause.

"So where are you, then?"

"Arkansas," I said, relieved enough that I stumbled into inaccuracy. "Well, no, actually I'm back on the road now. I'm about —" I checked the GPS and groaned, "—I'm *still* fifty miles from Badlands National Park at the moment."

"Ah, man, I've heard such great things!" he exclaimed, launching into a long diatribe on the history of the park. I listened without comment for a time, knowing it was wise to let him run himself out. John could get on some long tangents; I was just thrilled it was in an innocuous direction. "Did you know it was used as a bombing range in World War II? They still find undetonated bombs sometimes."

"I'll be sure to watch my step," I said archly.

"The park also falls within Lakota territory, so make sure you're not wandering off the trails," he said seriously, explaining how clueless tourists would sometimes stumble into people's backyards.

"Are you googling all of this right now?" I asked finally, incredulous. "How are you such an expert?"

"Oh it's all my roommate. Do you remember Hector? He's from out in that direction and knows everything there is to know about that area. He did the junior rangers program in the summers when he was a kid and now he's getting his degree in forestry so he can work in the parks for real. It's pretty cool."

"This is the guy that tried to free climb your dorm building freshman year?" I asked, searching my brain. John laughed.

"I forgot all about that! He was trying to impress a girl, I think. What a maniac." He sobered suddenly. "You know, if you need a place to stay out there, his family owns a ranch in Montana. I'm sure they'd love to have you. He's there now, I think. His mom probably needs help with the place now that his dad has passed away."

"A maniac *and* a cowboy, huh? " John laughed again.

"God's thrown a lot of interesting characters my way, what can I say? I can't complain."

"Hmph," the sun was now directly in my eyes. I would need to get sunglasses at some point. I hated to do it, because I always lost them almost immediately, but this was getting ridiculous.

"Speaking of, how's your relationship with God going?" John inquired, conversationally. My truck hit a bump in the road and the vehicle jolted abruptly.

"What a casual inquiry," I replied, laughing in a startled sort of way. There were many reasons I fell out of touch with my family. These sorts of questions were one of them.

"What an obvious side-step of the question," he challenged. I sighed and rolled my eyes, sun glare and all.

"God and I are fine, John." I lied outright, with a heavy sigh. I was actively regretting picking up the phone.

"Oh that's convincing," he replied sarcastically. Some sort of large insect exploded on my windshield, leaving a streak of electric yellow across the glass. "I had hoped your adventure would've softened you up some."

"Softened me up?" I repeated, puzzled.

"Yeah, it's like what we were talking about in small group last week," I heard a click as John apparently closed the door to his room. "A person has to be ready to receive God's love, otherwise it's like a seed falling on rock. It can't take root and grow."

"The parable of the sower, right? That's a good one." I knew I still didn't sound convincing.

"Right," he continued, "and I know you know all of this stuff already, but maybe it hasn't taken root. And you're *such* a teacher, that I thought maybe leading bible school would . . . I don't know . . . "

"*Soften me up*," I finished the thought through gritted teeth. I hadn't mentioned anything about bible school, and John being privy to that information meant one thing. "So you all have been talking about me, huh?" The sun glared, and I did too.

"Mom and Dad gave me the update yesterday. I asked, they didn't just volunteer," he said, turning defensive, "It's not like you ever tell me what's going on, if I even hear from you. And there's obviously *something* wrong. Mom and dad are worried. Have *been* worried. And I have too." I scoffed, a desperate, angry noise that couldn't fully hide the tears of frustration welling up in my eyes. This was just so annoying.

"What on earth have I given anyone to be worried about?" I took offense at his implication. Sure, I wasn't overly-communicative, but I had been so careful. With the exception of the past week or so, I had appeared utterly well-adjusted, damn it. I *had.*

"You're not happy," my brother answered with overdone gentleness, as one would speak to a spooked horse. "You just seem tired, and that's not you. You've been pulling away from the family, and it seems like you don't have a relationship with God anymore."

I felt a sudden strong inclination to throw my phone out the truck window, to lay it to rest in one of the many pastures whizzing by. Seconds ticked by as I tried to think of what to say, drawing deep breaths and letting the small, angry tears dry against my temples.

"You were always so strong in your faith, Vera," John ventured, breaking the silence cautiously, "and it's scary that it doesn't seem important to you anymore."

His words tapped a sad weariness that was all too familiar. I wanted to hang up, pull over, and nap in the sun until the end of time. I couldn't do any of those things now, though. I also couldn't have this conversation anymore.

"Aren't you majoring in philosophy?" I said finally, desperate enough for something to say that I resorted to brutality. "Don't philosophers believe that God is dead?"

There was a moment of shocked silence, then, surprisingly, a peal of laughter.

"Oh, you would quote Nietchze at me," John chuckled. I found I could smile at the sound.

"What's *that* supposed to mean?"

"C'mon, Vera, you're obviously a super cynical person now." I stuck my tongue out at the phone, annoyed at the accuracy but relieved at the lightness of his tone. "You know, the basis of that belief was fear," he continued, "Nietchze thought a belief in God made people subservient."

"And I take it you disagree?"

"Obviously." Now John seemed to be rolling his eyes. "I think people tend to become servants of a lot of things," he said gravely. "I believe God provides freedom from those burdens." I was silent again. "You there?"

"Yeah, I'm here," I said. It was time to bow out before I had to do any more thinking. "I might be out of cell range soon, though."

"I'll let you go then," he said, obviously unconvinced. "Just give it some thought, maybe."

"I will." But not by choice.

"And, hey, I'm going to send you Hector's number just in case you need help." He paused briefly, "Or, I should say, in case you for some reason decide to go against your nature and actually ask for help." I chose not to challenge him on that.

"Love you, kid."

"I love you too."

I pressed the red button with a vengeance, breathing out heavily. Conversations with my brother could be difficult, that was certain. I was about to heave the phone into the passenger's seat when it buzzed to life again in my hand.

One glance told me that it was a text.

Two glances told me the text was from Austin.

Dust rose as I brought the truck to an abrupt stop at the side of the road.

CHAPTER 12

4/29/2014

Okay, forgive me? I know that I've been inconsistent about writing, and I don't want to give it up, so I'll work on it. It's just that I'm so happy. It's hard to describe, and every time I try I get impatient because I'd rather be living it than just writing it down.

I was observing a class at a local middle school on Friday (adorable, by the way) and Austin surprised me by picking me up and taking me to a picnic on the beach. We ate dinner and watched the stars come out and it felt like the whole universe was watching us fall in love. I know that sounds cheesy, but somehow all the cheesy things I've ever heard now make sense?

My sides hurt from laughing, and my eyes itch from late nights talking about everything and nothing.

I brought him to church this morning, and it was perfect. He doesn't have a church, so he's going to start coming with me. I didn't go to the college group tonight—homework has taken me captive now that I've neglected it all weekend—but I'm singing God's praises anyway. I think He must love me a lot to have brought Austin into my life.

—◦—

OH, IT WAS CRUEL. As the dust settled, I stared out across the rugged countryside, dotted with bison. It was easy to imagine cowboys galloping over the horizon, driving cattle on painted horses. For the first time, I longed to be transported back to days like those, where messages would be passed across the wide open miles on horseback, and were thus treasured and significant. I couldn't imagine receiving anything from the pony express similar to the vague nonsense that now beamed up at me on my phone.

Hey, what's up?

Emotions whisked across my heart like a dirt devil as I sat in the still emptiness of the South Dakota roadside. Questions howled in my head. Why would he care? What could he possibly mean by texting me now? What time even was it in California? I was trying to determine what time zone I was in when another thought occurred to me. What if he had texted me by mistake? How typical would it be for me to place so much significance on three words that weren't even intended for me in the first place?

I threw the phone from me and startled the truck awake with a savage twist of the keys. Motion, I needed motion. My foot struck at the accelerator and my tires squealed against what I was asking of them until they finally caught traction and complied. Several dizzying minutes later, I pulled past the Badlands National Park sign.

There was not altogether much to see at first. The sky was big and the pasture was green. In the distance, I could vaguely see what looked to be rock formations. It was beautiful to be sure, but nothing different than what I had been staring at for hours on end.

All at once, there was a gash of dusty white to my left and the land seemed to fall away into a massive gorge. Pulling into the small parking lot dedicated to the overlook, I stumbled out of the cab of the truck, legs a bit dead from the long drive, and made my way to the edge. The canyon was vast and deep, studded with banded, variously colored buttes and spires like the ridged spines of enormous reptiles. It was at once gorgeous and hideous, a joy to behold and a shock to the senses. My hand was on my chest and tears pricked at my eyes, the awe overcoming my reservations and thankfully eclipsing all other thought. It was entire minutes later that I blinked and glanced around me.

My only companions were a spry older couple that stood a few yards away at the overlook sign. They, too, seemed struck, and were simply gazing outward, their hands linked. I walked out along the path, careful to not contribute to any unnecessary erosion, and sat on the edge of the walkway, knees hugged to my chest. The older couple followed me, the man letting go of his wife's hand to briefly snap a few photographs. A breeze whispered past, a bird gliding overhead on its wake, and the three of us stood and looked. I took the heavy feeling in my chest and focused on breathing it out and away.

"Noooooooo!"

A high pitched scream shattered the stillness and pulsed in the warm air. I jumped in surprise, and, grateful I had not stepped off the path and was now tumbling into oblivion, turned to look back at the parking lot. A van had pulled in and was discharging a large number of children, many of which appeared to be slap-fighting one another.

"Kids, please!" A harried-looking chaperone pleaded, redirecting the roiling mass towards the overlook path. I traded a dubious glance with the older couple and we quietly made our way back up the path to our vehicles. The peace of the moment was effectively over.

-◄o►-

The visitor's station down the road held a number of treasures, disguised in part by a lot of colorful nonsense. There were Badlands posters and mugs, puzzles, and stuffed bighorn sheep. An array of T-shirts hung on the wall for easy selection and a fake fir tree bore a variety of Christmas ornaments emblazoned with the likenesses of bison and prairie dogs. One shelf held several boxes of a children's game called, incredibly, *Whose Butt?*, the object of which was to identify an animal based on a picture of its rear end. I managed to find and purchase a few postcards, a decent map of the park, and a pair of sunglasses. At the last second, I tossed in a small bottle of sunscreen, hearing my mother's voice in my head hissing warnings about melanoma.

Slipping my new shades on, I unfolded my map with relish, perched casually on the dropped tailgate of my truck. Small families filed past, tired and grouchy parents damp with perspiration, their kids chorusing for ice cream and the like. They looked hot; hot and irritated. Conversely I, swinging my feet and utterly unencumbered, felt very cool. I had a map, and a truck, and my world was as wide open as the sky above me. I was an adventurer, simply doing what adventurers did. In that spirit, I circled a far-off campsite on my map and climbed back into the driver's seat.

The Badlands visitor's station had a small museum that I had perused, explaining the geology behind its formations, as well as detailing the wildlife that called the park home. Most notable, and accompanied by taxidermy displays, were the American bison, bighorn sheep, and prairie dogs. Though the museum boasted the abundance of these animals, and gave recommendations of the best places in the park to go to see them, I didn't hold out much hope of it. I had seen plenty of domestic bison along the way to the park, but now, the only signs of life were tourists toddling in every direction, often in defiance of trail markers and road signs.

The sun was low in the sky when I reached the campsite, a small circular drive in the prairie already dotted with vehicles and tent configurations. I pulled into an open space with some difficulty and began unloading my gear, erecting my small tent quickly and puzzling out how to use my Jetboil for the first time. Freeze-dried food, despite what the back of the package will have you believe, is rarely good, but adventure lends a certain tang that can make even stale mush appealing. I ate quickly and found I was satisfied.

"James, Caroline, it's time to eat!" A man in the next space over called loudly from behind his small fire, peering out at the two figures playing in the grass a short distance away. The kids waved merrily back at him but remained where they were, standing wide-legged in the dust with their hands on their hips like superheroes. The man sighed and trudged out to his children. I heard him exclaim suddenly in surprise and watched as he yanked the two by their hands back to camp. "The animals are not toys," he scolded. Properly chided, the two sat meekly on their camp chairs and quietly received their dinner.

"What's over there?" I called, curious. Startled, he seemed to notice me for the first time. I was set up barely five feet away, but understood the oversight after half a day of observing families in the park. It seemed that the price of bonding with one's children in this way was being driven to distraction at every minute.

"Just groundhogs," he answered, wiping perspiration from his brow. James piped up from behind his hot dog.

"They're prairie dogs, Daddy!" he exclaimed, shaking his head adorably at his father's apparently inexcusable gaffe. The man put his stern expression back on.

"Either way, standing on top of their burrows so they can't escape is *not nice*."

I turned to peer out at where the children had been and noted a trail marker and what appeared to be a path. A glance at my map confirmed all the makings for a short hike up a nearby hill, perfect to watch the rapidly setting sun. I grabbed my backpack and took long steps to the trailhead, feeling the heaviness of my recently consumed dehydrated chicken and rice protesting with each stride.

The prairie dogs were just starting to poke their heads back out of their burrows as I was walking up. Far from the skittishness I expected, the one closest to me sat up even more and examined me with its dark, unblinking eyes. I crouched down a few feet away and examined it right back. Light brown fur, wiggling nose, and roughly the size of a teddy bear, the oversized rodent was positively huggable. Seeming to come up with its own, less positive, conclusions about me, the prairie dog started to emit a high-pitched yipping noise, summoning about ten of its brothers and sisters to peep out from their own burrows and join in the chorus. In the stillness of the early evening air, the noise was piercing.

"Okay, I'm going." I waved to the little animals and continued along the path.

Fifteen minutes later, the trail began to get steep and narrow, and I found myself tripping over and brushing against the scrubby vegetation on my way up the hill. I wished I had changed out of my shorts. My legs had little protection in case I came upon one of the rattlesnakes that called the park home. Moreover, each bush and clump of tall grass came preloaded with a colony of insect-life designed to make my life miserable. The horseflies were bad enough, but the mosquitoes were large enough to carry me away if they learned to cooperate. Already feeling itchy, I kicked into high gear and charged recklessly up the hillside, snakes be damned.

Tumbling out of a particularly thorny bush, I stumbled into the clearing that I had hoped would be at the top, and was hit full in the face with a blood-red sunset. Regaining my balance, exhilarated by the run and the utter beauty filling my eyes, I found the silent reverence with which I had greeted Badlands earlier suddenly insufficient. A crazy urge struck me and I gave into it with wild abandon.

Arms out to embrace the scenery, I laughed and twirled like an itchy, bizarre Maria Von Trapp. It was the same warm sort of lightness that had nearly lifted me into the air the last night of Bible school, and I welcomed it back. My face was to the sun and I was far from everything that worried me and I was grateful, so grateful. Much of the past few years had been a testament to the contrary, but this moment pulsed with the sentiment I had thrown happily at Pastor Andrew only a few days before: everything was so wonderful sometimes.

Badlands in its majesty watched without judgement. The young couple that I had failed to notice on the other side of the summit, watched with plenty. On the cusp of my seventh or eighth twirl, my eyes finally fell on them, and I stopped short.

"Oh, sorry!"

My face reddened like the dying sun as their undeniable posture registered: he, on one knee, her, hands on heart, face glistening with rapturous tears. They were beautiful and I was ridiculous and trampling on a very intimate proposal.

I turned around in a panic without another word and rocketed myself back into the bushes. The couple's laughter pealed like bells behind me, worsening my embarrassment, but reassuring me that I hadn't, perhaps, entirely ruined the moment. I made my way quickly down the hill, managing to trip over the same root I had stumbled on previously and reached level ground as darkness grew around me.

The mosquitoes were out in earnest now, and were sizeable enough that their bites produced sharp pinches on my arms and legs. Bemoaning the miserable itching that was bound to ensue, I kept my pace quick and eyes on my feet to avoid tripping, falling in a hole, or stepping on something with teeth. So all-consuming was my concentration that I almost didn't hear the cry of warning in time to look up.

Before me was a vast, dark, furry wall. I was close enough that it filled my vision entirely, and I blinked, not comprehending for a second before scrambling away in sober understanding. Backing up quickly, I saw that it was a bison standing directly on the trail, facing away from me. Its tail swished slowly as it turned its shaggy, massive head. One dark brown eye met mine.

"Back up!" A woman's voice called softly somewhere behind me, and I obeyed, slowly backing up until I was well over the recommended one hundred yards away. The bison turned its head forward again and continued slowly along the path.

"Thank you," I breathed, turning gratefully to my saviors. It was, predictably, the couple I had interrupted earlier. They grinned, no doubt recognizing me as well.

"No worries," the man said casually. "You were booking it fast enough that Frank was probably in more danger than you were."

"Frank? Is that the bison's name?" They nodded.

"Frank likes to hang out near this particular campsite for some reason," the woman explained. "We like to think he's a guardian spirit." We started walking slowly, keeping the same distance between us and Frank's retreating backside.

"So you've camped here before?" I surmised.

"Every summer," said the man, grabbing the woman's hand and swinging it lightly between them. "It's our sacred place."

They were dressed similarly, in an organic sort of fashion, with bandanas wrapped around their heads and matching stripes of sunburn across their cheeks. She looked at him with the sort of heart-stopping expression that daggered my heart cruelly. I looked down and twisted my own hands together self-consciously.

"Sorry about crashing your moment earlier," I said, "I'm assuming you said yes?"

"Of course," she replied. She showed me the rubber band that was now around her ring finger. "It's an inside joke," she explained, plucking at the band. "We decided a long time ago that we were well matched because we're both so flexible about everything."

"Congratulations," I said, because there was nothing else to say.

"And don't worry about it," added the man, in his easy-going way, "it's a good story."

"That it is," I agreed.

We had reached the campsite at last, Frank choosing to post up a distance from the farthest tent. I said good night to the happy couple and watched them float away in their cloud of happiness.

A mosquito landed on my cheek and bit hard. I crushed it against my face and wiped it away. In the flickering light of some nearby camp-fires, I saw my hand was smeared with blood. I zipped myself into the safety of my tent and watched the silhouettes of the little vampires as they landed futilely on the canvas. I was safe, but, unfortunately, the damage had already been done.

In the miserable, sleepless hours that followed, I slathered my flesh in aloe and tried not to scratch anything. As a distraction, I cracked open my National Parks Passport and flipped to the section on Badlands, reading the wildlife section with renewed interest.

Prairie dogs, it seemed, had a sophisticated language, beating out even the communication systems of chimps and dolphins in its intricacy. They were, I read, able to describe their predators in complete sentences as a warning to others, even going into details such as shape, size, and color. I thought back to the piercing yips the prairie dogs had broken into when prompted by my presence. It was fascinating to consider that they had been having back-and-forth conversations about me. It was even more fascinating that someone had both the time and patience to decode their language. I read on.

As it happened, I was very fortunate in my almost-run-in with Frank. According to the Passport, bison could charge at more than thirty miles an hour and do some real damage with their horns. Bison goring injuries reported in the last few years in the parks had exclusively been the result of guests getting within the recommended one hundred yard distance. I shuddered; I had been *far* closer than that. My parents would be furious if I were reckless enough to be killed by a cow.

My parents. I smacked my forehead and groaned. They had expected to hear from me by now. Struggling to wake up my dinosaur of a cell phone, I realized that I probably had no reception. They would have to wait a while longer. At least John could attest that he talked to me earlier today. The phone illuminated suddenly, coming to life with a brightness that made me squint. The screen displayed exactly where I had left it: the message.

"Hey, what's up?"

◄○►

6/23/2014

We skipped church today to get a good spot on the beach, and it was a good decision. It was spiritual anyway, somehow, the warmth of the sun and the sound of the waves, and holding the hand of the man I love. Because I do love him, and he loves me. He told me today.

He's going back home to New York tomorrow to visit his uncle and then he'll be out in the field for a week. Separation is obviously a reality of dating someone in the military, but it's miserable.

It's fine. I'll work and sleep and repeat ten times and then he'll be back and I'll be able to breathe again.

My eyes dripped. The mosquitoes outside my tent sang a ballad that the bites in my flesh seemed to throb in time to. I flipped the journal's pages, just two. I had stopped dating my entries. I likely didn't notice what day it was, but I knew that no more than two months had passed since the previous writing.

Tonight, on our bench underneath the magnolia tree, Austin asked me to marry him in the most "us" way possible. I turned to him and breathed my answer, falling into the sea-green eyes I would now be able to swim in for the rest of my life. He pushed a ring on my finger and kissed my hand.

This is it. This is all I need forever.

The handwriting was a bit shaky, probably from emotion, but also because the ring had been too big. It was several months later, when raising my hand in class had launched the ring clear across the room, that I would finally take it in to be resized.

How reluctant I was to take it off, that tangible evidence of his love. Closing my eyes, I could still remember the feeling, the miraculous joy and anticipation. It burned so clearly in the eyes of the couple that had come to save me from Frank. I turned my face into my sleeping bag and sobbed brokenly, praying uselessly that their love would stay perfect.

CHAPTER 13

I ROSE WITH THE sun, unsure of whether I had actually achieved sleep, and sat at a nearby picnic table, scribbling out a postcard to Julia, Ruth, and Danny. Frank lumbered over to join me, his hulking mass grazing peacefully at a safe distance, shaggy fur wet with dew.

Badlands at sunrise was, if possible, even more beautiful than in full light. The sun vaulted over the horizon, spilling rays of tangerine and marigold into the canyons. The strata of the rock formations caught the light and glowed bronze and what was previously earth was now molten.

I was staring open-mouthed at this marvel with all the grace that expression suggests when an errant fly took the opportunity to dive down my throat. I sputtered, looking around to ensure no one had been watching and hastily returned to my writing. The air began to grow warm around me, and this activated the new and enthusiastic mosquito bites that freckled my exposed skin. I scratched, miserable, and finished up my postcards with a new resolve. I suddenly felt too ridiculous to be a part of this glorious picture. I may have intended to stay longer, but the need to push on could not be ignored.

Packing up my tent took less than ten minutes and I found myself driving back to the ranger's station before most of my fellow campers had even stirred. I stopped once to consult my map, and once more to watch as a family of bighorn sheep hopped up an impossibly steep ridge. Despite such distractions and the long drive from one end of the park to the other, when I pulled into the parking lot, I found that the station would not open for another ten minutes. I made good use of the time and newfound service by sending an update to the family group chat and diving into my backseat in search of a stamp for Danny's postcard.

Days on the road, combined with impromptu purchases had turned the backseat of my truck into a disorganized pile of stuff, and I was upside down amongst the bags when my phone pinged a reply to my message. Extracting a crumpled book of stamps from the outer pocket of my duffel bag, I experienced a moment of panic when my attempt to right myself was not immediately successful. Stuck in a ludicrous position, rear in the air and feet resting atop the steering wheel, I wondered feebly if I should press on the horn and summon help. I would likely die of embarrassment to be rescued for such a reason, which was maybe not any better than suffocating under my duffels.

For a solid minute I was still, reconsidering most every choice I'd ever made and trying to force down a sort of hysteria that could have resulted in either tears or laughter. Fortunately, a mosquito bite itched on my cheek and I found I could move my right arm enough to scratch it. This movement shifted a few bags enough to loosen the crush around me. I was able to do a complicated wriggling motion before I was free enough to reach the headrest and haul myself backwards into the driver's seat.

The front door of the ranger's station was now propped open, an older man in uniform reaffixing a ring of keys to his belt. I waved sheepishly and grabbed my National Parks Passport before hopping out of my vehicle, hoping he somehow hadn't seen my predicament.

"Thought you mighta been in trouble there for a minute," the ranger chuckled, dashing those hopes immediately. A mailbox stood at the entrance, and I slipped the postcard inside as I followed him into the station, with the distinct feeling that it had been more trouble than it was worth.

The man went about opening the cash register and I wandered around on a different sort of stamp hunt until I found the small table littered with ink pads. I fumbled to open one and sent it clattering to the floor. Crouching down to clean up the mess, I shoulder-checked the table by accident and it scraped noisily on the tile, nearly falling over on top of me with the jostling. I couldn't help it: I swore quietly under my breath. What was *wrong* with me today?

"Don't hurt yourself, now," called the man from the register, greatly mistaken as to what I would find humorous at that moment. I ignored him and tried for quiet dignity as I straightened and mashed the Badlands stamp into the open pad of purple. I marked my passport precisely and snapped it closed, saying nothing as I turned and carefully strode to the door. A poster warning guests about the park's rattlesnakes and scorpions glared at me from a nearby wall. I glanced at it coolly on the way out, feeling there was some implicit insult there. Obviously, I was more of a danger to myself than anything else.

When I was finally resettled in the truck and with my seatbelt safely on, I checked my phone. Two texts, both from John.

"Hector and his mom expect you there by six."

He followed up with the ranch's address, somewhere outside of Bozeman, Montana. I scratched a mosquito bite on my thigh in an irritated fashion, and considered scripting a scathing reply. I had told him I would be camping the next few days, after all. It was not only a huge presumption on his part to make plans for me, it was insulting that he thought I'd need them.

At that moment, the bags in the back shifted ominously with the rumble of the truck's engine, and I decided I didn't have much room to be offended. Sighing, leaving any remaining feelings of cool competence behind, I put the truck in drive, and tapped out three words before tossing the phone theatrically into the tangle of the backseat.

"On my way."

◄○►

I'm getting to the point that I'm not sure if it's going to get better. I started off this year so badly and now it's too late to turn things around. Next year I won't skip teaching expectations and procedures and I'm sure that will make all the difference, but it's not much comfort given that it's only October now and I'm miserable. I'm not making the difference I thought I would. I don't think I'm very good at this at all.

I cry every morning because I don't want to go to school. Every day is just a struggle to get through and every weekend is just a dread-filled countdown to the next week. I can't remember the last time I wasn't panicked. It's getting really bad.

I don't know what I'm doing, and I don't even know enough about what I don't know to ask for help. I know that sounds stupid.

I need Austin. This deployment is so hopelessly long. I know better than to complain, but I don't know how to get through all of this without him. Ten months is a long time without your best friend.

◄○►

I had just passed the Badlands exit sign when I pulled over to sheepishly retrieve my phone amidst the crush of bags. It had a GPS, after all, and I didn't actually know where I was going. Punching in the address, I was gratified to see that the drive could be done in a day, and was glad I had gotten such an early start.

Though I needed to be mindful of time, I found myself stopping a short distance from the park in Rapid City. It just seemed like a shame to simply drive past Mount Rushmore without taking a look. As it turned out, it was a shame either way.

I remembered the Alamo—not in the patriotic sense, but as a ten year old on vacation with her parents being somewhat disappointed. If you've ever been, you know what I mean, because your trip probably looked somewhat like this:

You go to San Antonio, and you spend the day enjoying the swelter-ing and vibrant city. You explore the river walk for hours, maybe even take one of the barges with some other tourists and cool off with a cup of Bluebell Ice Cream that makes you forget the stickiness of the sweaty people you were just crowded on a boat with. You go to museums, eat in-credible food, shop in the Market Square and load up on Mexican vanilla (if you happen to, like my mother, be unable to resist a bargain). Then, you walk on already aching feet to one of the nation's icons, a place of legend that you had studied in school, and when you find it, dwarfed by the massive buildings that surround it, adobe gleaming dully in the dying afternoon sun, you are thoroughly underwhelmed.

I experienced this sensation again, a decade-and-a-half later, having paid an extravagant price to park and walk past the bookstore and guided tour buildings to peer up at the presidents on the hill. And I do mean *peer*. I hadn't realized that the monument pavilion was at such a distance, but I supposed it was wise to not have thousands of people walking over Thomas Jefferson's face every day. I stood and squinted for a while, sun-glasses having gone predictably missing, until it seemed silly to drag it out much longer. I stopped briefly at the bookshop for my stamp—the Passport included National Monuments—and, feeling only marginally better, climbed back into the truck for the long drive.

I wish there were more to say about the push between Rapid City and the ranch. It was beautiful, to be sure, in that perfect way that almost makes you want to shield your eyes, as that level of perfection couldn't possibly be meant for you. The sky was wide and blue and the road, wide and generous. Occasionally I would see cattle and horses. Once, I swear, a bald eagle flew overhead. I scrambled to take a picture on my phone for

Austin, a thoughtless impulse that earned me an hour of an awful, hollow feeling in my gut.

Eventually, the length of the drive drove me to listen to podcasts for the first time, and, boy, were they fun and useless. Did you know that bears have a nasal mucosa area one hundred times larger than a human's? Bears can smell actual fear. I mean, probably.

Bear podcasts kept me fairly entertained throughout a day behind the wheel, with just a quick stop at a drive through for nourishment and far too many french fries. I was chewing on my last few, in fact, when I finally pulled into the long dirt driveway that led to Ramos Ranch. Glancing at the clock, I was gratified to see that the time was a handsome five fifty-five. Putting my truck in park and looking out the windshield, I was equally gratified to see a man in boots coming towards me. He was, in truth, also handsome.

"Are you Miss Vera?"

The man was older, possibly in his fifties, with the strong, lean build and crinkly, piercing eyes of Clint Eastwood. He opened the driver's side door and extended a hand to help me out. I quickly brushed the crumbs from my shirt and hopped down, staggering a little after so long in the same position. He steadied me with a warm palm to the shoulder and I giggled a little foolishly.

"I am," I said, sounding so shy that I blushed red and hated myself. "And you are?"

"Matthew," he replied, looking away kindly while I willed my blush to fade. He checked his watch. "Hector and Mrs. Ramos have been expecting you. They're putting dinner on the table now. You come on with me for now; we can get your bags later."

I nodded, internally giving myself a stern talking-to. It was unlike me to go gooey over a man's appearance, even if that man happened to look like a particularly dreamy cowboy. I firmly steered my attention from his square jaw to my surroundings as I followed him up the drive.

He led me into the main house, an impressive log cabin construction with dark green shutters and a wrap-around porch with porch swings so wide and welcoming I was tempted to set up camp right there. The wide double-doors opened into a generously couched family room, guarded on every side by stuffed elk and moose heads. We crossed the room beneath their perpetual gaze and entered a large dining area. A commanding dining table rested there beneath a massive chandelier made of a cluster of antlers. Already the table groaned beneath huge platters of the heartiest foodstuffs known to man, and I stared, a little frightened by the abundance that I had not expected. A tall, striking woman walked in then, removing an apron, and brightened at the sight of us.

"Vera! Welcome, welcome!" She opened her arms wide and embraced me tightly enough to elicit surprise, then pulled away slightly to examine my forearms, spotted from mosquito bites, and ravaged by hours of idle scratching on the road. "You have not been taking care of yourself," she scolded, reproving in an affectionate sort of way.

"Ah," I said, sheepish, but warming to her instant familiarity, "I bought sunscreen but not bug spray." She shook her head in the loving disappointment of a maternal figure and gestured to a nearby chair.

"Why don't you relax for a minute? We will be eating shortly." She turned to Matthew, "Can you call the others? I need to find my son."

"The other's?" I asked, as Matthew turned and disappeared back out the door.

"We're a family here at Ramos Ranch," she smiled, "Everyone has a place at the table."

This proved to be true. A short time later, I found myself wedged between two huge ranch hands, whose names I had been told and then promptly forgot. Matthew sat talking quietly with some of the older hands down the table while the younger, summer hires joked and laughed at the other side. It truly felt like a big family, rougher than most, perhaps, but companionable. I soon felt very comfortable, stuffing myself with roasted chicken and potatoes and basking in the warm attention of Mrs. Ramos and the somewhat cautious notice of Hector.

"What a journey you've had!" Mrs. Ramos exclaimed as I finished my quick summary of the past few days. She had a heart-shaped face and pretty, smiling brown eyes. Her son was like her in looks, a bit more tanned, maybe, with a shadow of stubble across his jaw. He was more reserved than I had expected from John's stories and had met my eyes only twice so far. "What a fearless young woman you are! I could expect that of John's sister, of course." Hector looked up at that.

"Mom, you're gushing," he said, exasperated. "She doesn't want to hear all that; I know *I* don't." Mrs. Ramos looked immediately crestfallen at his reproof and my heart went out to her.

"No, it's okay, really," I reassured her. "I appreciate the compliment though, honestly, I am decidedly *not* fearless." My brain struggled not to summon thoughts of Austin's text. "I could brag about my little brother all day, though." She smiled at me and nodded.

"When my husband passed, he sent me the most beautiful condolence letter," she said, with not a little emotion. "And he's taken care of my boy," she added tremulously, "even when he's been stubborn and reckless."

"That does sound like John," I said. Her reaction may have seemed overdone for someone she'd never met in person, but it was just like my brother to make such a strong impression. He had an almost magical ability to endear himself to people wherever he went and, it appeared, several places he hadn't. Mrs. Ramos dabbed her eyes with a napkin and put her hand over mine, pressing it warmly. Evidently, I was accepted simply by association. Hector, rolling his eyes, was finally driven to addressing me directly for the first time.

"What did you think of Badlands?" he asked, with an air of steering the conversation into less sentimental waters.

"It was amazing. I've never been anywhere so stunning," I replied. "I think I could spend my whole life there if I could avoid the mosquitoes. And running into bison," I added as an afterthought. Hector nodded, as if I'd given the right answer.

"Some of those bison can sneak up on you," he said. "When I was in high school there was one that would always guard the junior ranger's campsites at night."

I could hazard a guess.

"Frank?" I asked.

Hector laughed in reply and his eyebrows, tensed over the bridge of his nose, relaxed. It was a startlingly good laugh, deep and strong, and I felt some of my own tension melt away with the sound of it, just as his own frostiness had started to ease.

"So he's still at it, huh? That's good to hear."

Propelled more easily by the new subject, we chatted at length about the sights and history of the park, and I found a kindred spirit in Hector and his admiration for nature. He spoke of the parks and his experiences with a deep respect, and had a wide range of knowledge from years of hiking, camping, and volunteering. It was easy to imagine him spending his life as a park ranger.

The ranch hands at the table, not burdened by conversation, were done first and pushed back from the table with the satisfied sounds of hard work well rewarded. With brief but sincere thanks to Mrs. Ramos, they departed the dining room, Matthew looking back to nod politely to me on his way out the door. We heard the crunch of gravel as they made their way behind the house, ostensibly to the as yet unseen stables to complete evening chores.

"Those calves are going to need branding soon," Mrs. Ramos commented to Hector. "I'm sure Matthew would appreciate your help with that." He nodded.

"I'd planned on it already, Mama." He kissed his mother on the cheek and took her empty plate. "I need to repair some of the fence line out there too." He glanced my way, considering me for a hesitant moment. "Sun's up at five thirty, if you're interested."

"I'm sure Vera will want to rest a bit," protested Mrs. Ramos. She looked at me, embarrassed. "Please don't feel the need to strain yourself." I was already on my feet, however, gathering the last of the dishes and following Hector into the kitchen.

"I'm happy to help," I called to her, "I'm not the least bit tired anyway."

Enlivened by the good food and company, I found this to actually be true. Plunging my hands into the warm soapy water filling the farm-style sink, I felt at ease. The memory of Austin's text, sitting unanswered on my phone, lingered annoyingly in my brain, but I scrubbed extra hard at the dishes until both they, and my thoughts, were clean again.

Chapter 14

February is always hard, but this one has been longer and colder and darker than I think I've ever experienced. It's hard to write when there's nothing good to say. Work is about surviving now, and I can at least say I'm doing that.

Austin's Uncle James committed suicide last night; I just got the call. James had always struggled with depression and Austin had just convinced him to start going to therapy right before he left on deployment. We had a lot of hope it would help.

This is such a shock. Or, will be, once I tell him. He still doesn't know, and the sun's not up in his part of the world for several hours. I should let him sleep, right? That would be the kindest option. Or is it wrong of me to withhold that information? It's all so confusing.

This man raised my husband. Austin's father walked out when he was eight, and, when his mother died a year or so later, James took him in. He's the only family Austin has.

How am I going to tell him that he's gone?

◄○►

T HE NEXT DAY I found there was little time to ease into the realities of a cattle ranch.

"I didn't agree to this," I protested, revolted by the task Hector had set me to.

I was standing ankle-deep in the dirt outside a small pasture that had been set aside for the distasteful tasks we were to perform that day. I looked beseechingly at Matthew, who was busy leading calves into the pen.

"Sure you did," retorted Hector. He adopted a high-pitched, eager-to-please sort of voice, "*I'm HAPPY to help!*'" Matthew snorted as I swatted off Hector's hat in retaliation. It landed in the dust, kicking up a cloud that coated my legs in a dirt-orange hue.

"Your mom just said branding," I protested, "no one mentioned anything about *castrating*." A bull snorted from a nearby pen and I shivered. Neither he nor I wanted what was about to happen.

Matthew picked up Hector's hat and dusted it off on his jeans, fixing me with a steely eye that seemed to analyze my entire being with some dubiousness. I knew I was whining, but I crossed my arms and frowned at him anyway, already beginning to sweat in the early light. The two had questioned my choice of long sleeves, but I had brushed them off, claiming—truthfully—that I was always cold. As beads of perspiration began to trickle from my temples, I knew the rising sun would be calling my bluff, even if none of the ranch hands did. He finally smiled and plopped the hat back on Hector's head, pushing the brim down and towards his face until he stumbled back a step, a real older-brother move.

"You're not castrating anything," he said reassuringly, guiding me to the pen, "Hector's just giving you a hard time." He gestured to the small group of calves huddled on the other side of the fence, fur gleaming darkly in the sun. "These are all females anyhow."

"Oh," I stared at the calf closest to me, her brown eyes large and intelligent, starred by long lashes. "So what's the job?" Hector stepped forward, slightly dusty, but dignity still intact.

"These calves are all about sixty days old, so they are due for their brands and vaccines. I'll be handling the needles, but we think you should be able to do the branding." I stared at the calf. Her eyes seemed to grow larger, until I could see myself in them. I was suddenly very dubious of my abilities.

"I don't want to hurt them," I said.

I hated how soft that sounded, but hated the idea of singeing innocent flesh more. Hector grabbed an electric razor and began shaving down a patch of fur on the calf's hip. She mooed nervously but remained still and obedient under his firm hand. He then picked a brand from out of the nearby bucket, holding it up so that I could examine the brass backwards R.

"It won't hurt them. We freeze brand here," he said, grabbing a metal pole from a nearby bucket. I could see a fine mist rising from it. "The brand is cooled with the liquid nitrogen back there and has to be held to the hide for a short period of time, I'd say about fifty seconds." He touched the brand to the calf's hip and pressed firmly, working it slightly back and forth. He counted out under his breath and then dropped the brand back in the bucket and retrieved another. "Each calf needs two R's for Ramos Ranch. I like to overlap them a little."

"Gotta get those style points," Matthew added.

"And that doesn't hurt them?" The little calf trotted away with Matthew's capable guidance for vaccination. Hector shook his head.

"It doesn't burn the skin, just makes the hair grow back white where the brand was."

"That's okay, I guess." I reached hesitantly for the electric razor and situated myself in front of a new calf. Matthew, returning from the pen, peeked over her back at me, then at Hector. The two men stood still, watching, it seemed, for me to make a mistake. The pressure of their skepticism toughened my resolve, and I gripped the clippers firmly as I began.

The whole process took a little over an hour. I made few mistakes under Hector's careful instruction and even helped Matthew to administer some of the vaccinations. The two offered no words of praise or encouragement, but I understood the implicit compliment: I was doing well, so nothing needed to be said. I should have taken that attitude for my own, but as my confidence grew, so did my mouth. Truth be told, I may have bragged a little. Matthew was quick to put me in my place.

"Well," he said, in the wake of my boasting, "sounds like you'll be up for castrating the bulls tomorrow after all." He was probably joking, by the twinkle in his eye, but I shut my mouth after that just in case.

After lunch, which was an abundance of sandwiches, Hector and I headed out to repair the fence line, a task which was easier said than done. There were miles upon miles of fence, ranging mud and dust, stream and knee-high grass, and every inch needed to be carefully inspected. Any gaps or weaknesses in the barbed wire would need to be repaired to dissuade any predators tempted by the juicy livestock. Any loose fence posts needed reinforcement, so that a mischievous cow wouldn't knock it over in an ill-advised bid for freedom. Hector was meticulous in his inspection, and not overly chatty, and I trailed along behind him with the pliers, feeling more unnecessary than helpful. With little instruction needed, our progress along the fence was largely silent, and I found myself falling back into my solitary musings until Hector finally spoke up.

"So how long do you think you'll be staying for?"

I looked at him in surprise, wondering where that had come from. He had his eyes on the steel wire he was twisting and didn't meet my gaze. I frowned. I thought I had done well on my first day ranching, but maybe needing to teach me was more of an inconvenience to the operation than I thought.

Or maybe it was my presence in general. I had assumed, based on John's reassurance, that I was welcome, but my interactions with Hector so far hadn't exactly confirmed this. Aside from warming briefly to the topic of Badlands last night, his behavior towards me remained largely confusing. He had picked up this cowboy sort of gruffness this morning that alternated between wry teasing and ignoring me entirely. His face betrayed nothing as I studied him now, watching him squint a little as he clipped a few wires to barb them.

"I don't know," I admitted, taking the pliers back from him, "Not long." I opened and closed the pliers nervously. My gloves, borrowed and too large, fumbled the tool and I dropped it in the dust. "I hadn't really planned on coming at all. John sort of went ahead without me in arranging all of this."

"He does that," Hector replied, retrieving the pliers and straightening. We advanced another two feet before he found something else in the fence he didn't like.

"He mentioned your mom has needed some extra hands since your dad passed," I watched as a shadow seemed to pass over Hector's face. "I'm really sorry about that." He shrugged.

"It was a few years ago. We've adjusted," he spat casually into the dirt and pushed back his hat to wipe his forehead. He played cowboy pretty well, but it didn't entirely suit him somehow. "Matthew has had to take on a bigger role, obviously. We've also downsized a little, so we don't actually need as many hands as we have now."

"Oh." I felt, suddenly, very much out of place. Was I just imposing on this family? Discomfort crashed over me and I began to wrack my brain for some excuse, any, to get back on the road immediately. Hector glanced at me, and was immediately contrite.

"No, don't get the wrong idea," he said, correctly interpreting my face. "You're welcome to stay however long you want to. My mom has been dying for some company. Cowboys aren't the best conversationalists." He paused. A bull stood placidly a few yards from the fence, eyeing us calmly. "I'm not either, to tell the truth, but I'm sure you've figured that out by now."

Seeming more personable than he had all day, he gave me a hesitant smile that I returned with interest. Perhaps what I had taken for chilliness was just introversion. I had been too wrapped up in my momentary insecurities to even consider the possibility, which reflected more about me than it did him. Chastened by the realization, I hurried to extend kindness.

"I don't mind. I appreciate any company at the moment," I assured him. "The solo portions of my trip have been less than wonderful so far." In a few sentences, I filled him in on some of the less glamorous moments of my journey from Jonesboro to Badlands, which I had neglected to mention the night before out of embarrassment. He laughed as I recalled the letdown of the giant fork and the disastrous proposal I crashed.

"Sounds eventful," he said. "You might find it a little slow here in comparison." He hooked his elbows carefully over the recently repaired strand of barbed wire and absently examined the bull. I did the same, gazing out with sympathy: this bull was slated for castration come morning. "I usually have to take off every few weeks to break the monotony."

"What do you do?" I asked.

"Camping," he said. "Yellowstone's not a bad distance from here. I usually manage to get some good hiking in. Matthew and a few of the others sometimes come with me."

"That sounds like a good time."

"It is. I've been trying to get my mom to go, but she always makes an excuse at the last minute. I think it reminds her too much of my dad; they used to go backpacking together all the time." He straightened up and took off his hat, fanning his face casually. "It's a shame, because I think it'd really be a good thing to get her off this ranch."

"Does she get lonely?" It was a beautiful place, but I could see the ranch being pretty isolating after a time.

"It's not that, exactly," Hector shook his head, squinting as if trying to see the right words through the glare of the sun. "There are just so many memories here, you know? It's like she's trying to hang on to them by not making any more." He pushed off the fence and turned back the way we had come. "I think we can probably stop for today."

The crickets had begun to sing and I looked up in surprise to see the sky streaked through with pink. We began walking back in silence, inhaling the sweet smell of sunbaked grass.

It had been an early morning, and a long day besides, but I felt good. I spent ten months of the year leaving my classroom in exhaustion, having worked much the same hours, but this was tiredness of a different kind. It was a sweet and slow weariness that seemed to know a good meal and pleasant company were ahead, and any additional work could wait until morning. I took a deep, calming breath as the air turned golden around us.

"Hey, Vera?" Hector turned to me as we walked.

"Hector?" I answered. The tough-guy cowboy persona was gone suddenly, replaced by camaraderie with a touch of nerves. It suited him.

"John didn't send you to, like, convert me, did he?" I looked over at him, puzzled.

"*Convert* you? To what, the metric system?"

"No," he snorted and rolled his eyes, trudging heavily in step with me. "You know what I mean." I shook my head, honestly bewildered. "Like...to Christianity? Or spirituality or something?" He chuckled a bit at the look on my face, "You sure you're John's sister?"

A momentary silence fell between us as his words hit harder than he probably intended them to. I frowned, almost embarrassed. I hadn't been like John in a long time. If he had intended for me to proselytize to his friend during my stay, he was sure to be disappointed.

"Has he been, um," *Obnoxious.* That was the word that had come to mind during John's most recent come-to-Jesus talk with me over the phone. I searched for a kinder descriptor, "...persistent?"

"Kind of? I dunno," he shrugged and shook his head, "It's probably not worth talking about."

"Right," I drawled, sarcastically. "Sounds like it." The path had begun to transition from dirt to gravel. "But you might as well tell me about it now that you've said something." Hector swatted at a fly that was circling us and considered before drawing inhaling heavily.

"So, my dad was pretty bad off for a long time." He let out the breath in a long sigh.

"Like, sick?" I guessed. He nodded.

"He was diagnosed with Parkinson's when I was eight," he added, spitting the name of the disease like it was bitter in his mouth.

"That's so young," I said, shocked. "For both of you, I mean."

"Yeah," he nodded again. "He managed it for a while, but by my freshman year of college he was getting really bad." He kicked at a rock in the path and it flew with surprising precision, striking a far-off fencepost. He raised both hands in a mock celebration that contrasted oddly with the glum expression on his face. *Goal.* "The disease starts to take your mind in the last stages. John heard me trying to talk with him over the phone a lot, and eventually I had to tell him what was going on. It was rough."

"That must've been awful for you."

"Yeah," he shoved his hands in his pockets and examined his feet moodily.

"Did you end up going home?" John hadn't mentioned any of this.

"Nah," he said, face dark. "I was a coward." He grimaced painfully, eyes still on his feet. "I was in denial, I think; he'd been sick for so long. Not that it matters," he added, chastising himself, "Mom needed me. But I stayed until the end of spring semester. Dad was pretty much gone by then."

"I'm so sorry, Hector." I hardly knew what to say. He was squinting his eyes and sniffing forcefully in the way that boys do when they want to seem tough but need to cry. I wanted to give him a hug but didn't know if that would just make him more uncomfortable.

"Anyway," he continued, with the air of getting it over with, "I pretty much spent freshman year making every bad decision I could." He had finally taken his eyes off his shoes, and was squinting up at the sky, now shot through with orange and purple. "John seemed to understand, as squeaky-clean as he was. I probably wouldn't have passed my first year if he hadn't gotten mom to send a letter to the dean. That's the only reason why they waived my exam grades. He was always helping me out, even when I didn't want it."

"That sounds like John," I said, suddenly proud of the exact characteristic that had been so irritating to me earlier.

"Yeah," sighed Hector, "he's a good friend. But . . . " he seemed to struggle for words here, "He started, I don't know, *ministering* to me afterwards. Do you know what I mean?"

"Uh huh." Did I ever.

"Once I was back on my feet, so to speak, I really just wanted to act like everything was normal, but John kept dangling religion at me," he huffed, sincerely frustrated. "There wasn't a single Sunday last year that he wasn't trying to haul me into some pew," he shook his head wearily, "like that would solve any of my problems."

"Yeah, that also sounds like John," I sighed. "He's a good kid, but he pushes it sometimes."

"When he called me about bringing you out here, I kind of figured it was another plan of attack," Hector admitted gravely. I burst out laughing at the thought. It was all so ridiculous. After a moment, Hector joined in. "John's my best friend, and I know I owe him a lot," he continued, smiling a little, "but I'm not really cool with him evangelizing my family while we're vulnerable."

"I completely get that," I assured him quickly. "I lose patience with that sort of thing myself." Then, figuring I may as well be honest, "And I can't say I'm in any position to lecture you on faith. Mine's shaky at best. John gets on me about that too." I was stricken momentarily with guilt at the admission. Hector, however, was all relief.

"Well, that's good," he replied. We walked a few more minutes in an easier silence before a question occurred to me.

"So, were you scared?"

"Scared?"

"Yeah," I said, grinning, "That I was going to push you in a river and baptize you or something?" He laughed.

"Naw," he said. Our feet crunched on gravel. We had arrived at the driveway to the main house. "John just always hits me with these deep questions out of nowhere. About life, death, meaning . . . It's . . . startling." I smiled. I could definitely relate.

"Are you afraid to think about those things?"

He looked at me, and in his gaze was, unquestionably, a challenge.

"Aren't you?"

CHAPTER 15

If I could take his pain, I would do it without question.

He's untethered, drifting around the house aimlessly like a ghost. When I speak to him, try to bring him out of it, he looks at me like he doesn't even know who I am. It scares me, and I can't snap him out of it.

I was so happy he was able to come home, even if it was for a funeral. But he's not home. Not really.

What do I do?

—◦—

W E ENTERED THE HOUSE through a side door that led into the beautiful and spacious kitchen. Open shelving lined walls that gleamed with intricate tiling. The butcher block counters glowed a warm, red-brown and held colorful pots of trailing plants at every corner. The center of the room was dominated by a huge wooden island, nearly the size of the dining room table, with a natural-edge. It hosted a large stove-top and was circled with rustic wooden barstools.

Mrs. Ramos was sitting on one of these stools, phone to her ear. A large pitcher of something rested at her elbow, and she gestured to it when she spotted us, smiling an invitation. Hector moved quietly to the cupboard for glasses, and I knew that he had also noticed that his mother's eyes were rimmed in red.

"Of course," she was saying, as I settled onto a stool at a distance. Hector poured me a glass from the pitcher and slid it to me down the counter like an old-fashioned bartender. I took a cautious sip and was grateful to find it was as delicious as it was refreshing: lemonade with subtle touches of berry and something else. *Rosemary*, I concluded, taking another discerning sip. Hector settled beside me and took a swig from his own glass, his eyes fixed on his mother as she finished her phone call.

When Mrs. Ramos finally sighed her goodbye, her emotion was obvious. She hung up the phone with a regretful tap of the end button and placed it shakily back in its cradle. Tears oozed from the corners of her eyes, and she pressed the heels of her hands to them, breathing deeply as we watched, concerned. When she emerged from behind her hands a moment later, however, it was with a smile every bit as wide and gracious as it had ever been.

"So how did it go today?" she asked.

"Fine," said Hector, cautiously. "Who was that?"

"Your Aunt Rosa," she said, exhaling the words as if to push them from her. "Nadia is going to be coming up for a visit soon." From the corner of my eyes, I could see Hector stiffen through the shoulders, flesh tensing into stone.

"For how long?" he asked through gritted teeth. Mrs. Ramos had risen from the counter and was at the refrigerator, pulling out containers of beef and bags of peppers.

"I'm not sure, *mijo*," she said. "As long as she needs to be."

"You mean as long as Rosa doesn't feel like having her around," he challenged.

"Hector," his mother began, her voice a weary caution sign.

"You know it's the truth," he persisted doggedly. "She pawns Nadia off on you, Mom. And you just let her take advantage of you."

Mrs. Ramos took a slow breath in through her nose and let it out through her mouth in a thin, weary sigh.

"I've made my decision, Hector."

Hector stared at her, something like anger working in the hold of jaw.

"Sure!" he exclaimed, "Why not?" He pushed away from the counter and the stool scraped gratingly across the wood floor. I saw Mrs. Ramos flinch at the sound. "You know, why not just adopt her? What's another problem on top of everything else, right?"

He took his glass and headed up the stairs, his tread quick and heavy as he made his retreat. The uncharacteristic outburst seemed to restart Mrs. Ramos' tears, and she wiped them away impatiently as she continued gathering ingredients. My presence at the counter was regrettable to both of us, but I couldn't think of a way to leave graciously. After a few awkward moments passed, I fell back on my usual tactic.

"Let me help with something," I stood and relieved her of an armful of groceries. She seemed too preoccupied to give much instruction, so I began chopping the vegetables, creating thin, uniform strips of the peppers and onions. Mrs. Ramos circled the kitchen distractedly for a few moments before she finally sank back into her chair and indulged herself in a tissue. For a few minutes, there was only silence, punctuated by the rhythmic ticking of the clock and my knifework.

"My sister is an addict," Mrs. Ramos offered suddenly. I worked to keep the knife chopping steadily, nodding at her to continue. "She has been in and out of treatment for twenty years, but she's never stayed clean for very long."

"I'm sorry to hear that," I replied, awkwardly. It wasn't a conversation I had expected or prepared for. I seemed to be having a lot of heart-to-hearts lately, but I sure wasn't getting any better at them. "I'm sure that's been hard on you."

"It's worse for her daughter."

"That's Nadia?"

"Yes." Mrs. Ramos absently pulled my empty glass to her and poured the rest of the lemonade inside. "Sweet, beautiful Nadia." Her voice carried more than a hint of regret. "She has had a terrible life, and her mother has hurt her so badly."

"Then it's good that she's coming here," I said, electing to be supportive. "Being with family is important." Hoping that Mrs. Ramos had intended to make fajitas with the ingredients she had gathered, I rummaged for a large skillet and placed it on the stove to preheat.

"She's kind of a handful," she replied dully. "She's never had any real parenting and it shows. Hector could tell you stories . . . " She trailed off and sighed. "He's probably right. I'm not up to taking on my sister's problems," she sniffed sadly, "But I can't bear to turn away Nadia. She's someone I can still help."

The last word trembled in the air. I thought of what Hector had told me, how long she had cared for her husband as he deteriorated from incurable disease. She had done it all by herself, facing each day knowing that she couldn't save him. It made sense that she would want to help Nadia. For that matter, I realized suddenly, it made sense that she wanted to help *me*.

She had risen from her spot at the counter and now relieved me of my place at the stove, taking the package of beef from my hand and replacing it with the glass of lemonade. She was shaking some, I noted, and I was filled with a compassion that drove away any previous feelings of awkwardness. *Who helps you?* I wondered suddenly, and then, just as quickly, resolved to be that person.

"Kids who have undergone trauma, like Nadia, I'm assuming, need a lot of care and consistency," I said. "I've worked with quite a few troubled kids at my school, and I know how difficult it can be."

As we whirled around the kitchen preparing dinner together, I spilled a few harrowing tales of previous students that had been uniquely challenged in life, and therefore tremendously challenging to manage and teach.

I dredged up the student I had taught my second year, who came to me in sixth grade as a fourteen-year-old that had yet to learn to read and threw fists to distract from this fact. I pulled out the slip of a girl my year teaching seventh grade that had fished through my wallet for items to steal.

"I didn't have any cash," I laughed, "Imagine hoping to find money on a teacher! But she took all the cards that were in there. The debit and credit cards I could freeze and replace pretty quickly, but I do miss my library card."

I touched on the sexual harassment that became daily when teaching boys who had come from households of abuse, and the single-minded drama and violence coming from girls who had suffered the same.

I was surprised to find tears in my eyes in my recounting. The ache in my heart as I dredged each one from the dark, cramped space where they lived was an irritated pain that seemed to change into something else entirely when it was allowed to stretch.

"You cared very much for these children," Mrs. Ramos noted, sagely passing me my own tissue.

"I guess so," I said, and then laughed at the surprise in my own voice. "I mostly spent my days so frustrated there wasn't room to feel anything else." I paused, struck by another thought. "They're kids, you know? And they were all so damaged and challenged in ways that weren't fair. They needed someone to do right by them."

"And that fell to you," she said.

"Yeah," I replied.

The meat was sizzling now, and Mrs. Ramos was darting back and forth from spice cabinet to pan, sprinkling in different substances with a trained eye for approximate measurement. I found the tortillas and began to slip them into their basket.

"Nadia is like that," she said suddenly, above the singing of browned beef. "She's had to be the adult in many situations, and it's hurt her badly. It's hard sometimes to know what is coming from a place of trauma." I nodded. There was noise coming from the dining room; the cowboys had arrived and dinner needed to be served.

"I'll call Hector," I volunteered, and slipped out, but not before Mrs. Ramos paused me with a gentle hand on my forearm.

"Thank you, Vera," she said, brown eyes warm as she looked into mine. "I'm so glad you're here with us."

My face warmed a little at the attention, but I found myself smiling as I took the stairs two at a time, arriving a little breathless at Hector's door. It was ajar, and I knocked on the frame before leaning, freezing as my surroundings registered. It was a lot to take in.

I invite you to meditate for a moment on the term "nature enthusiast." Let your mind conjure up words and images related to all that the name implies. Then, if you will, take those concepts and mold them into the form of a bedroom for a teenage boy. This, I believe, was the process of whatever interior decorator had designed Hector's bedroom.

Leaves of all shape, size, and color dotted the ceiling as less specific children may have blanketed theirs with glow-in-the-dark stars. The walls were covered corner-to-corner with impressive, framed posters of National Parks and monuments. The Grand Canyon graced the wall to my right with earthy majesty; Devil's Tower loomed over his headboard. His bedside table held a lamp fashioned like a pine tree and an impressive model of a grizzly bear made out of legos. The desks and shelves, all painted a subtle hunter green, were lined with books and manuals on forestry and wildlife. A forest ranger hat, in the recognizable Smokey the Bear style, hung from the same hat rack that held his dusty cowboy number. Hector's interests were well represented in this space.

At the same time, a discerning eye could make out the few items that didn't blare obviously upon first arrival. These didn't totally match their surroundings, and interested me intensely as important pieces to the puzzle that was Hector: the Star Wars action figures that battled across his desk, the box of stationary (open! used!), the small picture of himself kissing the cheek of a glowy-eyed girl.

"Is dinner ready?"

To my credit, I did not jump, though in my inspection of the room I had completely forgotten its inhabitant. He was lying on his twin bed, hands behind his head, apparently looking up into the foliage on the ceiling as if lost in thought. The look on his face was undoubtedly sour, though his tone spoke no ill-will towards me as an intruder. He was clearly still upset over his cousin coming to stay. After my conversation with Mrs. Ramos, I was less than sympathetic towards him, but couldn't see any real benefit to pointing out what a baby he was being.

"It's a feast," I said, striving for casual neutrality. I scooped a stormtrooper from his desk top and twirled it between my fingers, smiling mischievously. "I didn't know you were a Trekkie!" He frowned, successfully distracted.

"It's *Star Wars*," he corrected in a wounded tone. He got up and retrieved the figure from me, placing it carefully back on the desk. "And, yes, it's sort of a new development."

"This is my brother's influence, isn't it?"

"It's the one conversion he's managed," he smiled wryly. "I hadn't seen any of the movies before, so it's been an education."

"I bet."

John's fanaticism had become a bit of a joke in our family. As a child, he tortured us with repeated watchings of T*he Phantom Menace* until the tape tragically—some might say *suspiciously*—unraveled in the rewinder one day. He had dressed up as Darth Maul that Halloween, the red face paint leaving his skin pink for a week afterwards. He had a large collection of Star Wars T-shirts and, the last time I could recall seeing him, he had been wearing a little number that spelled 'Pew Pew Pew' across the front in the movie's famous font. I had teased him for it, but he replied that I simply couldn't appreciate good cinema as a book-addled English teacher. He had a point, I supposed. In spite of all my exposure, or perhaps *because* of it, I could never really get into the movies like he could. I caught up the picture frame next.

"Is this your girlfriend?"

"That's Hallie," he replied, his cheekbones pinkening slightly. He took the frame from my hands and returned it gently to its place. "And, yes," he added, with dignity.

"Is this the one you climbed the building over?" I asked, with a flash of memory. He laughed, surprised.

"John told you about that? No, that was Claire. Or maybe Katherine?" he thought a moment and then shrugged. "Either way, not worth it." I opened my mouth to ask *so many* questions, but he shooed me towards the door before I could form any words. "Enough invading my privacy; let's go eat."

Dinner was a relatively stiff affair. Mrs. Ramos put on a face of ferocious cheer that could not distract from the tears that hadn't yet stopped flowing. Hector reverted to a quiet sulkiness and I joined the cowboys in eating with great gusto so that I could escape in a matter of minutes. Stomach grumbling its protest about my rate of consumption, I retreated back into the kitchen and began washing dishes with my ears tuned on high. I was soon rewarded for my eavesdropping.

"Hallie can still come to visit, Hector," Mrs. Ramos was saying, indignantly, "For goodness sake this house is big enough for ten extra people, let alone two."

"It's not about capacity, Mom," he replied. "Nadia is *a lot*. I don't want Hallie to have to deal with that. I don't want *you* to have to deal with that!"

"And what would you have me do?" she asked. I could hear tears in her voice once more. "Leave her on the street? She's *family*."

"So's Aunt Rosa," he shot back, "And we've just sat back and watched her ruin her life." There was a significant pause. "I'm sorry, Mama," Hector murmured. He had gone too far.

"I have tried so hard to save my sister from herself," his mother replied. Her voice shook now, dangerously. "Your father and I, we—for *years*, we—"

"I know, I know," muttered Hector. "You couldn't have done anything more. I know that. I spoke without thinking. Sorry."

"But we can do this kindness for your cousin, at least," she added. "And I need to do that. I *need* to, okay?" There was another pause, and a barely audible sniff.

"Okay," he said. "But I'm telling Hallie to cancel her flight." There was another long pause. My fingers, submerged whole minutes now in the soapy water, sported a pruney texture reminiscent of the canyons of Badlands. "And, Mama, I need you to remember that I'm going back to school soon. And after that . . . I don't know where I'll be, but it probably won't be here."

"I know that," she replied stiffly. I could practically hear Hector's head shaking.

"No," he argued, "Look, I—" he sighed, frustrated, "I should have come home when you needed me, I know that and I'll never stop being sorry." His voice, hoarse with emotion, was barely a whisper. Abandoning all morality in my curiosity, I drew my hands from the sink slowly and crept a bit closer towards the door, still just barely able to make out what he said next. "I was not the son I should have been. But I can't take his place here. You know he wouldn't even want me to. And he definitely wouldn't want you to be stuck taking care of *another* person, especially when it means you're not taking care of yourself. You know that, right?" Mrs. Ramos didn't reply. "Please just think about it."

Hector sighed heavily and I heard a scrape of a chair. I hurriedly clanged some pans together and was the picture of absorbed busyness when he came through the door, empty plate in hand. He smirked at me with a sort of grim acceptance, as though he knew I was listening, but said nothing. He handed me his plate and disappeared again.

Upstairs, I heard him retreat back into his room, this time closing the door firmly behind him. I finished the dishes and put away the left-overs in silence, turning off the lights to the kitchen and making my way to bed soon after. Mrs. Ramos never emerged from the dining room.

Chapter 16

I'm writing this alone in bed. That wouldn't be so unusual, except that Austin got back from his second deployment a week ago. But here I am, alone in bed.

He's been taking his laptop out to the couch every evening and surfing the web for hours while watching old movies on mute on the TV. Eventually, he falls asleep right there in the living room and then will leave for work before I can even get up in the morning.

It's been weird and kind of hurtful, honestly. He says he's been doing extra assignments for work, but won't elaborate. He talks to me so little these days.

◄○►

NADIA ARRIVED WITH A literal bang.

I was in the living room, being eaten alive by one of the far-too-comfortable couches after an unsuccessful day of trying to learn to ride a horse bareback. Matthew had assigned me the oldest, gentlest mare with the widest back, to no avail. No sooner would one of the ranch hands boost me up than I would slide unceremoniously over the other side and into the dust. The ground was not soft, and my companions were unrestrained in their laughter. So, after a few hours of it, I had retired for the day and sought out a sympathetic seat to minister to my bruised backside and ego.

I was just slipping into a weary nap when the front door opened and then was ferociously slammed closed. Peering out from my nest, I beheld a butterfly of a girl, small, ponytailed, queenly, sling a huge duffle bag into the living room and charge into the kitchen yelling wildly.

"*Auntie, I'm here!*" She screeched into the broken peace with a gusto surprising coming from such a tiny frame. On the wall, even the moose heads seemed to wince at the noise. The front door opened and closed again, much more gently this time. Matthew entered, looking uncharacteristically harried. It appeared Nadia had slammed the door in his face.

"Mrs. Ramos is at the stables, Nadia," he called at her. He rolled his eyes at me. "I was trying to tell you that when you ran off."

"So I've traveled all this way and no one is here to greet me?" she huffed, striding back into the living room. She posed with her hands on her hips and pouted. "That's rude. I'm not feeling very welcomed, Matthew."

"That'd be understandable, except you weren't supposed to be here until tomorrow," he replied. "Your cousin planned on picking you up at the train station. Did you change the tickets your aunt sent you for an earlier train?" She considered him a moment, chin thrust out in defiance.

"I caught a ride," she said finally, airily.

"I saw that," he nodded, "that was a nice Firebird. Guy driving it was kinda scruffy, though. Friend of yours?"

She just smiled, plunking herself down into an armchair and turning her eyes away from Matthew. He was, apparently, dismissed. Exasperation written in every line of his face, Matthew gave me a brief wink and walked back outside.

"And who are you?" She locked on me as the door shut. I was on my own. Her eyes, large and dark, lit up suddenly. "Oh, are you the girlfriend?" Her lips upturned in a catty smile. "Auntie Sofia mentioned you'd be here, I just didn't believe Hector could actually find a girl who'd want to live in the boonies with him." She examined me closely, eyebrows arched. I, for the record, was speechless. "I didn't think you'd be so old. Or *married*," she added, eyes lighting on my ring. I found my tongue.

"I'm not Hector's girlfriend. She's not coming out anymore, I don't think. I'm—," I cast about for a simple way to characterize my connection, "I'm a family friend, and," I couldn't help but add the last, "twenty-three is *hardly* old." Nadia was unimpressed.

"Got a name?" she asked archly.

"Vera," I said. She made a scoffing sound, as if my name didn't impress her much either. I was beginning to feel some sympathy for Hector. This girl had turned the full force of her attitude on me just for sitting there. "And you're Claudia?" I asked, bowing to an infantile urge to jab back. She laughed in a long, shrill cackle and wiped a tear from her eye in a showy fashion, smiling sardonically at me

"She said, 'and you're Claudia?'" she mocked me, to no one in particular. "No, sweetie, my name is Nadia. You're going to need to learn it."

"I'll see what I can do," I smiled sweetly. What a *piece of work*.

Hector, to my enormous relief, chose this moment to walk in the door.

"Hello little cousin," Nadia said grandly, "I have arrived."

"I see that," Hector replied, "And, last I checked, I'm four years older than you." He didn't smile or offer words of welcome. He also didn't give her room for reply, addressing me next. "Vera, can I get your help?" He turned and exited as quickly as he had appeared. I popped up and followed him up the stairs gratefully.

"I guess I'll just stay here *alone*," Nadia called at our retreating backs, with all the brave suffering of a martyr at the stake.

"WOW," I whispered to Hector, once we were safely on the second floor. He nodded significantly.

"Don't let her bait you," he warned. "She'll bring you down to her level if she can."

"I can see that," I replied. We stopped at a linen closet and he reached inside, passing me a pile of folded sheets.

"She's going to be in that room," he pointed to a spacious specimen down the hall. It was on the opposite end of the house from Hector's domain. It was also, most notably, right next to my room. I gave him a look. "Hey," he shrugged, "It was mom's call."

"Right."

"We need to make up the bed and make sure there are towels in the bathroom. At least you won't have to share that with her." He rolled his eyes. "She takes *long* showers."

We entered the room and stripped the bed of its comforter, laying the cotton sheets down one at a time. I was impressed to see Hector tucking the sheets into hospital corners and folding the towels neatly on the foot of the bed.

"Should we leave a mint on her pillow?" I joked.

"Only if you feel like doing that every day of her stay," he replied seriously.

We finished up quickly and hung around at the top of the stairs, reluctant to descend within range of the abrasive visitor until I began to feel foolish. She was, after all, only a girl. What happened to my well-meaning resolve to be helpful to Mrs. Ramos? All that compassion from yesterday, and here I was, folding at the first sign of conflict. I frowned at the thought. I needed to be better than this. With that in mind, I hustled down the steps to find the living room empty.

"Nadia?" I called uselessly. An elk head on the wall examined me in a sympathetic manner. The house was still, but for Hector's footsteps coming down the stairs after me.

"Oh no, she's gone," he said in a monotone, mocking my concern. He turned to the fridge and fished out a can of cola.

"Where would she go?" I asked. The property was huge and perils many for those without caution or sense. I was uncertain that Nadia possessed either of those traits. Hector shrugged, not quite unworried, but certainly relieved to avoid his cousin for the time being.

"She goes where she wants," he said. "She could be in the crawlspace, for all I know." The air was split suddenly by piercing shrieks from the direction of the stables. Hector took a slow sip of cola. "Found her," he said. I took off running.

◄○►

I wish I weren't so emotional. It would be a nice break for myself, and would help my relationship too, I'm sure, if I weren't so paranoid.

Austin has been so different lately, withdrawn, and I'm starting to feel like this is more than just residual sadness from James's death. I'm afraid he's hiding something from me.

I checked his search history. I know, that's such an invasion of privacy and I am ashamed. He just spends all his time now on his phone or his laptop, and I don't know what's going on. I found nothing, and you'd think that would make me feel better, but it made it worse. It's not that there was nothing to worry about, there was just nothing to find. He had wiped his search history.

I know he doesn't deserve to deal with my insecurity. It's not just the technology, I seem to always find something about his behavior to pick apart these days. It'll be him being at work later than expected, or changing the cologne he wears, or even just a new phrase or expression he'll start using out of nowhere.

He explains it all to me and I'll feel better in the moment, but it never lasts and then I'm freaking out on him about something else. And I know he's getting impatient with it all; I sure would be.

—◄○►—

When I arrived at the stables, gasping for air, the shrieks had devolved into what I suspect they had been the whole time: hysterical, coquettish laughter. Nadia was sandwiched between the broad side of a black horse and one of the younger ranch hands, a summer staffer, laughing flirtatiously with both hands on his biceps. The boy was clearly enamored at the attention and flexed in a way I'm sure he thought was subtle. Nadia, spotting my approach, turned to the horse and placed his hands firmly on her waist.

"Spot me like a gentleman this time, Jason," she giggled, pulling herself up onto the horse with graceful ease and settling herself on its back with poise. There was no saddle or reins, and her clothing was far too tight to be comfortable or functional, but she balanced like a pro and seemed at ease. Clucking her tongue softly, they trotted around the paddock with smooth grace and familiarity. I hadn't needed to worry about Nadia being trampled to death by farm beasts; she clearly knew a lot more than I did. The ranch hand leaned against the fence with his hands in his pockets and watched her with clear and soppy admiration.

"I can babysit her, if you've got things to do, Jason," I offered. He didn't acknowledge me. "Jason?" I ventured. Again, he didn't stir, seeming transfixed at the sight of Nadia. "Jason!" I waved my hands at him. He finally blinked and turned to look at me.

"Oh, my name's Will," he said, eyes sliding from me back to Nadia, who was galloping now, dark and lovely hair streaming behind her in the early evening air.

"Oh, sorry" I replied, confused, "Didn't I just hear Nadia call you Jason?"

"Yeah," he sighed. His boyish face, bearing the blonde type of facial hair that is at the same time invisible and altogether *too* visible, took on a rosy, sappy smile. "She can call me whatever she wants."

"Gross," I said reflexively.

He gave no reply but leaned hard against the fence, one dusty boot on the bottom board as if ready to hoist himself over into the pen. Atop her steed, Nadia waved and winked in his direction. Will went visibly slack-jawed; eyes starry and blue and glued on the girl in front of him. It would have been cute had it not been so irritating. Luckily, Matthew approached during this exchange and clapped a work-hardened hand on

Will's shoulder, jolting him back to reality with a suddenness that was certain to be unpleasant.

"Might want to check on your steers there, Will," he said gruffly, "I think you've caught enough flies for one day."

Will, who had, previously, been open-mouthed, straightened up and nodded. We saw him shaking his head roughly to clear it as he walked away. Matthew kept a strict eye on his retreating form until he was out of view and then joined me at the fence, scowling across the paddock at Nadia and the prancing horse.

"Well that was something," I said.

Matthew chuckled and shook his head. He turned to lean his back against the fence and took off his hat, wiping his forehead with a sodden bandana. It had been a long day of work for him, as I'm sure they all were, and it had become clear from my short time at the ranch that he was the one who held everything together. He worked harder and longer than the rest, but still made time to check on Mrs. Ramos and mentor Hector, as well as help me now. I felt a sudden surge of warmth for the old cowboy. He was one of the few who hadn't laughed at my equestrian attempts from earlier.

"I tell Mrs. Ramos every summer that I'm done hiring teenagers, and then I go on and do it again the next year," he said. He laughed again. "Distractible things, aren't they?"

"I think Nadia is uniquely skilled at being distracting," I said, trying to be fair. The summer staff worked long hours with little opportunity to socialize or even leave the ranch. A less dazzling stranger than Nadia would probably have caught Will off-guard. And the flirting likely didn't hurt either.

"That's one way to put it," he said flatly, a frown darkening his words. I wondered just how many of Nadia's visits Matthew had endured during his tenure at the ranch. The sky bruised pink and purple overhead as the evening rolled in. "So you're chaperoning her this afternoon?" I looked around. Hector had not followed me out of the house, and Mrs. Ramos was nowhere to be seen.

"I guess so," I said.

"Brave of you," he said. "I've known her since she was a little thing. She was a handful then. She just seemed to get wilder every year." He sighed, and I waited, hoping that he would elaborate. When he didn't, I ventured a question.

"Any advice?"

Matthew plopped his cowboy hat on my head and swiveled my skull gently to look back into the paddock. He pushed off the fence and began walking, bareheaded, back to the barn.

"Pay attention," he called over his shoulder.

I pushed back the brim of his too-large hat to see that the black horse now cantered around the pen riderless. Nadia was gone again.

◄◦►

It's odd and ironic, but work has really been good for me lately. My kids this year are awesome and funny and, frankly, trouble, but I don't mind the challenge of convincing them to learn. I'm overcoming the mayhem of last year and now I can actually contribute something. I've got all these books on pedagogy and I'm trying out new methods wherever I can.

It's pretty all-consuming, and that's what I want right now.

◄◦►

A quick look through the surrounding area confirmed that Nadia had not stuck around. Will was back with his steers, driving the animals with a melancholy look in his eye, and undeniably alone. She was not visiting any of the horse stalls or lurking in the barns. I decided to check at the house before I started to panic for certain. Even so, I ran on the way back, Matthew's hat flying off my head, angry and perturbed at how quickly I became winded.

I was still gasping for breath climbing the stairs to the expansive front porch, vowing to myself to start jogging the next day, to find Nadia and Mrs. Ramos seated together in a cluster of rocking chairs, watching the sun begin to set and laughing like little girls.

"Mama never told me that!" Nadia exclaimed, "You are so *bad*, Tía!" Mrs. Ramos batted her hand in Nadia's direction, a bit embarrassed but seemingly pleased.

"It was a long time ago," she said, chuckling. I collapsed into the porch swing at the corner, facing the two of them in their chairs. Mrs. Ramos was tall and strong to Nadia's short daintiness, but they were alike in dusky eyes and sudden, flashing smiles. I felt an odd pang of envy at their easy camaraderie and brushed off the feeling that I was intruding.

"What happened?" I asked. Nadia's smile blew off her face with the dry speed of a tumbleweed.

"Auntie, who is that?" she asked, pointing a polished nail in my direction. Her nose was crinkled in subtle disgust and she glowered at me in distaste, like I was a pile of bison dung, or an old shoe. I drew my feet up and crossed my legs, keeping the swing in a steady motion.

"Sweetie, this is Vera. She's the friend I told you about."

"We've actually already met," I explained. I tried to keep my expression neutral, but couldn't help adding a little jab. "I think she's gotten to know everyone on the property by now." Nadia rolled her eyes; her aunt looked at her reprovingly.

"Nadia, remember the conditions of your stay. You can't run wild again, understand?" Mrs. Ramos smiled at me. "Vera is my guest, and I thought you might like to get to know her while you're both here. You need more female role models, sweetheart." Nadia was distressed and her gaze turned watery in a matter of seconds.

"I'm not a baby," she whined, "I'm *sixteen* and I know how to take care of myself." She sniffed showily.

"Of course you do," her aunt said firmly, "but you will not be spending your summer running after boys and getting into trouble. That's why your mother sent you here, and I'm going to honor her intentions, am I clear?"

The girl was suddenly the picture of sweet compliance, putting one hand on Mrs. Ramos' arm, the other sincerely against her chest.

"Of course, Auntie," she said earnestly. "I'm so grateful to be here, and to you for letting me stay." She shot me a sweetly venomous smile. "I'm sure Vera and I will become great friends." Mrs. Ramos smiled widely.

"That's a weight off my mind," she said, sighing as she got to her feet. "Now, if you'll both excuse me for a minute, I have to get dinner on the table." Nadia was on her feet in a flash.

"No, wait! We can do it!" She seized my hand, pulling me along to the door in her wake. Her grip was a vice. "You sit there and rest, *Tía*, we'll take care of everything."

Mrs. Ramos smiled and settled back in her rocking chair, oblivious to the savage pinching my hand was taking as I was towed along to the kitchen behind the deceptively strong Nadia. Once we were through the doors, I extracted my hand with some difficulty and looked around, taking inventory of the kitchen

A sheet pan dinner was already in the oven as we entered the room, smelling as wonderful as usual. The timer had around ten minutes to go, which was enough time, I supposed, to whip up a side or two. I considered the options, flexing the circulation back into my fingers.

"Should we make a salad?" I suggested. Nadia was already at the fridge, rooting around inside.

"Yeah," she said, "go ahead and chop this up while I find some other things."

She turned and flung a cucumber at me with a force that was probably unnecessary. I caught the vegetable projectile with coordination that came from nowhere and took us both by surprise. I hustled to the knife block before she decided to throw one of those too and got to work.

Fairly confident with my knifework, the cucumber was sliced nicely in record time. Nadia, still by the refrigerator, tossed me a sizable carrot next, which I also, somehow, caught smoothly. We went through this routine several times with various veggies Nadia found around the kitchen. I was pretty pleased with the teamwork of it all until she passed me a potato, and I turned to question her choice.

Nadia was sitting on the kitchen counter next to a bucket of produce that she had pulled from the refrigerator drawer. In one hand was a cellphone, which she scrolled through in an absorbed fashion as she sipped from the large, brightly-colored glass in her other hand. I gaped at her.

"Did you make a *margarita*?"

"Mhmm," she replied happily. She held the glass out. "Auntie always hides the tequila in the produce drawer. You want some? It's good." She had even salted the rim. I held out my hand.

"Sure," I said, agreeably. She handed it over and I promptly dumped the contents into the sink.

"Well that was a waste," she said, frowning. "What's your problem?" I had to work hard not to sputter.

"First, you're underage," I began.

"Stupid reason, and barely," she interjected, "but okay, go on."

"Second, isn't your mother an addict?" She rolled her eyes.

"I am *nothing* like my mother, believe me."

"Finally," I continued, uncomfortably aware of how much I was sounding like *my* mother, "you just told your aunt you would help with dinner, and now you're leaving it all to me."

"But you're doing such a good job," she said, eyebrows raised. The oven timer went off.

"Please just finish the salad," I said wearily, "you just have to toss it all in a bowl and bring it out to the table."

She sighed in an all-suffering way, but slid from the counter and did as I asked. I cut off the timer and pulled the sheet pan from the oven, transferring its contents to a serving plate. Everyone was beginning to sit down at the table when we came out of the kitchen bearing food.

"What a beautiful salad, Nadia!" Mrs. Ramos was all praise as Nadia strutted in with the salad bowl, placing it at the center of the considerable table with the air of a high priestess placing her sacrifice on an altar. "Thank you for finishing up dinner. I can't remember the last time I got to sit on my porch in peace."

"It was no problem at all, Auntie," she smiled widely at me and took a graceful seat, shaking out her napkin and placing it delicately on her lap with dramatic flair.

I rolled my eyes and sat across from her, next to Hector. He was studiously avoiding looking at or talking to anyone, but nudged my arm with his elbow in a show of support. I nudged it back, trying to show my appreciation, and also communicate that I would be needing his help. He didn't respond, and I figured he hadn't really gotten the message. It was a lot to expect from an elbow bump, anyway.

Down the table, Matthew was nudging Will's arm too, albeit more roughly. The boy was once again transfixed, and jolted back to life only to take a heaping double-helping of salad, smiling shyly and Nadia all the while. She paid him little mind, but chattered brightly to her aunt the duration of the meal. She was charming, attentive, and intensely warm, once even getting up to refill Mrs. Ramos' glass with lemonade from the pitcher. Her aunt laughed and batted her away, with a smile so wide I saw her once reach up to massage her cheeks. Regardless of any previous trepidation, Mrs. Ramos was obviously overjoyed to have Nadia around, and Nadia definitely reciprocated those feelings.

She clearly admired her aunt enough to alter her personality entirely, and it was incredible how easily she did it. Her behavior was altogether different than what it was in the kitchen, or the stables, or even the living room where I first met her. I wondered which of the versions of Nadia I had witnessed so far was the real one, or even if any of them were.

When dinner was over and done, the dishes cleaned, and leftovers packed snugly away in the refrigerator for omelet ingredients the next morning, Nadia stretched showily, yawning in an overdone fashion that was comic and fooled no one.

"What a day," she said smiling, "I'm exhausted all of a sudden. You don't mind if I head to bed now, do you Auntie?"

"Of course not," Mrs. Ramos replied, embracing her warmly. "Your room is ready for you. We'll see you in the morning."

"Sweet dreams," she trilled, floating up the stairs.

We heard her door close and I breathed a sigh of relief, sagging slightly against the countertop. It *had* been a long day, and tomorrow promised to be any longer if just this afternoon had been any indicator. Nadia taking an early evening was a merciful reprieve, in my opinion.

But Hector and his mother were exchanging significant glances.

"What?" I said, aggravated. "Use words."

"That was too easy," Hector said flatly. His mother nodded.

"That was my thought, too," she said, "Think she's planning something?"

"Oh, come on," I cried out, exasperated. In my heart I knew they were right, but I was tired enough to want to see the best in Nadia, if only to rest easy for a moment. "You saw how she was at dinner. She clearly adores you too much to risk your disapproval."

"She cares, but that doesn't mean anything," Hector shrugged. "She's always an angel in front of mom. It's never stopped her from doing what she wanted the rest of the time." I was reminded strongly of her fashioning of the margarita earlier. With a sigh, I opened the fridge and peeked in the produce drawer.

"The tequila's gone," I announced solemnly. Mrs. Ramos groaned.

"I forgot all about it," she said, clapping a hand to her forehead. "I was going to get rid of it all before she got here."

"Looks like she's taken care of that," muttered Hector. He moved towards the door, then glanced back at me and jerked his chin in the direction of the stairs. "Come on, let's go to your room. That's probably where we'll find her." I straightened up and folded my arms, surprised.

"Why do you say that?" I asked.

"She's more likely to mess with your stuff than mine," he said over his shoulder, thudding up the stairs. Alarmed, I followed close behind.

"Why would she mess with my stuff?"

"You're new and interesting," he said flatly. "Also, I locked my door."

Entering the second floor corridor I saw that Hector's room was, indeed, shut tight. He examined the handle carefully and grinned.

"What?"

"I put some baby powder on the doorknob and in the keyhole to see if she'd try to break in." He moved back so I could see the shine of metal, clean of any trace of baby powder. "Looks like she made an attempt." I was horrified, but impressed.

"You booby trapped your door?"

"No!" he protested, "this is an indicator trap." He smiled. "The booby traps are *inside* the room."

"Right," I shook my head.

"Come on," he headed down the hall, "I have a feeling you won't be so judgmental in a minute."

I followed, concerned but not totally worried. Nadia could go snorkeling through my suitcases for all I cared. There was nothing she could have found that she could do much with, unless she had some sort of weird penchant for Walmart's generic brand clothing.

Of course, as we've learned by now, I tend to underestimate situations.

If Nadia had detonated a bomb in my luggage, she would have created less of a mess in the same amount of time. Clothes were everywhere they could be: the floors, the side tables, dangling from the tops of closet doors and shoved up under the bed. Nadia herself was shored up among my sheets and blankets. The tequila bottle lay open, almost empty, against a pillow to her left, convenient for a quick swig now and again, and to her right was a pile of my underwear, from the decidedly unsexy twelve-pack I had purchased in West Memphis. These articles she was shooting toward the ceiling fan by their thick elastic waistbands. As we stepped into the room, taking in the destruction, she managed to snag one on a rotating blade. It circled above our heads once, twice, and then flew off to rest in a saggy cotton heap at the far corner of the room.

"Ew, why are you here?" she said, pretending to have just noticed us. She sat up and drank from the bottle, gesturing grandly about the space with her other hand. "I require solitude."

"Vera requires her room," responded Hector. He kept his tone steady, almost bored, but his hands were in fists at his sides.

"Oh, is this your room?" Nadia asked me in mock surprise. "I thought for sure Auntie must have been hosting a hobo. You know," she tossed a pair of sweatpants to the floor, "by the looks of things." She gave me that same cat smile from earlier and I looked away, coaching myself. *Don't let her bait you.*

"Well," I took a calming breath and chose my words carefully, "it looks like you've made yourself comfortable in here." I glanced at Hector. "Would your mom care if we switched rooms?"

"I don't know," Hector played along, "let's call her up here and ask."

He turned, making as if he were about to summon Mrs. Ramos.

"Oh my *god*," groaned Nadia, "you're both so boring." She slinked off the bed, pulling most of the blankets to the floor with her in the process. "I'll leave, okay? But, oh," she smiled suddenly, "I need to text this *hot* guy back first." From her back pocket, she pulled my cell phone, holding it out so that I could see Austin's message from days ago floating across the screen. "You've left him on read for so long he's probably given up on you," her smile widened, "thought I might send him my number instead. I'm *very* responsive."

Beside me, Hector's arms shot out so quickly they were a blur. In a moment, he had snatched my phone from her right hand and upset the tequila bottle in her left, sending it splashing down her front. Cursing, she lunged at him with arms outstretched, but tripped as her foot snagged one of the piles of clothes on the floor. Hector sidestepped her easily and handed me back my phone.

"You should leave now," he told her, maintaining his level tone. "You're embarrassing yourself."

Nadia staggered upright, combing her long hair back from her face. There were vivid spots of red high on her cheekbones, from alcohol or anger, I couldn't tell.

"Some loyalty you've got, cousin," she spat, "though, after you abandoned your own mother to live it up at school, I guess I shouldn't be surprised." She shoved him hard on the way to the door. Hector's face had twitched at her jabs, but he let her pass. She paused at the threshold and glanced back at me, eyes glittering angrily, "Might want to password protect your phone, Granny panties," she hissed, "Married guys *love* me."

The door closed behind her with a vicious click.

"Whoa," I sank to the floor on my knees, staring blankly around the messy room before shaking my head and starting to gather my clothes together in one pile. "That got really personal."

Hector had dropped his calm demeanor and was staring at the door angrily, as if his cousin stood there still.

"She can't stay here," he growled. "That went too far." Privately, I agreed, but the way I had taken her bait at the beginning pricked at my conscience uncomfortably. I had done more to make things worse than I had helped so far.

"She was drunk," I pointed out. "She probably won't even remember what she did in the morning."

"She wasn't," he sniffed, "She's just genuinely that awful." He reached up and pulled a shirt down from where it was snagged atop the closet door.

"She just got here, though," I tried to sound reasonable. "She didn't expect me to be here and transitions can be hard for kids. Maybe tomorrow she'll be more toned down."

Hector looked entirely unconvinced, and kept the thunderous look on his face as he helped me clean up the room. We worked silently and the job was done within minutes. He turned to leave, then turned back.

"I recommend you lock your door."

CHAPTER 17

Hector didn't have to tell me twice. Twisting the lock firmly secured, I gathered clean clothes and proceeded into the bathroom attached to my room. Consistent with the lavish furnishing of the rest of the house, this bathroom provided quite a few amenities, including privacy and a clawfoot tub. I had yet to take advantage of the massive basin but, in light of today's bruises, both physical and emotional, I decided a soak was warranted.

The tub was soon full and steaming fragrantly, the surface of the water silky from the juniper-scented bath salts I had added. My right foot hovered above the water, ready to plunge in when it occurred to me that, besides my phone, there was another possession here that I wouldn't want to fall into unfriendly hands.

I lowered my foot back to the cool tile and hurried into the room, with the sick sort of swimming in my stomach that comes from a drowning wave of panic. Lifting the mattress up off the bed, I peered underneath and sighed out the flood of sudden tension. My journals were untouched where I had stashed them. I pulled the next one from my collection, a smooth diary of black leather, and hugged it tight to my bare chest as I trudged back to the bathroom and finally slipped into the tub.

If there's one thing that's different about me since the start of my last journal, it's the bitterness that invades my thoughts now. Even Austin, who gave me this new journal for my birthday, can be painful to think of at times.

Because he's never home.

Because he's hurt and won't let me help.

Because sometimes I doubt him.

I don't want to, and it hurts him more when I do, but I can't shake the feeling that something is wrong here.

It's my fault, I think. I used to be so much more independent, but now I can see I've been clinging to him a bit. I just got so fixated on my feelings, and I was—am—too embarrassed to share my fears with anyone else. So my friends and family have definitely gone on the backburner. I know that's wrong, but I'm also afraid that if they see me now they'll see right away how ragged I've become.

I'm so different than I was back then. That was when my heart was safely in my ribcage where I could keep an eye on it. Now he has it, and he says I'm paranoid, but I think he'll break it.

I sighed at the rambling confusion of that first entry and fanned through the pages, the journal exhaling puffs of desperation with the flip of each grimly-written page. The little book was full of more of the same types of reflections and, as time went on, entries became shorter and more frantic, sharp and staccato in a way that stabbed at the eyes.

I turned to the end of my second year teaching. The month of June that year had been studded with victories at school. Professionally, it had marked the start of my success as an educator. My journal didn't even mention the accolades.

A few pages were stuck together and I pried them carefully apart with damp hands. The pages had been wet before, crinkled as they were with previous moisture, and some dark smears indicated the start of something else entirely.

He's in California again, and I'm all alone. Then again, that's not much different than when he's here.

This love drains me. I never know how it might fail, or why, or how much it will hurt. I only know that it will. I'm so afraid of the things that I don't know, the things that I can't stop thinking about. I think there's a lot I don't know, and I think Austin has secrets that sully me entirely, and our marriage completely. I look at myself, and I don't look betrayed, disgraced, defiled, but I might be, I don't know.

I've started hurting myself. I know that's bad.

It's all bad right now.

Drops of water from my hands bring back to life the dusty streaks of dried blood. I touched one, a half fingerprint, knowing that the next day I had, perhaps, held the door for a group of chattering seventh graders in the hall on the way to the library. Those hands had maybe called my mother and chattered vacuously about nothing for a prescribed ten minutes. I had reached them out to embrace my husband, and he had flinched at the ugliness I had created before folding me into his arms.

God, Vera, he had said once, *Why do you do this to yourself?* He would kiss me gently then, soft touches on my lips and eyelids. *We need to find you some help*, he'd say, *this isn't healthy.*

Where were you last night? I had thought then. *Why haven't you been coming home?*

I had ached to say it, but hadn't. I folded to his tenderness and basked in his love, fears quelled for a time while I, at least for a moment, healed. And, of course, met the next dangerous day armed with scars. I set my journal to the side and examined them in the wavy visibility of the warm water.

I was scarred extensively and sporadically. They lined my hands in dainty, herringbone patterns, visible only in certain lights and when I clenched my fingers tightly. They streaked across my hips and pelvis, thick, gruesome ropes of scar tissue splayed like the swipe of a tiger's claw. Most I could conceal under clothes, long-sleeves being my best friends even now, but here, exposed under full light, I was a monstrosity. I closed my eyes and sank down, the water pressing blessed silence against my ears and closing over my lips like the reverse of a kiss.

◄○►

I woke late the next morning and descended groggily to the kitchen, where Mrs. Ramos and Nadia were drinking coffee together and laughing. Nadia's eyes flashed in annoyance at the sight of me, but she otherwise remained quiet as I helped myself to some orange juice and settled at the counter.

"Good morning," smiled Mrs. Ramos. "How did you sleep?" She was clear-eyed this morning, and seemed to be genuinely happy.

"Pretty well," I lied. In truth I had tossed for hours, but there was no real reason to bring it up.

"I was going to come get you in a few minutes if you weren't up already," she said, pushing a bowl of muffins my way. "Hector has gone out to help Matthew for the day, but I thought we could head into town for a while."

"There's a town?" I questioned.

Nadia let out a cough that I might have suspected was a laugh if she were friendlier. To my knowledge, there were at least fifty or so miles of farmland in every direction from Ramos Ranch. Unless you counted the odd gas station, there wasn't anything to visit that would constitute a town.

"Bozeman," Mrs. Ramos explained, smiling her understanding, "It's a little bit of a drive, which is why I don't go much, but it's cute. I have a few errands to run and I thought we might make a girl's day of it."

The smile became fixed painfully on my face. While I could see enjoying shopping with Mrs. Ramos, something told me a girl's trip with Nadia would be a disaster. Nadia definitely concurred.

"Auntie," she said, a whine of annoyance edging her words, "I thought we were going to have some time just the two of us."

Mrs. Ramos smiled kindly, rising from her seat and pressing a kiss to the top of Nadia's head as she walked her mug to the sink.

"I thought it might be good for all three of us to have some time together," she said, "And I'd like both of your opinions on something."

She left those words to hang in the air as she exited the kitchen. Nadia looked at me, eyes moving over my face and down my frame to take in my bedraggled appearance fully.

"Let's hope we're not going to the mall," she said drily, "You're in no position to give anyone fashion advice, Granny."

"If we are, maybe you could help me pick some things out," I answered sweetly.

I was determined to be pleasant. I could do that, right? If the day consisted of the makeover montages you see in movies, I could take one for the team for the sake of bonding. It might even be fun.

"Not likely," sneered Nadia, her lip curling as if she knew what I was thinking. She, too, got up and put her mug in the sink, leaving behind a damp ring on the counter and a generous sprinkling of crumbs from her blueberry muffin. She made to exit and then turned to deliver one last jab. "You know, I don't know what you think you're doing here. *I* sure as hell don't want you here, and you know what else? I don't want to be your friend. In fact, I pretty much hate you already. So just stay out of my way today, all right?"

With that declaration done and hanging in the air like smog, she turned again and left me to sip on my cooled coffee, stomach sour at the thought of the day ahead.

◄○►

As it turned out, our excursion to Bozeman wasn't for retail purposes at all, a fact Nadia bemoaned as we rolled through the cheerful downtown and out again into pastureland. We rolled past a few country clubs before turning onto a long dirt road.

"Are you taking us into the wilderness to murder us, Auntie?" Nadia inquired sardonically as the Ramos' truck spit pebbles from its tires behind us.

"No, Nadia," Mrs. Ramos laughed.

"Not even if I ask politely?" she muttered quietly so only I could hear her, wedged as I was between the two of them on the bench seat of the truck.

Nadia had protested the method of transport when she realized she would have to sit next to me, and acquiesced only when assured she would at least have the window seat. Now, it appeared she didn't appreciate the view at all. We came to a stop in a wide dirt parking lot and Mrs. Ramos killed the engine.

"So," she turned to us, appearing nervous, "I haven't talked to Matthew or Hector about this yet, but Edgar, my husband," she added, glancing at me, "had the idea years ago and it's chewed at me ever since that we never did anything about it." She looked at us expectantly.

"Okay," Nadia and I said together, both sensing her need for encouragement. I winced as I received a discreet elbow to my side for the coincidental moment of unity.

"We discussed it back when Edgar was relatively healthy because there was a major boom in demand, but then the economy tanked and it was all we could do to keep the ranch, especially with the hospital bills and needing to hire on Matthew for extra help," she continued in a rush, eyes darting between Nadia and I. "We've recovered everything and more," she paused, "financially," she clarified, "and now that they're popular again and I think it's the right time to bring them to Ramos Ranch."

"Them?" I asked. Nadia stuck her sharp elbow into my side again, harder this time. Letting out a quickly stifled cry of pain, I turned to see her attention fixed out the window at the field closest to us. There was something in the distance, and, unified again in our confusion, we squinted to make them out as they moved closer.

Coming over the horizon was a procession of oddly-shaped animals, tall and furry and somewhat monstrous in their weirdness, like long-necked Fozzy Bears. They galloped towards us on short legs and then stopped, leaning down to nibble delicately at an especially vibrant patch of grass.

"Alpacas," Nadia said flatly.

Recently sheared, the alpacas were odd and knobby-looking, with long necks that were skinnier than was comfortable to look at. We climbed out of the truck and approached the fence, gazing at the animals with widely varying degrees of warmth.

"Aren't they adorable?" Mrs. Ramos asked.

"They look like a cross between a poodle and a llama," I said, skirting the question.

"Nah," scoffed Nadia, "they're more like a sheep-giraffe hybrid." She looked sideways at Mrs. Ramos, "So you want to turn Ramos Ranch into an alpaca farm?"

"I'd like to farm them along with our cattle," Mrs. Ramos clarified. "There's a huge market for alpaca products right now. It's a good business move from that perspective."

"Are they a lot of work?" I asked, wary.

I had been helping out with the cattle only a few days, but had developed a deep respect already for how much there always was to do. Hector might not have thought they needed any extra help with the ranch, but from where I was standing, even Matthew was stretched as thin as he could be. I didn't blame Mrs. Ramos for hoping Hector might come home and help after graduating, but expanding the ranch would make it almost a necessity. I frowned. Hector would see this as an attempt to force his hand.

"That's what I'm here to find out," she replied. She pushed away from the fence and straightened her denim work shirt. "I have a meeting with the family in a few minutes, why don't you two look around?"

She set off up the drive, boots leaving puffs of dust in her wake. I looked back out over the field. More alpacas were joining the small herd that had approached earlier, perhaps turned loose after being shaved down at some barn hiding over the hill. A particularly big one, gray in the face but white everywhere else, stepped cautiously towards our section of fence to dine on a dewy cluster of clover. It raised its head and chewed and slowly, while I examined the weird, horizontal pupils of its blue eyes. I turned to Nadia.

"What do you—," I began, but she had pushed off the fence and was walking away, pointedly indifferent. "Where are you going?" I called, feeling even more stupid when she didn't reply. Frustrated, I turned tail and followed her as she disappeared up the drive.

Panting as the ground finally leveled off, I quickly found myself turned around. The driveway was straightforward, if steep, but the rest of the ranch was not. The property was vast, and dotted here and there with individual barns and paddocks that were more or less uniform, as well as a few other buildings that seemed to be for visitor purposes. Peering into the window of one, I saw a cash register and a rack of t-shirts and sweaters on display.

"Did you want to go in?" I jumped and unstuck my face from the window, turning to see a little girl of no more than nine standing behind me with a ring of keys big enough to tip her over.

"That's okay," I said, "I was just looking for my friend." She looked disappointed as she selected the correct key from amongst its identical brethren and unlocked the door.

"You sure?" she asked, hopefully, "We just made a fresh batch of jerky and I'm trying to sell it all before the day is over." I wrinkled my nose slightly. Alpaca jerky?

"Is it any good?"

"It always sells out quick," she shrugged. "At least, I hope it will to-day. I wanted to help with the shearing, but Papa said I had to work the gift shop instead."

"It sounds like a responsible job," I said, pulling an automatic reply from the teacher phrasebook lodged in my brain. She shrugged again, not much comforted by the fact. "You said there was shearing today? Where is that happening?" The girl forlornly pointed me in the right direction and I departed, deciding to drop in again later.

I walked for a long time before I came to the correct pen and stopped to watch for a while. The alpaca were orderly and docile, submitting peacefully to being shaved, even seeming grateful for it after the fact. When they were done they trotted out into the open sunshine and continued to feed. The whole process took about fifteen minutes per animal, and with five ranch hands in the pen, the herd was being taken care of quickly.

Looking around, I caught sight a long dark mane of hair that I quickly identified as belonging to Nadia. She was cozied up to one of the ranch hands, petting an alpaca sweetly while he worked and chattering to him in much the same manner. He pushed his ball cap back to smile at her and looped a finger through the belt loop of her jeans to pull her closer to him. I heard the now-familiar coquettish laugh from my spot fifty feet away. I was astounded and more than a little aggravated. We had been here, what, twenty minutes? It was one thing to have this disappearing act, but did she have to flirt so aggressively with strangers?

"Nadia!" I called. The laughter faded from her face as she looked across the pen and spotted me. She frowned darkly and turned, jumping the fence with ease and approaching me like a thundercloud.

"What's up?" she sneered, walking past me with a flip of her hair.

"You disappeared," I said, hating the implied whine within the statement. Somehow, despite my more advanced years, Nadia managed to make me feel like a pesky little kid.

"And?" she replied, "*Tía* said we should look around. She didn't say we had to be together."

She was right, of course. I wasn't sure why I had taken it upon myself to be her chaperone. She was certainly savvy in the ways of the world and I, really only a few years older, and very much a mess, was hardly qualified to look after anyone. Still, the looks this sixteen year old was getting from adult men raised goosebumps on my arms.

"Who was that guy you were talking to?" I persisted, trying to sound casual as we walked back towards the gift shop area. She smiled a nastily at me; she knew exactly what I was trying to ask.

"I don't know his name," she said carelessly.

"You both seemed pretty friendly."

"Yeah," she smiled wickedly, "I'm good at making friends, if you know what I mean."

"Yeah," I sighed, "I'm pretty sure I know what you mean." The sun was high in the sky and heat beat down on our shoulders. We moved to the side to walk in the shadows of the small barns we were passing. "Nadia," I said suddenly, "You know that was a grown man, right?" She quirked an eyebrow at me suggestively.

"I sure do," she drawled.

"And you're sixteen," I continued, authoritatively, "You really shouldn't be flirting with him."

She looked at me in surprise, and an odd disappointment twisted her mouth into a wry and painful smile.

"I know how old I am," she said slowly. She spoke with a sort of condescending pity, as if I were an idiot. "That means he shouldn't be flirting with *me*."

Before I could answer, we both heard Mrs. Ramos' voice. We turned to see her in the doorway of the little gift shop I had peeked inside before. She waggled a long strip of jerky in our direction.

"You've got to try this," she called, chomping into it.

After perusing the gift shop and receiving a thorough education about the myriad of products that can be made with alpaca wool and meat, we took an official tour of the farm together. Mrs. Ramos's meeting had apparently been encouraging, and she smiled the whole time. Nadia and I, having covered most of the grounds already, tried gamely to be supportive, but the burning sun did a lot to quell our enthusiasm over time. Our stomachs, too, were unsatisfied with a single stick of alpaca jerky each, and about an hour later they were protesting loudly.

"C'mon, Auntie," wheedled Nadia, "We should discuss all of this at home, don't you think?"

Mrs. Ramos, glowing with excitement and fairly bursting with ideas, was determined to make a day of it, however, which is why we found ourselves shortly thereafter at Miguel's, a local eatery, plates piled high with tacos.

"Are the owners actually Mexican?" asked Nadia. She was examining a picture on the wall of our booth, a watercolor of Disney's Three Caballeros. Mrs. Ramos frowned as she pondered.

"Probably not," she concluded, "I think we're the only Hispanic family in Bozeman. Montana is predominantly white, you know."

Our waitress, a pale redhead swimming in a serape and topped with a sombrero, paused to refill our waters.

"You don't say," said Nadia drily.

"So," began Mrs. Ramos, reaching for the basket of tortilla chips, "What did you think of the alpacas?"

Nadia and I glanced at each other.

"They seem pretty popular," I said. A bus full of older people had pulled up as we were leaving, no doubt ready to decimate the rest of the gift shop. I had heard that agrotourism was becoming more popular, and the farm had definitely tapped into it. "I think it—" Nadia cut me off.

"What's your plan here, Auntie?" she asked. She laid a hand flat on the table and shot her aunt a square look, as if this were a board meeting. "You know Matthew can't handle another herd of animals; he's going to need extra help." Mrs. Ramos reddened a bit.

"Hector might—"

"Hector has no plans to move home after graduation," she interrupted emphatically, gesturing wildly now with a half-eaten taco and sprinkling me with ground beef in the process. "He's going to wear a stupid hat and live in the woods. That's been his plan for forever and he's not going to give it up for you. You know that."

Mrs. Ramos bit her lip as Nadia's words piled on top of her. I felt I should say something, out of sympathy to Mrs. Ramos and loyalty to the slandered and absent Hector.

"You don't know—" I started, but Nadia was in command of the conversation, and took back her role as speaker with a look that cut like a knife.

"I do," she said, with finality, "Who are you again?" She glared at me until satisfied that I had been put in my place and turned back to her aunt. "Listen, *I* think your idea is brilliant."

"You do?"

"Absolutely," Nadia nodded. "Other than all the products you can make from them, alpacas are cheap to take care of. They mostly eat grass and hay, and their poop is, like, awesome compost, which'll be great for your garden. They also breed and give birth pretty much without help, which is a lot better than everything you have to do for the cattle." Mrs. Ramos and I exchanged glances, stunned at the deluge of information as Nadia continued. "You'll need to figure out shearing and processing, of course, but that shouldn't be a problem."

"Why not?" Mrs. Ramos asked faintly.

"Because I can do it," Nadia's teeth flashed in a smile and her eyes darted over to me, glinting roguishly. "I kind of interviewed one of the farmhands and got the lowdown on what it's like. He even let me shear one." She laughed, still eying me defiantly, "It was a productive conversation."

Mrs. Ramos was shaking her head. "We wouldn't be ready to purchase any animals for months yet," she said, "You'll be home long before then."

"Unless I move out here with you, Aunt Sofia," Nadia's smile suddenly became strained. Putting down her taco and folding her hands demurely in her lap, she looked at her aunt with pleading eyes. "I could help with everything and finish school out here."

"Your mother would never hear of it," Mrs. Ramos said. She was still shaking her head, and avoided her gaze.

"Mama wouldn't even notice."

"Nadia . . . "

"Well, she wouldn't!"

"*¿Qué pasa mis amigas?* How are we doing over here?"

Our waitress was back, waving a pair of maracas around for no apparent reason. Nadia scoffed and turned towards the wall, folding her arms angrily when Mrs. Ramos tried to reach for her hand. I forced a smile and disregarded the question.

"I think we're ready for the check," I said.

CHAPTER 18

W HEN WE GOT BACK to Ramos Ranch, Nadia set off for the barn
without a word and climbed atop a horse, jumping the fence and
riding off towards the outer fields. Mrs. Ramos and I looked at each other
wearily and turned towards the house.

I went upstairs and unlocked my door, falling gratefully into bed
where I dozed for an hour or two, flipping through my journal in brief
moments of wakefulness. My state of mind in these pages had become
worryingly consistent.

> I'm getting to where I don't want to write anymore. I get so tired of
> finding new and increasingly in-depth ways of communicating my
> depression and watching its voice claim these pages, while mine
> dies.

I had continued to write, though, but the entries had become spo-
radic, loose collections of lines.

> God, I need You. I know it's been a long time, but I don't know
> what to say or do. Please help me not to hurt myself tonight.

The last entry of the black leather journal hurt my heart.

> Why am I here? Why am I so unlovable, and so unloved?
>   How I wish to be someone else entirely, or maybe no one at
> all.

I was wiping away sorry tears when Hector appeared at my door.

"What's up?" he asked. He was in his barn clothes and brought the
smell of horses with him. Dead grass clung to his jeans.

"Long day," I answered, drawing a shaky breath, "Don't ask."

"Oh, I don't need to," he raised his eyebrows at me. "When I heard you had gone with mom and Nadia into town, I was worried you wouldn't come back." I laughed.

"I survived all right," I said, "but I think Nadia's mad at your mom now."

"So that's why she's baking," Hector slapped his forehead in epiphany, "That makes sense." He looked at me again, seeming to notice my reddened eyes for the first time. "You okay?"

"Yeah," I slid off the bed and glanced in the mirror, running my fingers through my hair in an attempt to clean up a little. Brown roots were beginning to peek through at my part and the redness of my eyes weren't doing the dark shadows underneath them any favors. I sighed at my reflection. "Is dinner ready?"

"Just about," he answered hesitantly, his expression just as much of a mirror, "But I'm sure there's time if you want to—"

"Dinner time, Granny!" Nadia's voice rang down the hallway. "Let's give that elastic waistband some exercise." She appeared in the doorway, small but imposing. "You too, little cousin. Everyone's at the table." Her wordless anger from earlier had apparently given way to a sort of sour bossiness that wasn't much of an improvement. With a few more sharp words, she ushered us out of my room and followed us down the stairs. Outside the dining room, I stopped briefly to run my fingers through my lank locks one more time. Nadia rewarded my delay with a forceful push to my lower back. "Don't worry, you look *great*," she hissed spitefully to me as I was propelled into the room. Too defeated to protest, I dropped wearily into my seat.

Dinner proceeded as usual, the only difference being the cookies, pies, and tarts Mrs. Ramos pressed on everyone for dessert. Hector had not been kidding; Mrs. Ramos was definitely an emotional baker. Everyone ate themselves close to bursting to oblige her, but mountains of the goods still remained at the end of the meal. We would be wading in sugary snacks for the rest of the week.

Nadia stuck around to pretend to clean dishes and then went charging up the stairs with a single-mindedness that put Hector on high alert. He glanced over at me.

"Did you remember to lock your door?"

I groaned. I hadn't, of course. Not only that, but my journal was still out on the bed for anyone to read, or ridicule, or, as would probably be

Nadia's course of action, publish on the internet. "I'll go check on things," Hector said, a grim look on his face.

Before he could go after his cousin, though, Matthew entered the kitchen with a bashful Will in tow. Matthew pushed the boy forward to the center of the kitchen and leaned casually against the counter next to me, cleaning under his nails with a pocket knife. He offered no explanation, but seemed to wait, as Will turned a hearty magenta before our eyes for some long, painful moments. Mrs. Ramos bustled in with a platter of leftover raspberry tarts in hand and pulled some plastic wrap from one of the drawers.

"What's wrong, Matthew?" she asked, wrapping the desserts.

"Young William here was on his way to meet your niece," Matthew said, not looking up from his work.

"Nadia just went upstairs," Mrs. Ramos said. "She's in her room."

"Oh, not anymore," he replied, his tone unchanged. "She left. Out the window, I suspect."

Hector scrambled up the stairs without a word. We heard his footsteps pound down the hallway, pause, and then return, heavily, to the kitchen.

"She's gone," he confirmed. "I guess she got her hands on some rope? It's hanging out of the window right now."

"She must have picked up rappelling since she was last here," Matthew added humorously. No one laughed.

"So where did she go?" I asked.

I looked at Will, who avoided my questioning glance and examined the tiled floor uncomfortably. His face was a concerning shade of strawberry.

"Given the circumstances, I think she's probably still on the property somewhere," replied Matthew. He looked sideways at me, half a grin quirking the corner of his mouth up. "You're welcome, by the way."

"Thank you," I said automatically, and then, "For what?"

"You gotta keep an eye on your things," he answered.

He reached into his pocket and tossed something onto the kitchen island. It flew, glinting and clinking, through the air to rest on the smooth countertop: my truck keys, last seen on the bedside table of the room I hadn't locked. Nadia had, I realized now, rushed us downstairs for that exact purpose. I reached for the keys and held them up, incredulous.

Hector actually cracked a smile.

"So it's grand theft auto now, huh?" he chuckled mirthlessly, shaking his head. "That's new. I didn't think she'd even gotten her license."

"She hasn't," said Mrs. Ramos.

"Doesn't matter," continued Matthew. "Young Will here was prepared to drive her wherever her little heart desired. Seems she promised him quite the night out," he added, chuckling darkly. He squinted at Will, a hard glint in his eye. "Ain't you *Mormon*?" The boy turned, if possible, a deeper pink.

"She said she needed a ride into town," he muttered. "I didn't know it wasn't her car."

"But you didn't ask, right?" pointed out Matthew helpfully. Will squirmed.

"Enough," said Mrs. Ramos. "It doesn't matter now. Will, where is my niece?"

He shrugged miserably and stared back at the floor as if very much wishing it would swallow him whole.

"Could she have gotten on a horse and ridden off?" I asked. Matthew shook his head.

"The rest of my team knows Nadia," he said, still looking at Will. "They know better than to let her take off without supervision after dark."

"Then she's on foot," I said, looking at Hector.

He seemed to be enjoying this somehow, relaxed against the doorframe with his arms folded, as if watching a show. When his eyes met mine, however, he sighed and straightened reluctantly.

"I guess we'll go track her down," he said. He kissed his mother on the cheek and motioned for me to follow. We left Matthew and Mrs. Ramos behind to deal with their regretful employee.

—◦—

"She can't have gotten too far," I commented, grabbing a jacket from the coat hook by the door.

The sun had set, and Montana nights, even in the summer, verged on chilly. We stepped out onto the front porch and scanned the horizon. Stars were just beginning to prick through the velvet of the sky and the air was still sweet with the smell of baked grass.

"Pretty romantic, isn't it?" We jumped as the voice came from somewhere to our right. I squinted and made out a dark form, Nadia, curled up on the porch swing with a bottle to her lips. She had dug up more booze somewhere, it appeared. She giggled as I clutched my chest, heart beating fast. "People always look so stupid when they're surprised," she said.

Hector had recovered quickly and his face had taken on the same blank expression he had worn before when dealing with his cousin. He walked over to her with heavy steps and settled into a rocking chair. I followed his example.

"Where were you going to go?" he asked. His voice was eerily calm. I recognized the patience of a teacher dealing with a particularly difficult student.

"There's a bar out in town," she shrugged. "I first noticed it when Jason was driving me in, and then I saw it again this afternoon on the way back."

"Jason?" Hector questioned. She rolled her eyes.

"Some guy I got to drive me up here yesterday. I didn't want to wait for the bus." She giggled a little. "He was kind of fun."

"Was his name really Jason, or is that just what you decided to call him?" I asked, remembering her rechristening of the hapless Will. Nadia actually rested her chin on her hand, considering this.

"You know, I don't remember," she laughed. "Does it matter?"

It didn't.

"Why *my* truck?" I asked. She laughed again, the sound throbbing against my temples with a drunken hysteria. The bottle in her hand was very nearly empty.

"We're supposed to be besties now, right?" she trilled, smiling at me mockingly. "That's what Auntie wanted, at least. Friends *share*."

A spark of anger ignited between my shoulder blades and moved up the back of my neck to lick at my ears. Her taunting was nothing I hadn't seen inside of a classroom, but it was different where it concerned my truck. She didn't know, or likely care, what having my own mode of transportation meant to me right now, but it didn't change how badly a possible accident could have gone for me. That truck was in Austin's name. If anything had happened, he would have had to get involved.

I knew I was turning red and grateful for the safety of a shadow that fell over my chair. Hector, possibly feeling the heat radiating from me in that moment, stepped in to take over.

"You crossed the line this time, Nadia," he said. "You messed with the ranch *and* with a guest," a grim smile cracked his lips. "I wouldn't be surprised if you get sent home tonight."

She scoffed, unshaken.

"Aunt Sofia wouldn't do that," she said. "She wouldn't abandon me. She *invited* me, at least. Granny—" she gestured vaguely in my direction, "—*just* showed up, from the sound of it."

"You were invited to stay," he replied. "Not to take advantage of our kindness." He paused, considering his next words. "You know, I thought it was a bad idea from the beginning, but even I didn't think you'd mess up so quickly." Nadia didn't blink.

"I guess that was your mistake," she sneered.

"You're right," he replied, terribly calm. "I somehow assumed you were a better person than you actually are. *My* mistake."

Nadia had opened her mouth to unleash what would have been an undoubtedly blistering retort when the front door swung open and shut. Matthew strode from the house and down the stairs without a word or glance in our direction, whistling cheerfully. Will followed close behind, face cast down as he hustled to keep up with Matthew's long-legged gait. He did not look at us, but carefully trained his gaze in every direction but the one Nadia was in, even when she called out to get his attention. Whatever that conversation in the kitchen had been, it had been effective.

Now the door opened again, and Mrs. Ramos emerged. She was exhausted, her tall, strong form a bit bowed with the strain of the day, the dim lighting of the porch casting the crow's feet beside her eyes into stark relief. Hector quickly offered her his chair, and seated himself on the railing of the porch facing in, his back to the deepening indigo of the horizon. We formed a tight circle on the porch, and the three of us sat quietly, waiting for Mrs. Ramos to speak.

"It's not good," she said finally.

The words were heavy, and seemed to strike a chord with her niece, who suddenly sat up straight and sober. I noticed her edge the bottle a bit into the shadows as she did so, on the off-chance her aunt hadn't yet noticed it. All was quiet for a grave moment.

"I think there's been a misunderstanding," said Nadia at last, making a valiant attempt to give her tone a bright levity, but a slight quaver in her voice gave her away. She was nervous. She took a steadying breath and put on a winning smile. "That boy had been staring at me all afternoon, Auntie, and I tried to ignore him the best I could. I think he may have exaggerated some things to—" her aunt put up a weary hand.

"No, Nadia, no," she sighed, cutting her off. "I understand what has happened, and it's not good." Nadia slumped back into the swing, crossing her arms over her chest. Mrs. Ramos's voice shook as she counted off the offenses. "Selling the ticket we sent you, arriving unannounced with a strange boy, disturbing Matthew and the operation of the ranch, stealing and consuming alcohol underage, manipulating one of our summer staff—who, by the way," she glanced up at Nadia here, "didn't have a driver's license either—into taking you off-property in a *stolen* vehicle. Nadia!" Her voice rose incredulously. On her swing, Nadia flinched and curled more tightly into her shadowy corner. "You arrived yesterday! It's been *barely* thirty hours!" She shook her head, "And don't think I haven't noticed how you've been treating Vera, who has done *nothing* to deserve it."

"Granny just can't take a joke," Nadia sniffed, "and she shouldn't even be —"

"Be what?" Mrs. Ramos interrupted again, daring her to say more, "Be here? When she needed a place and I invited her? How is that any different than your situation?"

"Well I'm family. And—"

"And family should respect one another, Nadia!" Mrs. Ramos exclaimed. She turned her rocker and peered into the shadow that held her niece. She was close to yelling now. "I took you in hoping it might help you to get away for a while. But you've taken that gift and thrown it in my face! And you put others at risk in the process!"

Tears oozed from her eyes. She drew a tissue from her pocket and stemmed the stream, rocking gently. For a few minutes, the only sounds were muffled sniffling and a chorus of cicadas. I was sure Nadia would chime in at any moment to somehow smooth everything over with her aunt, but she said nothing.

"So, what's the call, mom?" Hector asked finally. His tone was grave, but his eyes were bright, eager. His mother shook her head, and her voice shook too.

"I can't keep you here," she said to Nadia. "I told your mother you were welcome to stay, but, given the circumstances, I can't deliver on that promise. I'm sorry."

"Auntie —" Nadia began, a quivering plea in her voice.

"No," Mrs. Ramos answered, with finality.

An owl made its presence known in a nearby tree. I looked at Nadia and shivered. She had drawn her knees to her chest and was hugging them tightly. She was nodding in recognition of her aunt's decision. But her *face*, I shivered again at the emptiness, the despair. There was no self-pity in it, but a deep, aching tiredness.

She was too much. Too much to love, to keep, to bear. The world was large, and she again had to find a place in it, alone. I could see the weight of it bowing her head. *Why am I so unlovable, and so unloved?* A lightning bug lit on her shoulder, and I suddenly found my voice.

"Wait," I said. "Can we talk this over for a minute?"

CHAPTER 19

T HE THREE STARED AT me; Hector's eyebrows, surprised, had practically disappeared into his hairline. I was momentarily overcome
with the discomforting reality that I was intruding on a family decision,
but I cast it aside with another glance at Nadia. Her eyes were on me.
Wary, but not quite dead anymore. I cleared my throat.

"I think this deserves more thought."

"You're kidding," said Hector, shocked into laughter. His eyes bore
into mine. *Tell me you're kidding*, they seemed to say.

"I'm not," I replied. He sobered.

"Vera," he lowered his voice. "It's fine, okay? This is how it has to be."

"It's not," I returned, shortly. Reluctantly, I turned my eyes to Mrs.
Ramos, who sat quietly like a weary queen upon the throne of her rocking
chair. When she didn't say anything, I took a breath and continued. "She's
had a rough start, but I think if she is willing to correct it, she should have
another chance." I weighed my words carefully. "Throwing people away is
not good either." Still, no one spoke. Hector had climbed down from his
perch and now leaned back against the rail with his arms folded, a scowl
darkening his features. His mother rocked slowly, her face giving nothing
away. Nadia, for the first time, leaned out of the shadows. Her eyes darted
between me and her aunt. "Kids make mistakes," I pushed on. "And however grown she likes to act, Nadia's a kid. I think any further questionable
behavior would mean she would go home right away. But," I added, "now
that she knows there will really be consequences, maybe Nadia will be
more cooperative with your rules." I fixed my eyes on Nadia, who had
been nodding silently. "Will you?" I asked.

"Yes," she said quickly, looking at her aunt.

Her voice sounded different now, younger, stripped of any spite or flattery. Mrs. Ramos didn't meet her gaze, but rocked gently a few moments more. At long last, she sighed.

"It's late, and it's been a long day," she said. She pulled herself out of the chair with some difficulty and looked at me. "I will think it over and we'll talk about this tomorrow."

Hector, scowling, helped his mother inside and shut the door behind him with a firm snap. Nadia and I sat for a time listening to the symphony of crickets and cicadas that filled the air like a solid. Tears flowed like lava down Nadia's cheeks, and she offered no response when I announced I was going to bed. I left her there, on the porch, and ascended the stairs to my bedroom, wondering if I had done the right thing.

◄o►

It was a little past midnight when the lights in my room snapped on and my ears were assaulted with a shrill roaring sound. Sitting up, my eyes adjusting painfully to the sudden light, I beheld Nadia, still dressed, heavy mascara application evident in what was now thick tear tracks down her face, inflating an air mattress at the foot of my bed.

"What are you doing?" I croaked. Why did I continue to forget to lock my door? She put an open hand behind her ear, indicating that she couldn't hear me over the roar of the motor. Refusing to yell, I waited until the mattress was filled, mercifully only a few seconds later. "What are you doing?" I repeated then, calmly. She pushed the hair off her face and threw a tangle of sheets over the mattress.

"I'm moving in," she said matter-of-factly.

"Why?" I asked, dazed.

"So you can keep an eye on me," she answered. She perched on the foot of my bed solemnly, face wild but eyes focused. "I want to stay here," she announced, "I *need* to stay here. And I have to prove to my aunt that I deserve it."

"Oh," I replied.

My brain was foggy with fatigue and I wasn't sure whether this new development was a good thing or not. A small part of me wondered briefly if this wasn't part of Nadia's plan: get me definitively on her side while I was sleepy and vulnerable. Perhaps she was plotting something even more nefarious, for which she needed access to my room. Nadia seemed to sense my skepticism.

"Look, Gran—Vera," she drew a deep breath. "I'm sorry. I know I've been a pain in the ass." I raised my eyebrow. "And I know you're thinking I'm only apologizing because I want something from you, and maybe that's true. But," she hesitated, and the words came out slow and painful, "I would be on a bus home if you hadn't said something, so I guess I owe you some respect."

"I deserved respect before that, too," I yawned.

"Right," her fingers traced the embroidery of my comforter. "I get that."

"You sure?" I settled against the headboard, "because you were seriously awful to me."

"I *know*," she rolled her eyes and focused them right back down to the fabric she was now twisting in her hands. Her brows furrowed in a frustration that, I realized, was more towards herself than me. "I think I was jealous," she said finally, still avoiding my gaze. "Aunt Sofia is my only real family, and I thought you were going to, like, take her from me or something. That's stupid, right?"

"Yeah," I agreed bluntly.

"And now I feel like I might actually lose her, and I need your help to keep that from happening." She finally looked me in the eye, tearful but determined. "You don't know how badly I need to fix this." I, uncomfortable with displays of emotion, was now the one to look down at the bedspread. "Please Vera," I heard her say. "Can we please start over?"

She had extended her hand and I stared at it for a second while I had an ethical crisis. It occurred to me that if Nadia went home, there would be justice in it. She had been cruel to me, and to Hector also, and a small part of me wanted nothing more than to return the favor. A larger part of me, however, deemed that impulse as petty and small, and it was that part that reached out and took her hand in mine.

"I'll help you," I agreed. We shook on it, and then Nadia cracked a real smile.

"Excellent," she said happily. "Shall we toast to a fresh start?" I saw the glint of a bottle as she reached into her bag.

"Nadia!" I gasped, grabbing it from her. I held it up to the light.

"Gotcha?" she chuckled hesitantly as the light revealed the bottle to be empty. I swatted her with a pillow and she slid off the bed, laughing.

"Wash your face and go to bed," I said.

I laid back down and pulled the blankets over my head as Nadia went about whatever her bedtime routine consisted of. Within minutes, the overhead lights snapped off and silence fell once more.

-◁◦▷-

What seemed like moments later, the lights were back on and I was being shaken unceremoniously from a very weary sleep.

"What?" I muttered, swatting away the aggressive hand and burying my face further into the pillow.

"Time to get up!" Nadia trilled. The comforter was yanked off, prompting me to curl into the general posture of a fetus against the chill of the room.

"You're joking," I said, raising my head and blinking at the clock. It was a few minutes after three.

"I think I have a better sense of humor than that," she replied. She was running a brush through her hair and was already fully dressed, blankets folded and piled neatly at the end of her mattress.

"Well this isn't funny," I said, letting my head fall back into its pillowy nest.

"C'mon Vera," she pleaded. "It's a new day, remember? I want to make a good start." She was sincere and I was reminded of my promise. I groaned and sat up, wincing as my bare feet met the cold hardwood floor.

"And what does that have to do with being awake right now?" I grumbled.

Apparently, a good start involved a lot of early morning physical labor. By four o'clock, I found myself in what felt like a fever-dream of chores, which I stumbled through with all the grace and efficiency one could expect of me, which was none at all. Under Matthew's critical eye, we fed and hauled water to endless rows of cattle, which yawned humidly in our faces as we filled their troughs. We swept out the barn, and then the expansive porches of the house, working up clouds of dust that stuck in our hair and eyebrows.

Later, we found ourselves busy in the kitchen, whipping up hearty breakfast foods for the family and ranch hands. I was sore and weary, longing for a shower to rid myself of the dirt I just knew was still settled in my ears. Nadia, for her part, actually whistled while she worked, with such a demented Disney-level exuberance that I, at one point, threw a fresh-baked blueberry muffin directly at her face. She caught it and took a bite.

"These are amazing," she commented with maddening cheer. "Good call on adding lemon zest. It really gives it something special."

I had thought of about five special things I could say in reply to that statement when Matthew entered the house, prompting us to bring breakfast out to the table. There was a flurry of feasting in which an improbable amount of food was consumed in about fifteen minutes, and then abandoned as the ranch hands made their way back to work for the day. Soon, all that was left at the table were Nadia, myself, and the Ramos family, as well as a solitary strip of bacon. We stared at it in order to not stare at each other. Finally, Nadia cleared her throat.

"I think it's right that I start this off," she began bravely.

She looked at me and I smiled at her in a weary but supportive sort of way. This was something I had coached her on as we were sweeping out the barn this morning.

"Maturity is the name of the game here," I had said then. "You need to show her that you're taking responsibility for what you've done and you're able and willing to control what you do next."

"What if she cuts me off?" Nadia answered. "Or Hector butts in again? When I get angry I shut down."

"They won't do that," I promised, though I had no way of knowing whether they would or not.

Luckily, however, the two behaved just as I hoped: Mrs. Ramos silent and serious, Hector sulky, but also silent. Nadia took a deep breath and continued.

"I'm sorry for yesterday," she said. "I'm also sorry for last summer, and the one before. I made a lot of bad decisions. My mom—" I kicked her under the table. We had discussed this, also.

"Offering excuses, no matter how valid, will not be effective at this point," I had stressed. Nadia, sufficiently reminded, changed tack quickly.

"I caused you a lot of trouble and pain," she said, "*both* of you. And you didn't deserve it." Her lip trembled. She looked at them both beseechingly. "If I've overstayed my welcome, I understand, but I hope you'll let me stay. This is the only place that's ever felt *safe* to me, and going forward I promise to be better." Silence descended on the table for a long moment. "Vera said she'll help me," Nadia added, tone revealing desperation. Hector shot me a sharp look. I put my hands up.

"I know this is a family thing, and I'm not a babysitter, but if you need someone to confirm she's acting right, I don't mind," I said, ignoring his glower. Mrs. Ramos was shaking her head.

"This is more or less what I had proposed when you got here, no?" she questioned her niece. "I told you to stick with Vera and stay out of trouble and you said you would. And that was a disaster from the start. What's the difference?"

"Me," said Nadia, quickly. "I'm different. I was insulted that you thought I needed a role model, Auntie, and I fought it. I'm not going to do that anymore."

Mrs. Ramos sat back in her chair and appeared to be thinking hard, emotions worrying deep lines into her forehead. Nadia, eyes a little panicked, swiveled her gaze to her cousin, who sat like stone beside his mother. I looked at him too and raised my eyebrow, silently demanding his input.

"I don't buy it," he finally muttered, when she caught his eye. "You've always been a nightmare, no matter how much your 'auntie' cried over you. So I have the same question as my mom: what's the difference?"

A tear tipped over the edge and spilled down Nadia's left cheek. She took in a deep breath, examining her hands self-consciously.

"Mama is in jail," she said quietly, not looking at anyone. "She and her boyfriend were arrested for possession at a party two days ago. That's why I decided to come early." She looked up, eyes starry with tears. "It's her third strike. If I can't stay here, I'll be put into the foster system until I turn eighteen."

My mouth dropped open in surprise. Across the table, Hector slumped back into his chair, eyebrows drawing down furiously. Mrs. Ramos rose wearily from the table. She pulled open the dining room door and turned to us.

"Hector, do you mind showing Vera the garden? She mentioned she had some experience with growing vegetables and I thought she might enjoy looking at our plots." He glared at her.

"You expect us to go look at squash right now?" he asked.

"Please," she said. "I need to talk with your cousin alone."

She waited, holding the door open. Hector looked at me, rolled his eyes and pushed back from the table. I followed him out into the backyard.

"Sounds like she'll get to stay," Hector laughed humorlessly. He kicked the grass and a clod flew through the air into the small garden in front of us. His aim really was impeccable. I shrugged.

"If she gets herself straightened out, will that be such a bad thing?"

"Maybe not," he said, "but she won't." He leaned against the fence and squinted into the garden plot. "She used to steal toys from me and bury them out here when we were little." I raised an eyebrow at him. "I know," he said, acknowledging the look on my face. "Army men, slinkies, it was like a mass grave for the cast of Toy Story out here."

"Why on earth would she do that?" He shrugged.

"Spite? I don't know. Why does Nadia do anything?" A bee started circling his head. "I know she's messed up but, man," he swatted at the bee, "does she have to mess things up for everyone else, too?"

We entered through the gate and walked amongst the rows of vegetables. The sun shone down strongly on our heads. Looking sideways at his long-faced expression, I took a guess at Hector's real hang-up.

"Did you already tell Hallie not to come visit?" I asked.

"Not yet," he mumbled. "It's not going to be a great conversation."

We stopped at a small patch of earth at the edge of the garden. The soil had been turned several times, and now created a narrow mound that was darker and richer than its surroundings. I bent and poked through the pile until I found its contents: several large sunflower seeds, a few already showing signs of sprouting. I sighed with relief as I poked them back into the earth and straightened up, dusting off my hands at my sides.

"How about you put it off, then?" I suggested. "See if this new Nadia thing sticks. Maybe it would be okay for her to come after all." Hector was still looking dubiously at the soil.

"Yeah," he said. "Maybe."

—◦—

Despite all the doubts still held by the household, Nadia was a model citizen in the next week. She worked harder, longer, and (to my detriment) rose earlier than anyone else, and often did so with a smile. Mrs. Ramos, ever the tender optimist, was convinced by the third day, when she rose to find the house scrubbed as if by magical elves.

Nadia had woken me wielding a mop with such determined ferocity that I sprang from bed lest she punch a hole in a wall by accident. She had very little knowledge of how to clean, and was intent on slopping bleach over everything until I confiscated the bucket and instructed her on the merits of floor wax and soap on surfaces that required milder solutions. She listened attentively and carried out the chores with such ruthlessness that grime seemed to make itself scarce simply to avoid her. When Mrs. Ramos walked into her gleaming mudroom that morning, she pulled us to her in a delighted embrace and declared that she wanted to adopt us both. Nadia's shining eyes showed just how much the light-hearted announcement meant.

Matthew was the next skeptic to fall, after a day fixing irrigation lines out on the ranch. Nadia showed herself to be a fast learner in this field as well, and Matthew's diligent double-checking of her work yielded little to be corrected. He took off his hat and scratched his head when he found that we were done before lunch, and shook his head in wonder when I caught his eye. Nadia was grimy and sunburnt at this point, and perhaps wouldn't have mesmerized a young ranch hand as easily as she had Will just days earlier. Matthew's face, however, offered a grudging respect, which was a far harder and more valuable prize to win.

"You might get to take a break now and then if I stick around, Matthew," she grinned winningly over her shoulder as she skipped off to weed the garden. "We might even be able to handle some more animals."

There may have been times I felt ill-used as she dragged me around, seeing to chores and manual labor, but Nadia was careful to pay me back however she could. I fell asleep on the porch one afternoon, exhausted by a day under the sun, and came to find that she had wrangled Will into giving my truck a much-needed oil change. Any concern I had over seeing the two working in close proximity was alleviated by Matthew, who had slipped into the rocking chair beside mine, and pushed me a glass of lemonade to sip as we watched them complete their work.

My horseback riding deficiencies, too, fell victim to new-Nadia's determination and after more than a few brutal lessons, I was able to climb up to a seated position without aid and even ride at a gentle canter. I was far from the "horse-girl" ease and connection with all members of the equine family that Nadia clearly had, but I was happy with the process and grateful for her tutelage.

She even managed to acquire a bottle of blue-black hair dye, claiming that seeing my roots was giving her a headache. She helped me to apply it with a careful precision I hadn't bothered with the first time around, and I didn't worry once that she had impregnated the dye with Nair, or something similarly terrible. The result was downright professional and I found myself offering her a very uncharacteristic high-five. We had, as Mrs. Ramos had hoped, become something like friends.

Our new friendship wasn't without its tests, however. As determined as Nadia was to throw off the hindrances and mistakes of her past, my lack of forthcoming about my own grated at her immensely. Once, having gone to shower after dinner, I came back to the room to find her lying on her stomach on the air mattress, nose deep inside one of my journals. The pile of notebooks had stood untouched on my bedside since Nadia's transformation and, being one of my few personal possessions that hadn't yet been plundered, they had apparently caught her eye.

"Why am I the only one that can't have secrets?" she whined, stung, when I snatched the journal from her hands.

"This isn't yours to read, Nadia," I replied firmly, ignoring the inquiry.

"*Sorry*," she said, not sorry at all. "You're just so mysterious. You can't blame me."

"Yes I can," I snapped. I turned the light off and climbed under the covers. For a moment, the only sound was the slow-leaking of air from Nadia's mattress.

"So are you here because of your husband?" she asked suddenly, a loud voice in the dark. I didn't answer. It seemed she had managed to read a bit after all. "Did he hurt you?" she persisted. I let the silence envelop the ring of her words and lay still. It was quiet for a long time.

"Yes," I said finally, quietly. There was no reply at first, and until I had almost assumed she had fallen asleep.

"I'm sorry," she said then.

We didn't discuss it again.

Hector held out for longer than anyone else, and stomped around the house like a monster the entire week. He growled in reply to Nadia's polite inquiries and sneered at her attempts to be helpful. To me, he wouldn't speak at all, and only acknowledged my existence in a dark scowl that would appear on his face when I entered the room. I was, apparently, a traitor. He ignored all my attempts at conversation as well as my questions about Hallie's arrival. When I stopped by his room to deliver laundry and corner him into talking to me, he actually marched me back through the door and closed it behind me.

Admittedly, this stung. I grew to miss his friendship, and generally found the arrangement awkward. I was, essentially, his guest, and his newfound disgust called into question my even being there. Pulling out my phone one afternoon, I did the unadvisable and called John for advice.

"The guy can hold a grudge," he acknowledged, as I bemoaned my current predicament. "I borrowed a pen from his desk drawer once without asking and he threw a fit. Did you know he booby traps all his belongings?"

"They're indicator traps," I said knowledgeably, "but this is so much worse! I feel weird staying on now. Do you think I should just leave?"

John considered this for a moment.

"I don't know," he finally admitted. "It sounds like your stay has been a blessing. But what do you think? Are you ready to go now?" I furrowed my brow as I considered the question.

"I don't know," I echoed, truthfully. "It wasn't exactly my plan to be here at all, but I'm not sure where to go next."

"Have you prayed about it?" I let that question hang unanswered until he tried again with a less complicated suggestion. "Why don't you talk with Mrs. Ramos about it before you make any decisions?"

I mulled this over for a few seconds; it sounded reasonable.

"You're right," I said, "I'll do that. Thanks, kid."

"No problem, dweeb," he replied cheerfully, "And Vera?"

"Yeah?"

"*I'll* be praying for you."

◄○►

I brought it up that night at dinner.

"Absolutely not," Mrs. Ramos said firmly. I glanced at Hector, who was staring solemnly at his steamed carrots.

"I really don't want to cause any trouble," I probed further.

"And what trouble have you caused, exactly?" Mrs. Ramos chuckled.

I fell silent, not sure how to answer without making things awkward. Hector started shoveling down his vegetables without a word. Nadia, who had been sitting uncharacteristically still up to this point, burst out with the pressurized force of a vigorously shaken can of soda.

"It's me," she said, tears springing to her eyes, "*I'm* the one that's caused all the trouble." She got up from her seat and began tearfully collecting dishes. "Vera shouldn't leave; I will."

"Nadia!" exclaimed her aunt, with bewildered laughter, "No one is suggesting *anyone* leave." She looked around the table, confounded. "What on earth is this all about?"

Matthew, as usual, had all the answers.

"Think our boy here might need some adjusting," he said. He reached over and laid a rough, heavy hand on Hector's shoulder. Hector shrugged it off irritably and put down his fork.

"Just because trouble comes visiting doesn't mean you need to offer it a seat," he retorted, unmoved. "Isn't that something you've always told me?"

Matthew whistled.

"Sure is," he said, "and I never would've bet you listened. But here's the thing, cowboy," his eyes lit across Hector, Nadia, and then myself. "The same thing can be said about anger."

A reverent silence followed, as everyone struggled to find something to say. Matthew leaned back in his chair with drink in hand, sipping comfortably on his lemonade. Hector was making a valiant effort to look unaffected, but the tan on his face was looking rosier than usual. Mrs. Ramos sighed.

"I don't know what to do," she said, looking at him sadly. "I know you're angry about a lot of things, but we're doing the right thing here. You know that, don't you?" Hector maintained stony silence. She sighed again. "If your father were here, he'd take you out to Yellowstone," she said. "That always helped you both to clear your heads."

"I don't see what's stopping you from going now," said Matthew. Mrs. Ramos looked at him, surprised. He raised his hands. "I don't mean to put my oar in on how you run your family, Ma'am, but you know this is my family now too. Has been for a while. And it seems to me like you might all benefit from a trip to Wonderland."

He drained his lemonade and set the glass firmly on the table with the weight of a judge's gavel. Catching my eye across the table, he gave me a wink and settled back in his chair.

"I don't know," said Mrs. Ramos, worriedly, "there's a lot to do here."

"Oh, don't give me that," Matthew scoffed, "if we can take on a herd of alpacas, you can leave the ranch for one weekend." He smiled as her mouth dropped open in surprise. "Don't think I haven't noticed Nadia trying to work me on the idea."

"It's just something I've been thinking over," Mrs. Ramos protested, stricken.

He waved her words away.

"I'm not saying I disagree with the notion, it's just something we should talk about as business partners," said Matthew, a twinkle in his eye. "But we can discuss it when you get back." Mrs. Ramos lapsed into an anxious silence. "Sofia," he pressed gently, "It will be fine."

Finally, she looked up, eyes wet.

"This weekend will be as good a time as any," she said. Her eyes met Hector's. His expression had softened somewhat, a glow of cautious hopefulness lightening his features, and this more than anything seemed to give her resolve. "You'll get everything ready?"

He nodded and she rose, sweeping her way out of the dining room.

"This is big for her, you know," Matthew said, nudging Hector. "I know you're upset about your girlfriend, but it's worthwhile to get your house in order before you invite anyone inside."

Hector nodded again without saying anything, then exited in the opposite direction.

CHAPTER 20

"Do you think there will be bears?"

Nadia was again on her air mattress, slowly squeezing the life from it with her slight weight, and flipping through my National Parks passport to find the section on Yellowstone.

"Probably," I replied. "I'd rather not think about that part, actually."

"Well, if we see one, we can just run downhill," decided Nadia.

"Why do you say that?"

"Bears can't run downhill," she said knowledgeably. I snorted.

"That's a myth." She sat up, the mattress squelching in protest beneath her.

"Says who?" she challenged.

"I listened to a podcast on bears on my drive out here," I said. "Bears can run thirty-seven miles an hour, and, while they can't run as fast downhill, they could still outrun *you*." Nadia snorted her skepticism.

"I'm pretty fast though."

"Not that fast."

"I'm Vera," mocked Nadia in a nasally voice, "I know everything in the *world*!" I threw a pillow at her. It missed by about three feet and flumped to the floor in a defeated fashion.

"I'm glad Matthew got Mrs. Ramos to go," I said. "I think it'll be good for her to get away."

"No kidding," Nadia agreed, "I don't think she's really been anywhere since Uncle Edgar died."

She sat up and cast the passport aside. It landed open and face down on the cluttered floor a few feet away, a small tent in the jungle of Nadia's various belongings.

"What was he like?" I asked. "You know, before he got really sick?" I realized suddenly that I had never even seen a picture of Hector's father, let alone heard anything about him other than sad references. Nadia considered the question.

"Strong," she said finally. "Real outdoorsy, you know? Even when his tremors were getting bad. And weirdly spiritual about it."

"Religious?" I questioned. That would further explain Hector's complicated feelings towards faith.

"Kind of?" Nadia shrugged. "I don't know. I've been here for Christmas a few times and we always went to church out in Bozeman, but Uncle Edgar was more about nature and the richness of the earth and how we're all *connected*." She laughed and then sighed. "I'm thinking this might be a little intense," she added, "for my cousin."

"I guess we'll just have to be sensitive then," I said. "And *you'll* need to be nice to him." Nadia huffed and tossed my pillow back at me. Her aim, far more accurate than mine, propelled the feathery mass directly into my face.

"I'm always nice."

‒◦‒

It was an early Friday morning when we finally rolled off the ranch in the Ramos' old Chevy van. I had gaped at the evident oldness of the thing, but shut my mouth promptly when informed that it was a nineteen ninety-seven model. It was, as Nadia pointed out helpfully, younger than myself.

Hector insisted on driving and his mother perched herself gingerly in the passenger's seat, seeming fragile amidst the weighty bulk of the vehicle and the piles of camping material it held. Nadia and I were stuffed somewhere in the back. We were unable to unearth any functional seatbelt, but it hardly seemed to matter, so immersed were we in duffle bags. Looking around at my cramped nest, I was reminded unpleasantly of my near-burial in the Badlands ranger station parking lot.

"We intend to hike with all this stuff?" I called out nervously. There were four of us, true, but the sheer volume of equipment was less than encouraging. My back was aching already.

"Probably not," Mrs. Ramos offered a wan smile over her shoulder. "We'll get our packs organized once we're there and know more about what we'll be facing."

"What does *that* mean?" cried Nadia. She was much less confident this morning.

"Some trails might have snow," Hector answered, keeping his eyes on the road. "They'll be able to tell us more about what we'll need once we get to the ranger's station. No worries."

He had been far more cordial in the days leading up to the trip, a spark of adventure growing steadily in his eyes. He had a lot of knowledge that he was not loath to impart to us whenever the occasion struck. Come to that, he had a lot of knowledge that he was not loath to impart regardless of the circumstances.

He had met me as I was exiting the bathroom just that morning to remind me that, when backcountry camping, the expectation was that you pack out any waste you accumulate. "That includes feces," he added, face bright as the sun that had not yet risen. I had just grunted in reply and returned to my room to ready for the day. Ordinarily it might have been a bit annoying, but it was reassuring given the circumstances, and certainly better than the cold-shouldering of a few days previous.

I fell asleep quickly amongst the luggage, to be woken some time later by a gentle nudge. I blinked confusedly through sticky contact lenses to see Mrs. Ramos, who had reached back to wake me. She smiled.

"Sorry," she said. "I thought you might not want to miss this." She gestured out the window and, following her gaze, I caught my breath.

All I registered at first was that there was snow. It wasn't a uniform layer, but patches of the stuff clung to the rocks and crevices around us, casting the gray blue of the sky in an even chillier light. I shivered a bit in my tank top, grateful for Hector's hectoring over packing warming layers. It certainly appeared we would need them.

I was struck next by the weird sensation that we were flying, a feeling I couldn't quite place or explain until Nadia, who had been sleeping against the right-side window, woke and launched backwards towards the center of the vehicle with a yelp.

"We're going over the side!" she cried.

Mrs. Ramos shushed her hurriedly, and I saw Hector's jaw tense, mirroring his fingers, which had already been clutched white around the steering wheel.

"We will if you don't *shut up*," he snarled. "I need to concentrate."

It was now clear why. While we weren't falling into the massive gorge to the right just yet, a closer look out Nadia's side revealed that there was little more than a few feet of room and a small barrier to prevent that particular fate. That barrier, too, was broken in some places, and missing altogether in others, and Hector seemed to be going impossibly fast to navigate the dire squeeze the road was presenting.

"Welcome to the Beartooth Highway," Mrs. Ramos said, smiling, as her son sped recklessly through the treacherous terrain.

"It's beautiful," I managed, wishing with all my heart that I had stayed asleep.

"Yeah, when do we get off of it?" Nadia squeaked.

Mrs. Ramos checked her map. "Not for a while," she said. "The highway itself is around sixty-seven miles, and we're not even halfway through." She traced the route with her finger. "We should stop in a few minutes, though, to check out the highest peak, don't you think?" She directed this question at her son, who nodded stiffly, not taking his eyes from the road.

We endured what felt like a lifetime of twists, hairpin turns and switchbacks. There were an unfortunate number of cars coming from the opposite direction going even faster than we were, and taking up more than their fair share of the asphalt. Nadia grabbed my hand hard as a red Lamborghini careened past us, causing the top-heavy van to rock slightly.

"There sure are a lot of sports cars," I noted, trying to direct my thoughts away from sudden death.

"I noticed that too," agreed Mrs. Ramos. "Maybe they're filming a commercial up here today. It's a good landscape for it."

We climbed and twisted. I tried my hardest to keep my gasps to a minimum. Nadia wasn't particularly helpful on this front, reaching out to clutch my arm at every turn of the wheels. At last, Hector pulled over into one of the larger lookouts and put the car in park.

"We're at ten thousand feet," he announced. He exhaled heavily and smiled as he unbuckled his seatbelt and pushed open the door.

We piled out with wobbly legs, breathing the thin air gratefully. The earth fell away below us, and we could see mountains peaking for miles and miles in all directions. It was cold and clear. Incredibly, wildflowers of yellow and blue peaked out between patches of snow. Mrs. Ramos and Nadia wandered away to take pictures. I found I was rooted to the spot.

"It's a big world, isn't it?" Hector had joined me where I leaned against the front of the van. The land tumbled down into oblivion before us.

"Huge," I said, staring into the chasm.

"It's easy to forget," he said, crossing his arms in front of him. "There's not much like this in North Carolina."

"There's not much like this anywhere," I said. I turned to look at him carefully. "Thanks for bringing me on this trip. I think I've needed to get out."

Hector laughed. "It's not like you've been much of a homebody this summer."

"I'm serious," I persisted. "I know this isn't what you envisioned for your camping trip, and I'm grateful you let me come. It means a lot to have been included."

He sobered. "Don't mention it." His hands hid themselves in his pockets awkwardly. "My dad always made sure to take Beartooth Pass to get to Yellowstone's entrance. I loved it, all the switchbacks, every time we almost drove off a cliff." He shook his head. "It's easy to feel invincible when you're a kid."

"And when you don't have to drive," I added.

He laughed. "Yeah, that too." He stared for a minute into the distance. "I'm glad Mom's here, at least." I glanced at him and smiled.

"Me too," I said. "I think she's really happy to be spending this time with you."

"And Nadia," he added, heavily.

"And Nadia," I agreed. A chilly wind came and lifted the hair from our necks in a momentary bluster. I shivered and rubbed my arms. "I'm sorry if I've been overstepping, Hector. I know you didn't want Nadia around any longer." He was quiet for a long time.

"You know," he said finally, "I'm starting to realize that what I really want is for my mom to be happy again. Maybe that's why Nadia is here." He glanced at me shyly. "Maybe that's why *you're* here." I turned fully and looked at him in amazement.

"Why, Hector," I said, pretending to be scandalized, "that sounded positively *spiritual*!" He scoffed.

"Don't get excited," he said gruffly. "I'm just trying to be a good son for a change."

"John is going to be thrilled," I teased.

"Don't start with me," he replied gruffly, but the smile had returned to his face. He elbowed me amicably.

"Guys, there's a beaver up here!"

Nadia's voice cracked like a whip in the high altitude. We turned to see her crouched in front of a rock, trying to coax whatever was behind it to come forward. Mrs. Ramos was bent double with laughter.

"Nadia, that's a *marmot*!"

"A varmint?" she asked, bending closer.

The small, brown creature darted away quickly, running full speed towards the edge of the cliff. Nadia let out a panicked squeal as we watched the animal disappear over the drop off.

"Did you really drive that thing over a cliff, Nadia?" asked Hector. He was laughing.

Nadia was staring blankly at where the fuzzy thing had disappeared. "I don't know," she said, "Did I?"

"Not at all," Mrs. Ramos looped her arm around Nadia's shoulders and steered her back towards the car. "Marmots are good rock climbers, and they burrow. It probably just made a run for home."

"That said," added Hector, "we need to talk about how close we should get to wildlife once we're out there."

"I can lead that one," I volunteered, "there's a section on it in my Parks Passport. Besides," here I gave him a strained smile, "you need to be able to concentrate on the road." He grinned wickedly.

"Have at it, Teach," he said, unlocking the van with a musical tone from his key fob. We piled in with almost as much trepidation as difficulty, having to once again find our place amongst the bags. Once settled, Hector started the engine, made a regrettable joke about forgetting to put the van in reverse, and we were off.

As it turned out, teaching from the passport was an excellent distraction during our treacherous final hour through Beartooth Pass. Nadia was ravenous for information and Mrs. Ramos was polite and inquisitive, claiming she needed a refresher course after a few years off from adventures like these. I, as usual, learned more and better from teaching the information than I had from reading through it the first time, and was reasonably confident by the time we pulled up to the gate and showed our passes to the bored-looking youth standing vigil.

We drove on down mercifully wide, winding roads as the day ripened around us. Puffs of steam wafted up from the horizon in some places, evidence of some of the park's hydrothermal areas. At Nadia's insistence, we stopped briefly to stare open-mouthed at one of the hot springs, colored brilliantly in jewel-bright hues. These interested me particularly, and I peppered Hector liberally with questions. He had just begun to explain some of the finer points of thermophiles when an excited Nadia dragged me by my elbow across the road to a patch of sluggishly bubbling mud pits.

"The earth is alive!" she exclaimed, her eyes bright with the sort of childlike wonder I had not thought her capable of. I found it hard to be impressed with this feature, watching the pale glubbing of the mud in front of me.

"Those are mudpots," noted Hector, anticipating the question as he checked his watch. "We really need to get to the backcountry office before all the permits are gone. We can check out the tourist stuff later."

"What do you mean tourist stuff?" demanded Nadia indignantly.

This question was also answered before she had even finished voicing it, as a large bus pulled up and unloaded legions of people like a clown car. The chattering of multiple languages filled the crisp morning air and we quietly took our leave, arriving at Hector's beloved backcountry office a while later.

Hector and Mrs. Ramos spoke at length with the ranger at the window, and she obligingly provided us with permits, maps, and a bear box, with the condition that before heading out we complete a viewing of a program called "Bear Aware." We watched the short video crowded around a beat-up tablet in the grass, and I was hushed several times as I tried to interject my own bear knowledge over the narrator.

A flurry of packing and a quick lunch followed the presentation, and we drove the short distance to the trailhead imbued with the ranger's last-minute reminders, which were still ringing in our ears by the time the van came to a stop. A week of hurried and concentrated planning had finally come to this: it was us and the trail.

CHAPTER 21

I'LL SAY THIS ABOUT backpacking: it's best appreciated when it's done. We had not gone more than a few steps down the trail, the trees closing in behind us and silence pressing on our ears as if we had plunged underwater, when my body's small aches and annoyances began to sing. The right strap of my pack had begun to dig into my shoulder with just the right amount of pressure to numb my right arm. The sock on my left foot had slipped down enough to expose the back of my heel to the rubbing friction of my shoe. My bear spray, strapped excessively to my side, slapped obnoxiously against my thigh and was loud in the relative quiet of the park.

Not that the quiet remained for long, anyway.

"Hey bear!" Hector called out. A few minutes later, he repeated the sentiment, "Heeeeeeey bear!"

"I know we're supposed to do that as we hike so we don't startle them," panted Nadia, who had fallen a few steps behind me, "but is it really the move to let them know we're here?"

"It's a good thing to do," Hector assured her, calling back from his position in front. "Bears don't want anything to do with people. If any are in the area, they'll clear out when they hear us coming."

"Not always," I countered, "Some bears have been known to stalk hikers, and they move quietly enough to be invisible."

"You know what?" called Nadia, "No more podcasts for you."

When we came to a small, trickling stream, we stopped for a quick rest and some electrolytes contained in not a little chocolate. The granola bars had grown gooey as the air warmed around us, and we carefully licked the melted portions from our fingers as we breathed in the mountain air funneling through the valley where we found ourselves. It was undeniably beautiful, the sun beaming down, gilding the pines in a bright, vigorous way. The streams babbled brightly to us as they passed. A sharp pain came over me suddenly, and I had to close my eyes to it. It was all *too* perfect.

"You good?" Hector was staring at me. I nodded and tried to wave him off. Unconvinced, he passed me a packet of moleskin, and I kicked off my shoes gratefully.

"How'd you know?"

"Mom saw you limping," he said. Mrs. Ramos had insisted on bringing up the rear, saying that she didn't want to get in the way with her slower pace. I now suspected she simply liked to keep a sharp eye on everyone at once.

"You need to speak up if you need anything," Mrs. Ramos said, adjusting the straps on her pack. "Don't be brave about it; even the little things grow serious over time. That goes for both of you." She glanced pointedly at me and her niece.

Nadia raised her hands, as if to ward off the implication. "Hey, you know I won't think twice about complaining. It's Vera you need to worry about."

She had stripped off her socks, and flung one, damp and woolen at me. It missed, and landed heavily on a rock where it lay like a tired, deflated eel.

"Don't do that," advised Hector. Nadia had wandered to the stream and was preparing to dip her bare feet into the merry flow.

"They feel so gross, though!" Nadia protested, a definite whine in her voice.

"You'll feel worse hiking with wet socks," he assured her. "Besides, we don't want to pollute the water source. If you need to wash up, take a cup of water and biodegradable soap, and rinse well away from the stream."

"Oh right," Nadia rolled her eyes, "I forgot we were hiking with a bona fide forest ranger."

"Not yet," Hector grinned, "but soon."

We continued on in our previous formation: me, leading Nadia, the two of us sandwiched by the Ramos's. We talked for a time, but conversation became less possible as the incline steadily grew more intense. Much of the day, we simply took turns calling out to the potential bears in the area, and hiked on in relative silence. Unlike Badlands, there was an abundance of vegetation and roots to navigate. Also unlike Badlands, there was no large wildlife to be seen. I remarked on this to Hector at one point.

"The further we get from the trailhead, the more likely we'll be to see something," he said over his shoulder. "This part of the trail is actually pretty well trafficked, and the animals don't want anything to do with people for the most part."

When the sun began to slant through the trees in distinctly afternoon-like angles, Hector announced that we had arrived at the first campsite. There were several clearings in the vicinity, mostly leveled off, and Hector examined each critically before choosing the one that was furthest along the trail. It was a good spot, studded with large boulders to one side that provided privacy from other hikers that might come along, as well as enough open space to stretch out in the sun and nap, as Nadia did immediately.

"You're not going to help me put up the tent?" Hector asked, unloading the poles from his pack.

"You've got this," replied Nadia lazily, "You're a power ranger, remember?"

"A forest ranger," he corrected, "and that doesn't mean help wouldn't be nice."

Nadia didn't reply, apparently already asleep. I dropped my pack heavily and stretched. My muscles were already sore, and I hated to think what they would feel like after a night on the ground. Together, we took our water bottles down to the stream and filtered some water for a refill.

"All right," Hector said, stepping back from our work. "I think that's good." He dried his hands on his pants and then bent to his pack to grab a Ziploc from the side pouch. "I gotta go take a dump."

"Hector! *Language!*" his mother sputtered. She had been drinking deeply of her freshly filtered water and now coughed forcefully, aghast at his statement. "There's no need to be crude!"

"We are *literally* in the wilderness, Mother. No one cares about manners here."

"I do; correct yourself."

Hector sighed exaggeratedly. "Fine," he fought a smile that threatened to inch up his face and reached up to grip the bill of his hat. "Fare thee well, honorable matriarch, and you, gentle lady," he swept the ball cap off his head and leaned into a low bow. "I must go forth on a solitary quest to oust a monster, a creature so ponderous, nay, so *odious . . .*"

His mother threw a roll of toilet paper at his head. "Begone, vile offspring. Take care not to slay any monsters upwind this time."

Hector caught the roll and started off, his ears looking a bit pink from behind. "It was *one time* . . . " We laughed as he walked away.

"That boy," sighed Mrs. Ramos, brushing a tear of laughter from the corner of her eye, "He's so grown up in some ways, but in others . . . " She smiled at me. "I can't resist taking him down a peg sometimes."

"I don't think he minds it," I replied. "He's so at home out here."

"He is, isn't he?" said Mrs. Ramos reflectively. "I'm glad we did this. I had forgotten how much closer we would get as a family on these trips."

I knelt at my pack and unbound my sleeping mat and bag. Hector had already put his out as well, and on his high-altitude sleep system sat the squat, plastic bear box we had received at the backcountry office. I picked it up and brought it to Mrs. Ramos.

"Oh, we need to find a place for that don't we?" she said, pausing her own unpacking. "Would you like to go see to that now?"

"Let's do it," I said gamely.

"Hey," Mrs. Ramos nudged Nadia with her toe. She squirmed irritably on the ground a moment before peering up at her aunt. "We're going to stow away the bear box. Do me a favor and help your cousin set up the tent."

"Fine," she yawned, before hauling herself to a seated position.

"Play nice," Mrs. Ramos warned, and together we headed off, walking perpendicularly to the trail and away from camp.

"It needs to be at least one hundred yards away, but I prefer to walk it out even further," she said, taking even, measured steps. "And we'll need to be able to find it again, that's the trick."

"Will we need to eat our food away from camp also?" I asked.

The ranger had instructed us to put all food items in the box, as well as scented substances like toothpaste and wet wipes. If bears could smell those sorts of items, we definitely wouldn't want any potential food smells hanging around camp.

She nodded. "That would be wise. We'll walk the Jetboils out here when the time comes and have a picnic." We walked for a while in silence before she spoke again. "How are you liking all of this?"

"It's not what I expected," I said, thinking the matter over carefully, "I camped at Badlands on a whim; I have a feeling I couldn't do that here."

"There's a bit more to it, isn't there?" she conceded.

"Definitely," I said, "And that's not really been my thing recently. Planning things out, I mean," I said in answer to her questioning look. "I probably wouldn't have done this by myself, but now that Hector's gotten us all through the process, I really like being out here. I'd do it again."

"I thought the same thing when my husband first brought me out," she replied. Her eyes took on a dream quality. "He would insist on prepping for a trip at least three months in advance, and wouldn't talk about anything else the whole time. He was forever researching new gear and repacking, and repacking *again*. Used to drive me crazy."

"So we got the condensed version," I surmised, seeing Hector's frenzy over the past four days with new eyes.

"Oh absolutely," she said. "But, wouldn't you know it? Every bit of the tedium, all of the endless conversations, it always ended up helping us out of what would otherwise have been a dangerous situation."

"Like what?" I asked, curious.

We had come to a stop at the edge of a small meadow. Long grasses danced in the slight breeze, edged in gold by the descending sun. At the center, a large conifer held court over the clumps of wildflowers at its base. I glanced at Mrs. Ramos and she nodded in affirmation. Our bear box would be living here for the night.

"Well, one summer we came out for a week, just the two of us." She tucked the bear box at the base of the tree, ensuring it was visible from the direction we came. "Hector was still a baby, and it was my first time being away from him. It hurt me, right here," she patted her chest, "to even think about it. My mother had come out to look after him, but still," she looked at me, "when you love someone like that, they become a part of you."

I knew this, and swallowed a lump from my throat, cognizant of the pang living in my own chest. Bear box hidden, we turned to hike back.

"Edgar, of course, wouldn't talk about anything else, and I just couldn't bear to participate. I remember he asked me, once, if he should purchase crampons for us. I had just put Hector down for a nap, and was watching him sleep, the sweet little thing, and this man decided it was an appropriate time to bother me over traction devices for our shoes."

"What did you say?"

She chuckled, "Would you believe it? I yelled at him. Woke Hector right up, which I also blamed Edgar for. I told him he needed to take his camp talk and shove it if he wanted me to go at all."

"That's a little harsh," I said, tripping on an exposed root.

"He just kissed me on the cheek and went on with his preparations, in silence this time. He didn't bother me again, but he did go ahead and buy those crampons, along with extra thermal gear and hand warmers, and put them in our packs. And, can you guess what happened?"

"It snowed?"

"We woke up to a foot on the ground in mid-July. He fitted the crampons over my boots and I didn't slip on ice once on the way back. When my toes went numb, he activated some hand warmers and put them between my double-layer of socks."

"So he really knew what he was doing," I said.

"He took care of me," she answered, "He did that for everyone he loved, for as long as he could." She smiled. "And so I try to honor him now by doing the same, whenever I can."

By this time we had arrived back at camp. The tent was set up and appeared sturdy. To our surprise, Hector and Nadia were perched together chummily on one of the boulders, poring over his ranger handbook. He was explaining, with great enthusiasm, the massive caldera that Yellowstone sat upon, ready to erupt at any moment. To her credit, Nadia was doing her best to look interested instead of just terrified. Mrs. Ramos clapped her hands eagerly.

"All right, children, shall we wash up and get ready for supper while there's still light out?"

We did so, cleaning carefully away from the water source, per Hector's instructions. That evening we dined on rehydrated lasagna, which wasn't half bad after a day of exertion, and followed with a quick brushing of teeth, spitting into the woods before stowing our toothbrushes and toothpaste back in the bear box. Tired after the early wake up and travel, no one much wanted to sit around afterwards, so we all crawled into the tent and, despite cramped quarters and the sounds of bugs bouncing off the canvas, quickly fell into a sound sleep.

Chapter 22

THE COLOR OF THE tent dyed the morning light a flare orange, and I squinted at it before navigating over Nadia and Mrs. Ramos to step out into the dawn. The air was chilly, and I shivered in my thermals while I tried to blink the world into focus. My eye doctor would have been appalled to know I was sleeping in my contact lenses, I know, but I didn't much want to stow my only means of vision overnight in the bear box. That said, contacts get sticky and slide to the corners of your eyes when you sleep in them, so I don't recommend it.

When my vision finally cleared, I saw Hector around the side of the tent, also blinking, although, in his case, it was out of disbelief.

"They put it literally three feet from us."

He reached down and picked up what I recognized as a bear box. I was mystified for half a second until I realized that it wasn't ours. This one was dark green, and labelled with a different number in white spray paint.

"Who?" I asked. He turned to me, a bit wildly.

"I'd say probably someone a hundred yards in *that* direction," he replied, pointing down the trail in the direction we came yesterday.

"Oh," I said calmly, seeing his agitation, "I'm sure it was an honest mistake."

"It doesn't matter," he said angrily. He tucked the box under his arm and struck out along the trail. "That's too dangerous to let slide. I'm going to talk to them."

He turned on his heel and strode purposefully off down the trail, the anonymous bear box held in his arm like a football.

"Okay, but we can do this calmly, right?" I called.

Hector didn't answer and was soon out of sight. Concerned, I grabbed my jacket and hurried after him.

We walked for five minutes in silence and Hector didn't stop his angry march the whole time. I grew nervous when we neared the other camp, parked alongside the trail at the very beginning of the designated campgrounds. Two young men were already out of their tents, stretching. At our approach, they turned and waved in a friendly fashion, beaming at us as Hector moved in like a thundercloud.

"Hector," I grabbed his arm and gestured to their tent, "they might not speak English." A Cambodian flag fluttered merrily in the breeze where it was pinned to the canvas.

"I don't care," he said, pulling away from me, "I'll make them understand."

And he certainly tried his best. At first, the two simply took the bear box from him with bowing motions, clearly trying to thank him for delivering it to them. He shook his head and explained more loudly, with big gestures of his arms that would not have made sense in either language. When, confused, they opened the bear box to show its contents to us, he turned away with a huff and gave up, throwing up his hands in frustration and marching back up the trail. I gestured at the two in what I hoped looked like a conciliatory fashion and followed. The men waved cheerfully at our retreating backs.

"Don't say anything," Hector warned as I caught up to him.

"No, that was really good," I said drily. "If the forest ranger thing doesn't work out, you should look into international relations." He glowered but didn't dignify me with a response.

We packed up camp quickly and journeyed out to the meadow to retrieve our bear box, still sitting obediently at the base of the tree, to scarf down some oatmeal before we got on our way. The trail curved alongside the mountain today, meaning our hike would be fairly level before we started our descent the following morning. It was happy news to hikers that awoke feeling aches that howled in our joints like ghosts of exertions past.

We hobbled along in a similar formation to the day before, talking little and taking frequent breaks for snacks and hydration. Mrs. Ramos was diligent about refilling our water bottles with freshly filtered water from the mountain, and Hector was diligent about scolding us when he felt we weren't emptying our bottles fast enough.

"Dehydration is a merciless teacher," he chided me. I tried not to let my face twitch as, over his shoulder, Nadia mocked the stooped posture he had adopted to speak sternly to me, wagging her finger in my direction like a disappointed grandmother.

We saw little more than trees until midafternoon. I had begun to wonder when we would be stopping for the day, when Hector did just that, with an abruptness that caused me to run into him from behind and topple over backwards, taking Nadia down with me. Mrs. Ramos, more poised and alert, remained on her feet, and urged us to get up in low, urgent tones.

"Be still!" Hector hissed, alarmed by the crunching of the leaves that resulted. I carefully leaned forward to peek cautiously over his shoulder. In the brightness of the mature sun, I could just barely make out the retreating backside of something large and dark. It was well over the distance away recommended by the National Parks Service, but it was easy to understand Hector's caution.

"What was it?" I whispered, as the form faded away into the foliage.

"I'm not sure," he admitted, breathing out his relief. "It could have been a bear, or maybe a moose? I couldn't really make out anything other than its size."

"It was big," I acknowledged. "Do we need to turn back?"

He scrutinized the path in front of us. "I'm not sure," he said finally, "It was heading for a higher elevation. I think it just happened to cross the trail when we got in view." For the first time, he turned bodily to look at the three of us. "I think we should be fine to keep going?" Our fearless leader sounded less than secure.

There was a dubious silence.

"Aye, Captain," Nadia, to our surprise, shouldered past and started down the trail. "Hey bear!" she called, as if greeting a friend by her locker. "Hey bear?" she cried again, a few minutes later, as if clarifying something from a distance. "Hey, bear!" she persisted minutes after that, as if challenging a bully to a fight. We laughed at her theatrics until hiking robbed us of breath again.

The designated campsite for that night lay so little used that we might have missed it, had it not been for its excellent added feature.

"A fire pit!" cried a delighted Mrs. Ramos, crouching to examine the depression in the clearing, light with ash. "I had hoped there'd be at least one this trip."

"But we don't have any firewood," I pointed out, a bit disappointed at the fact. One of the reminders the park ranger had emphasized over and over was that the natural foliage should not be harmed as a result of hiking or camping. Any campfire would have to be kindled with wood that was packed in, and then suitably smothered according to Smokey-the-Bear procedures.

"Yeah we do," Hector reached for a hidden zipper at the bottom of my pack and yanked firmly. The previously unknown compartment opened wide and dropped a load of neatly chopped firewood in various thicknesses on the forest floor like a weird pinata.

"That's been in there the whole time?" I cried, incredulous. My pack, now freed of its splintery burden, was easily ten pounds lighter.

"Thanks for taking one for the team," he smirked. He and Mrs. Ramos began setting up camp with the well-coordinated speed of experts. Nadia bent down and gathered the kindling at my feet.

"And y'all think *I'm* sneaky," she said, rolling her eyes.

We ate dinner the prescribed hundred yards from camp, a watery chili this time that was only welcome as it was warm. The falling darkness had the air turning cooler than my current layers were fit to combat. A campfire would be a wonderful thing.

Mrs. Ramos, as it turned out, was in charge of that particular installation. With deft hands, she carved slivers of wood, tossing the thin curls into a pile before using her Firestarter to kick up a spark. The dry wood caught eagerly, and with hands cupped to protect the little spark from any errant breezes, she blew lightly until the glow became a small flame that could hold its own.

"You make that look easy," I said, impressed. She shrugged modestly.

"When Edgar got sick, our first clue was that his hands would shake," she straightened up and dusted off her knees, surveying the flames with a critical eye. "I learned so we could keep coming out a little longer."

"Can we *not* take that particular turn down memory lane?" Hector had just emerged from the tent, where he had been setting up his sleep system. He gave me a sharp look, as if I had been responsible for prompting the sad nostalgia, which I suppose I had. I moved forward to warm my hands over the fire and gamely changed the subject.

"If bears weren't such an issue, we could have roasted marshmallows," I grinned at him in a pacifying fashion. "Don't s'mores sound good right about now?"

Hector dropped his attitude as quickly as he had put it on. "I thought we could tell stories around the fire like we used to," he said eagerly, pulling out a small, worn book. "I brought dad's old collection of myths and lore."

"Oh, Hector," his mother protested, "No one will be able to sleep tonight."

"On the contrary," interjected Nadia. She was flat on her back with her eyes closed beside the fire. Her pointer finger raised resolutely in the air stated that she would be able to sleep no matter what.

"Let's do it," I said quickly. "Storytime sounds perfect to me."

We settled around the fire, wrapped against the creeping chill with our sleeping bags. The shadows deepened at our backs as Hector flipped open the worn tome and began.

"It's only fitting that I tell the story of a creature that haunts the lonely places," he said, creepily. His voice became the hoarse whisper of an undertaker suffering from a head cold. "It's a beast of Algonquin folklore, and there have been sightings all over the world, including in this very park."

"Skin walkers?" said Nadia. She was still reclined on her back, eyes closed, but was apparently listening.

"No, shut up," Hector said, breaking character momentarily, before continuing in his raspy tones. "According to legend, the wendigo is cursed to roam endlessly, feeding its hunger with human flesh, where it can get it. The wendigo is said to be able to grow as tall as the trees, emaciated and starving, with antlers sprouting from its skull and yellow fangs, bared in its bloody, lipless mouth. It leaves footprints of blood in its wake, and a heart of ice rests in its chest."

Nadia had sat up by now, and was watching her cousin skeptically. "So it's a scary deer-man that eats people? Cool. Where's the story in that?"

"Be patient, Nadia," chided her aunt.

Hector continued as if the interruption hadn't occurred. "The Algonquin claim that this creature has the ability to possess the people who cross its path. Young men who become lost in the woods often fall victim to this fate, and bring the hunger of the wendigo back with them. They feed and then move on to rove the wilderness for all eternity."

The dark had fallen in earnest, cloaking the outside of our small circle in velvety blackness. *Prone to wander, Lord, I fear it.* The words, sung in my father's rich baritone as I had heard it in church years ago, crossed my mind randomly, unbidden. I shivered despite myself and shifted closer to the fire. *Where did that come from?* Hector continued his story, flipping a page in his book without even looking down.

"In the late 1800s, a man named Swift Runner was out in the woods when he crossed the path of a wendigo. He was a trapper by trade, and was often alone in the forest for long periods. One day, though, he wandered off the trail and found himself lost. Try as he might, he couldn't remember where he had come from, or the way back. He was alone for three days and two nights before he finally stumbled back into his small village. His young wife and children were overjoyed to see him, but something was different." He paused significantly, and nodded at us, as if answering an unposed question. "One by one, he slaughtered and ate his wife and children."

"Men," scoffed Nadia. I laughed and Hector silenced us both with a look.

"He stored their flesh in the snow and feasted in the dead of night, gorging until he was sick," he continued. "No matter how much he ate, though, his hunger was never satisfied."

"Sounds like Will on taco night," Nadia snorted. Mrs. Ramos laughed in agreement.

"Can I continue, please?" Hector waved his book for attention. "One by one, the children of the village began to disappear. The villagers had their suspicions already, and conducted a raid on Swift Runner's home. Inside, they found piles of human bones." Hector paused dramatically. Mrs. Ramos rolled her eyes at his theatrics. "Swift Runner was arrested by the Canadian authorities and convicted right away. Those who were present at his hanging swore they saw the figure of a strange man, tall, thin, with antlers, watching the execution from the tree line."

He took a bow and then sat, snapping his book of lore shut decisively, though he had not looked at it once since he began telling the story. I imagined Hector as a child, crouched around a similar fire, begging his father to tell him a story. Edgar must have indulged him often for Hector to have memorized the tale like that.

"Well that was stupid," grumbled Nadia, obviously shaken, but trying not to show it. "Where do people come up with this stuff?"

"I think I've heard of wendigos, actually," I said. "Isn't wendigo psychosis an actual condition?"

Hector nodded, pleased. "It's a syndrome that makes you crave to consume humans, and, ironically, the fear of becoming a cannibal. It's rare, but it has been diagnosed most often in Canada and the northern United States."

"In other words, places where heavy snowfall can isolate people and lead to starvation," added Mrs. Ramos, "hence the regional lore."

"It's interesting, isn't it?" I asked, "how people tend to create monsters to explain awful behaviors?"

"What do you mean?" probed Hector.

"Well, like your mom was saying, there were conditions in place that led some people to acts of desperation to survive, like cannibalism," I said. "But because it's such an unimaginable thing, it's easier to say they were possessed by monsters than to accept that a person could be driven to eat their wife and children."

"I think plenty of people would rather die than kill their families," argued Hector.

"You're right," I conceded, "but obviously there are those that would. Plenty of people do terrible things for less. It's not because there are monsters, it's because *they're* monsters." My commentary was met with silence.

"That's pretty cynical," said Mrs. Ramos finally.

"It's not though," Nadia said, glancing at me thoughtfully, "It's spot on."

There was a still moment where the only sounds were the hearty cracklings of the campfire. The light created a bright circle around us, but cast everything outside of it into such deep shadow that we couldn't see anything else. We were warm and snug in our golden bubble, but, peering uselessly into the darkness outside, it was easy to imagine unseen creatures prowling the perimeter. Mrs. Ramos seemed to feel the same way.

"It's my turn to tell a story, I think," she said, with an air of changing the subject. She shook her head at Hector, who was attempting to pass her the book of lore, and scooted closer to the fire, extending her hands to warm them before the flames. "I'm not one for horror stories, so I think I'll switch up the genre. This is one I know by heart. It's about me and your mother," she looked at Nadia, "when we were around your age."

"So we're moving from legends to ancient history," teased Hector. Mrs. Ramos smiled but didn't comment as she began to tell her story.

When she was young, she explained, her parents moved the family to Salinas, California. It was a beautiful place, and excellent for farming, which is what her parents did, but it was in no way perfect.

"This was the seventies," she said, "and at that time there really wasn't much for kids to do. The little ones ran and played outside, but Rosa and I felt too grown up for that. That's when we discovered the rodeo."

She described sneaking into the rodeo for the first time with her sister. She had been captivated by the energy and power of the bucking horses, and enthralled to watch the young men try to ride them without being flung into orbit.

"I liked the bull riding events the most," she said. "They were the most exciting to watch. Rosa, on the other hand, was more interested in the cowboys."

"Of course she was," sniffed Nadia, rolling her eyes.

"We went back as often as we could," Mrs. Ramos continued. "I don't think we ever paid admission, because Rosa had this way of walking like she owned a place and no one ever questioned us. Eventually, we got a little bolder about it."

Soon, the two weren't just sneaking into the stands, they were going down behind the chutes where the bulls and horses would be released. Rosa, who was sounding more and more like Nadia to me, made a game of charming every man on the floor. Mrs. Ramos, awe-struck and a bit shy, hung back and watched the events from the closer vantage point, eyes wide and thrilled.

One day, while Rosa was busy flirting with a cowboy from Texas, one of the competitors was thrown from his horse and landed badly. He laid there in the dust while his horse was wrangled safely away, and was so still she feared he was dead.

"I'm not sure what happened," she said, "but the next second I was in the ring at his side, even before the medics were able to reach him with the stretcher. I held his hand and brushed the dirt off his face, and I remember thinking he was the most handsome man I had ever seen."

She paused, her eyes misty. Nadia, Hector, and I exchanged glances and gave her a moment before bringing her back to earth.

"Did he wake up?" asked Hector. Mrs. Ramos smiled at him.

"He opened his eyes and laughed," she answered, "this deep, exhilarated laugh like that had been the most fun he'd ever had. And then he looked at me, and it was all over."

"Wait," said Nadia, slowly, "was that Uncle Hector?"

She nodded, still smiling, and Nadia and Hector exclaimed as one.

"You've never told us that story!"

"Your father wasn't overly proud of his rodeo career, short-lived as it was," she said, addressing Hector. "He preferred to think we had met in a more dignified way, when he wasn't flat on his back, but I didn't mind." She looked deep into the fire. "You don't forget falling in love, and, even all those years we watched him deteriorate, that memory kept him alive in my heart. Those eyes, and that laugh."

Hector was staring into the flames now, too. It was, I reflected, a side of his father that he probably hadn't had a chance to see. Edgar's diagnosis had happened when Hector was still so young. Was he grieving at how little he had gotten to know his dad? Or was he treasuring this new story, just as Mrs. Ramos did? Either way, he was at a loss of what to say now. Nadia, however, moved and settled next to her aunt before the fire, wrapping a thin arm around her frame and hugging her tightly.

"It's a beautiful love story, Auntie," she said softly, giving her aunt a kiss on the cheek. She looked round at me and quirked an eyebrow. "What about you, Teach? You got any stories in your arsenal? Romance or horror, we don't mind."

Truthfully, my story encompassed both of those genres, and I fully intended to take both of them to my grave. It came as a surprise, therefore, when my mouth opened and words came out.

"When I was in school," I began, "there was this huge magnolia tree nestled up against the library. It was the perfect place to sit and study, because you were sheltered by the stone walls on one side, and the branches screened you from the rest of campus on the other. It also had this bench underneath with these wide arms that could hold your books at the perfect angle for reading while you were taking notes. I was there all the time."

"Of course you were," scoffed Nadia, "What a nerd." I smiled and continued.

"One day, before my sociology test, I went to my tree for a quick hour of studying and there was someone already there. He was stretched out on my bench fast asleep." I looked up from the fire and saw that Mrs. Ramos had turned to face me, legs crossed like a child during story time. "For some reason, this made me really upset. It was the one spot on campus that I didn't have to share, and here was this guy, not only in my space, but using it *wrong*."

"So you woke him up," concluded Hector. I was gratified to see the corner of his mouth twitched up in a smile.

"Vera? No, surely not," chimed in Mrs. Ramos, "She's too sweet."

"I did," I admitted smiling. I looked at Mrs. Ramos, "I used to be a lot feistier."

"That's hard to imagine," said Nadia. I shrugged and continued.

"I had brought an apple as a snack, so I took it out of my bookbag and tossed it at him. He woke up all startled and I told him it had fallen out of the tree."

"And he bought that?" laughed Nadia.

"No, not at all," I answered. "Like I said, it was a magnolia tree and I had gotten the apple from the cafeteria so it still had a produce sticker on it." They laughed. I chuckled a little too.

"So how did mystery man respond?" asked Nadia.

"Very gallantly," I recalled. "He made space on the bench and suggested we share it so we could both study. I guess he'd been using the spot for the past year or so, and we'd just been missing each other. He was nice, but then he took a bite of my apple and made a face." I laughed again. The memory was as fresh and tart as the granny smith had been. "It was a green apple, which is my favorite fruit. He told me that they weren't fit for eating and of course I had to correct him. We argued for a really long time; I was almost late for class."

"How'd you do on your exam?" asked Mrs. Ramos, smiling as if she already knew the answer.

"I really don't remember," I admitted. "But I went back to the tree the next day, and he was there again. We started meeting there to study and argue, and eventually we weren't studying anymore," I smiled, "we never stopped arguing though." The fire was aging, burning low. The tinder beneath it glowed dark and hot, and my heart felt the same way, love giving way to the perpetual bruise. I would finish this part quickly and leave it at that. "A few years later he met me at the bench and tossed me a green apple. I caught it, and saw that he had replaced the produce sticker with a custom one. It had a message asking me to marry him."

"Ugh!" Nadia flopped on her back and fanned her face with her hands, "that's so goddamn romantic!"

"It is a great story," agreed Mrs. Ramos, looking at me carefully. "Did you accept his proposal?"

I nodded and scratched at my forearm self-consciously. They were all looking at me, I knew, but I couldn't stop the frown that warped my mouth, or the tears that had come uninvited. I still wasn't sure why I had shared that story, but I knew I didn't want to share any more.

An owl took the opportunity to hoot loudly in a nearby tree, reminding us of the time. The nocturnal shift had begun and good campers would heed the clock and retreat to the safety of their tents. Nadia was the first to jump up.

"I'm going to call it a day," she said, slinging her sleeping bag over her shoulder. She considerately avoided looking at me as I dried my face, and I was grateful. "I enjoyed story time, even if Hector's was kind of weird. If anyone gets hungry tonight, I formally request that no one eat me, 'kay? Thanks so much."

She disappeared into the tent. Mrs. Ramos followed her closely, delaying only a moment to give me a quick hug and kiss on the side of the head. This, too, surprisingly, I was grateful for. Hector lingered behind to observe as I put out the campfire, ensuring I quenched it properly. A good weekend didn't need to be spoiled by unwittingly starting a forest fire. I carefully spread dirt over the fine ash that remained and leaned back on my heels, certain no sparks remained to wreak havoc in the night.

"Do you need to talk to someone about your husband?" I froze, still crouched at the edge of the fire circle, hands gritty and dry with dirt and ash. "I wouldn't think a story like that would make you so sad." Ice clambered up my spine at the question in his words, and the char of the fire lay burnt and useless.

"Ah, that's okay," I laughed nervously. "Storytime is over for tonight, I think." My heart was thick and heavy.

"Nadia told me she's worried about you," he said softly. I stood up and looked at him. He wouldn't meet my gaze, a good thing, as one empathetic look might shatter me to slivers. "Look," he continued awkwardly, "obviously I've been caught up in my own stuff these days, but," he stamped at the firepit, unnecessarily, "I'm here if you need to talk."

"I don't want to talk about it," I said, shortly. I picked up my sleeping bag and struggled to zip it back together, no mean feat in darkness with hands numb enough to be mittens. There was finality in my tone this time, no more nervous laughter or deflection. Regardless, Hector persisted.

"I know," he muttered somewhere behind me. "But maybe you should, you know?" I felt a cautious hand brush my arm.

I was scrambling to get away. Picking up my things, I all but somersaulted into the tent, spreading out carefully next to Mrs. Ramos. I appeared to be asleep when Hector entered a few minutes later, but I wasn't. I didn't sleep for a long time.

◄◦►

I'm going to be a good wife from now on.

*Austin needs help and, though he won't admit it, or ask for it,
I'm going to give it to him. No more suspicious questions, no more
micromanaging of his time, no more problems from me. I'm going
to love him as best I can and have faith that, if I do this right, it
will all get better.*

I just have to hold on.

◄○►

As our hike the next day was downhill, we made the distance in roughly
half the time of our ascent on Friday. Gravity helped, but perhaps even
more so did the newfound confidence that lengthened our strides. No
more did we stumble over exposed roots and jump at our own shadows.
We pummeled the silent woods with our robust calls of "hey bear," and
any beasts of the forest would have been unfortunate to get in our way.
We emerged, victorious, at the trailhead and piled jubilantly back into the
faithfully waiting van. It was nearly noon, and we were discussing a cel-
ebratory lunch at one of Yellowstone's restaurants when Nadia piped up.

"Not to be rude," she said, rudely, "but we're not exactly pine-fresh
these days. How about we find a shower before we inflict ourselves on the
civilized world."

She had a point. A quick perusal of the park map revealed some pay
showers not far from our location, and we descended on the place with
hunger-fueled urgency.

"Is there anything in the world better than hot water?" Nadia sighed,
somewhere to my left. The female washrooms had been full when we arrived, and Mrs. Ramos, Nadia, and I had to wait in line before three stalls
opened. It was admittedly worth the wait and, watching dirt stream down
my legs and swirl into my own shower drain, I silently agreed with her.

"Let's be quick, Ladies," reminded Mrs. Ramos, voice echoing from
a stall somewhat further away. "Hector is probably having to wait for us."
The men's room, not as beset with bathers, had permitted him to walk
right in with his shower kit.

"He can wait," called Nadia flippantly, "perfection takes time." But
she was done in five minutes along with the rest of us.

We collected an impatient Hector on our way out, his irritation
soon quenched by the modest mountain of chicken and waffles he consumed within the hour. Later, hunger sated by foods deliciously innocent

of the dehydration process, we collectively agreed to forego any further activity in lieu of getting home at a reasonable hour. I was initially a bit disappointed to miss out on more of the vibrant, glowing thermophiles, but was reassured by the gobs of people present at every roadside turn-off that it was better to skip the experience for now.

"Early morning is the best time to get out to see the springs anyway," Hector commented to me. He was at the wheel again and I had been named copilot while Mrs. Ramos attempted to sleep in the back. "There are less people, so you can take your time on the walkways. Sometimes you'll see bison wandering around too."

"Do the bison know to stay away from the hot springs?" I asked.

He grimaced. "Mostly. A baby bison did fall in one year. It made the news. If I recall, the water was around two hundred degrees."

"Ouch," I said, wincing.

"Hey, at least it was a fairly alkaline spring," Hector noted. "A guy fell into the Norris Geyser Basin a few years ago—completely disregarded all the signs. He was just trying to stick a finger in when he slipped and submerged. The pH of the water there is around a two."

"Which is, what, battery acid?" I ventured, trying to remember the acidity chart posted up in our school's science lab.

"Eh, more like vinegar," Hector admitted reluctantly, obviously still on a scary-story bent. "His body still dissolved in less than twenty-four hours."

"Could you two think of anything else to talk about up there?" Nadia grumbled behind us. She was as curled up as her seatbelt allowed in the back seat, gazing out the window. Dark rings under her eyes revealed how much she had tossed and turned last night, though I knew already firsthand, having been already awake to witness it.

"What, you don't have the stomach for it?" Hector taunted her.

He was smiling again. Matthew would be pleased with his progress when we got home. While this idea of his had given Mrs. Ramos some much-needed bonding time with her offspring, it had also improved the cousins' relationship incredibly. Hector had even trusted Nadia to take point on our way down the mountain that morning, a position he did not take lightly.

"It's not my first choice of topics, no," she replied, a trifle icily.

"Well, if you're going to whine about it, then you choose," I offered. "What would you like to talk about, Nadia?"

At first I thought she would ignore me and lapse back into silence, but then I heard the nylon creak of a seatbelt being pulled out to its limit. Nadia had leaned forward, bracing her elbows on the center console. Propping her chin on her hands between the two of us, she cocked her head and eyed me seriously.

"Let's talk about you," she said, softly enough that I knew she was trying to be sensitive.

"Me?"

I laughed uncomfortably and glanced accusingly at Hector. His eyes were firmly on the road, his grip on the steering wheel as tight as it had been going through Beartooth Pass, though we had opted for a less cinematic route back.

"You," she replied, firmly. "You've managed to get all up in our lives and now it's time for us to return the favor. 'Fess up, sis."

CHAPTER 23

S TRANGE HOW SILENCE CAN take on a personality. In the woods, the silence had been clear and brisk and free and open. I had welcomed it like a friend. In the van, silence was close and pressing and hot. It took up too much room, and I was stifled.

"Vera," Nadia prompted, more gently this time. I had not said anything for what seemed like hours. I couldn't imagine why we needed to talk about this now. "Start with something easy. Why did you decide to come out here this summer?"

That in itself was too big a question to fit in this small, suffocated space. I tried anyway. "My brother arranged it with Hector and his mom. I needed a place to stay for a while."

"Where were you before this?" Nadia persisted. "Before Badlands, I mean. We know that you camped there already."

"I was in Arkansas," I managed, sure that my heart was audible. They waited in silence. From the back seat, I could hear Mrs. Ramos sleeping, her breathing calm and steady and even.

I took a calming breath myself and went into more detail. I told them about meeting Ruth and Julia and Danny, helping set up and teach vacation Bible school, and working at the church with Pastor Andrew. Hector glanced at me a bit curiously here, my church work obviously not lining up with my previously stated doubts, but didn't interrupt. I was grateful. The more I said, the more there was to say, and I realized with regret that I had forgotten to get a postcard from Yellowstone to send back to Jonesboro. I had not been gone long, but the distance and distractions offered had put the place and its people almost completely from my mind. It didn't speak well to my person, I decided.

"Your parents called and reminded you to get going, so you put your church people and the hot priest in the rearview and headed west," Nadia summarized neatly. "But where are you ultimately going?"

"California," I said, automatically. It was an answer I had given before.

"Right, but why?" asked Nadia. I fell silent again, configuring and reordering words until my thoughts were a newsprint of nonsense. "To get away from Austin?" she pressed. "I saw your phone. I know he's been trying to reach you." The name shot through my brain like a neon bullet.

"Get away?" Hector asked, sending me a sharp glance to the side. "Is he coming after you?" No. That was an easy answer, but before I could give it, he followed up with another question. "Is he the one that hurt you?"

Nadia has once asked the same thing, but Hector was angry at the very concept. I felt a rush of gratitude to him that quickly cooled to icy dread when I saw where his eyes had fallen. I suddenly realized the implication behind his question.

I followed his gaze to my lap, where my hands curled, useless as kittens. The faint tan line where my wedding ring had been was gone. I had taken it off before a day of working with new calves and never put it back on again. The pale line that had remained burned away quickly after hours of working in the sun.

My arms were spackled with new freckles in testament to this as well, having finally discarded my long-sleeved tees in favor of lighter clothing. Now, in the discerning, clear light pouring in through the windshield, I could see that the spots and tan lines did little to distract from the series of scars, thick and thin, smooth and ragged, that worked their way towards my elbow like a ladder. The first day I had gone sleeveless, I looked in the mirror and concluded that they were not so visible anymore. Who would notice them in the sunlight, especially covered in dirt as I often was? I knew now: they weren't just noticeable, they were obvious.

They flashed silver and purple in the light, like strange fish scales and, likewise, a flash of panic sliced through me, recalling the countless eyes that would have observed them in the past week. Securing fencing, branding calves, those small acts of service had put me on display. Matthew, with all his kindness and watch over me, had surely taken note of the marks the moment I greeted him at the breakfast table. Mrs. Ramos, occasionally touching my arm in affection, had surely felt the uneven surface of my skin and had resolved to keep me close. Perhaps even Nadia, the troubled runaway I had so arrogantly seen as some sort of mentee, had gentled her approach in deference to my stupid plight.

And now even Hector had caught on, critical eyes grazing me as we stood above the cloud line in Beartooth Pass, as we filtered water in the stream, as we put out the campfire together. He had seen my scars and, worse, assumed they had been inflicted on me by someone else. His anger was a protective one, misdirected and ultimately useless. You cannot keep whole what is already broken.

To them, I was a victim, I was a worry.

I was horrified.

"Helloooo," Nadia waved a hand in front of my face, her nails dark with crescent moons of dirt that had not managed to be exorcised during her hurried shower.

"Sorry," I managed, smiling weakly. "I'm actually feeling a little carsick all of a sudden."

"Carsick?" questioned Hector, brow furrowed, "we're on a straightaway."

"I know," I answered, "It's weird, right? Do you mind if we switch seats?"

This I addressed to Nadia. She hesitated briefly but, perhaps something in my face—truly, I did feel sick now—made her unbuckle her seatbelt without a word and make room for me to crawl back. She settled herself next to Hector and I closed my eyes, trying not to listen to their whispered conversation up front. I held as still as I could, and did not stir again until gravel beneath the tires announced that we were back at the ranch.

◄○►

The next few days back passed quickly in a flurry of activity. Nadia, whose departure from the ranch had been put on hold indefinitely, flew about the property with renewed energy and an entirely new sense of joy. Hector, too, was in a better mood than I'd ever seen him. The positivity was welcome, as we all were being kept busy with a myriad of important tasks. Two events were coming up that required a lot of preparation and discussion, and generally raised a lot of excitement.

The first was that Mrs. Ramos was getting her herd of alpacas. Matthew had done enough thinking and walking about the property to come to terms with the idea, and had developed a few ideas of his own besides, none of which he shared until the ringing of the doorbell interrupted dinner two nights after our return.

"That's for me," Matthew said, leaping up from his seat with his characteristic, spry energy. At the table, we exchanged confused glances in his wake.

"I wonder what that could be about," Mrs. Ramos said, throwing down her napkin and rising from her seat as well. Hector, Nadia, and I followed her out the front door, where we found Matthew signing for a large cardboard box.

"I never thought you'd be an Amazon Prime member, Matthew," Nadia teased, examining the logo on the side. Matthew snorted.

"I'm not," he said, "this here's something I found on the eBay." He reached into the back pocket of his jeans and pulled out a knife, flipping it deftly in his fingers until the handle pointed out, which he then offered to Nadia. "Consider it my gift to you," he said, as she took the knife, confused. "Welcome to the family." He strode from the porch then, whistling merrily.

"Should I be scared?" asked Nadia.

She held the knife out between her and the box, as if expecting it to leap at her with wide, cardboard jaws. Hector took out his own pocket knife, shrugging.

"Let's see," he said, cutting through the tape.

The box held a wooden, one-wheeled contraption that wouldn't balance and stumped all of us until Mrs. Ramos, laughing suddenly with realization, reached out and turned it over so the wheel rotated at the top.

"It's a spinning wheel," she said, smiling. "It's for turning fiber into yarn."

"Yarn?" questioned Nadia. Her nose wrinkled delicately at the little machine.

"Yarn," confirmed Mrs. Ramos, "for after we shear the alpacas. I thought we might outsource that labor, but Matthew's right. We have the extra hands now to do it ourselves." She smiled brightly, "You know, I used to know how to knit but it's been years since I last tried my hand at it." She reached out and drew Nadia to her in a side hug. "It's easy once you get the hang of it, and then we'll be able to make sweaters and hats to sell." She clapped excitedly, warming quickly to the idea. "Oh! And blankets! This is wonderful!" She bent and gathered the little machine in her arms, chattering brightly about setting up a craft room as she carried it into the house.

Nadia's face had not yet transitioned from its confused expression. She looked at me and Hector, both of us trying to suppress our smiles.

"Yarn?" she asked again, so bewildered that we both burst into laughter.

"This is going to be so fun for you," I giggled, wiping tears from my eyes. Hector was fairly doubled over, hooting out his mirth like an overstimulated owl.

"Sweaters and hats and blankets," he gasped, clutching his sides, "I'm sorry, just imagining you here all winter *knitting* . . ." He could hardly finish the word. He finally grabbed the porch railing for support and heaved himself upright, trying to be composed. "Well, it's a tall order," he said, the corners of his mouth still twitching, "but I think you'll be up to the challenge . . . Granny."

Nadia gasped and spat something doubtlessly unkind in Spanish at him as she chased her cousin inside. I laughed to myself as I heard the thunder of pounding feet above my head. They continued until Hector reached his room and then I heard the slamming of the door that meant he had made it inside and locked Nadia out.

We all donated some muscle to enclose a space large enough for six alpacas towards the rear of the property, and Matthew arranged for a new barn to be put in for the animals to nest. He and Mrs. Ramos made several trips out to Bozeman to begin the buying process. It was all very time-intensive, but somehow was still unable to detract from the second big event at Ramos Ranch that summer: Hector's girlfriend was finally coming to visit.

After several stern conversations with Nadia, Hector had finally decided to bring Hallie out for a week, after which they would both be returning east for fall semester. He was alternately hot and cold over the idea, one moment grouching to me about how his family would conspire to embarrass him, the next getting caught humming as he made up the guest bedroom for her arrival.

Nadia, in a show of support, had scoured the internet to examine Hallie's social media footprint. She studied these pages as if preparing for a job interview, and peppered Hector with questions that only served to bewilder and irritate him.

"I have no idea if she's gluten-intolerant," he said, in response to one of Nadia's interrogations over breakfast. "Does it matter?"

"Of course it does, dear cousin," answered Nadia, with maddening patience. "Imagine if she's allergic to gluten and we offer her a morning muffin." She took a massive bite of the large poppy seed specimen in her hand. "On the one hand, she might turn it down and just think worse of you for not anticipating her needs," she explained. She swallowed hugely and took a swig of orange juice. "On the other hand, she might take a muffin so we don't think she's rude and eat it anyway. And you know what happens then?"

"What?" asked Hector.

Nadia leaned close and confidential across the kitchen counter. "Diarrhea," she said significantly. Hector stared at her in disgust.

"Nadia!" I protested. "What is it with you two and potty humor?"

"What?" She picked up her empty plate and took it to the sink. "It's worthwhile to be prepared for anything."

In all the excitement, you might think the cousins would be too distracted to bother me with any more painfully-intimate questions, and you'd be right for the most part. Since the drive home from Yellowstone, I had gone back to wearing sleeves and effectively avoiding any questions about my past and well-being. Then, Thursday afternoon rolled around and that comfortable reality was shattered in an instant.

The three of us were sharing a rare moment of downtime in the living room beneath the ever-watchful eye of the moose head anchored to the wall. Hector was lodged in an armchair typing away at his laptop, trying to edit the seat assignment on his flight reservation so that he and Hallie could sit together. It was not, it seemed, an intuitive website, and Hector broke the quiet often to loudly voice his disapproval.

Nadia was planted on the floor with a pair of knitting needles and one of Mrs. Ramos's old knitting pattern books spread out in front of her. She had worn the piece of practice yarn she was using down to just three threads in her many unsuccessful attempts, and she too declared her frustration without inhibition.

I, flopped on the couch, dozed lazily, weaving in and out of sleep despite the punctuations of noise until a new sound jolted me upright in a panic. If you've stuck with me this far into my journey, you probably already know what it was.

It was, of course, my phone.

From upstairs came the melody of my phone ringing its heart out on the nightstand, where it had sat undisturbed for days. It was barely audible at such a distance, but my reaction caught Nadia and Hector's attention and they tuned their ears to catch the last few notes.

"I'll get it," Nadia was on her feet in a flash, throwing her needles down on the floor with a faint clatter.

"Don't!" I cried out, voice desperate enough to stop her in her tracks. She turned and stared at me. Hector looked up from his struggle with the Delta website and examined me too.

"Maybe it's John checking in," he suggested lightly.

"Or your school," offered Nadia. "I know it's summer, but don't you still have, like, responsibilities?"

Either of them could be correct, but the sick sinking of my stomach robbed me of the strength it would take to risk it. I shook my head.

"Please," I croaked, "just leave it." Nadia walked back and sank into the couch beside me, peering into my eyes.

"Your pupils are actually dilated," she exclaimed, eyebrows raised in judgement. "Vera, this isn't healthy."

"I'm fine," I answered, hating how unbelievable the two words became when combined.

"So you're going to, what, never use your phone again?"

"Nadia," Hector cautioned.

"No!" she flapped a hand to quiet him, "I'm being serious. You said you're going to California for some reason, but obviously that's been put on hold. So what's the plan here? To just hide out until you feel better? What if that never happens?" Her voice raised an octave, words spilling quickly in anger. "Aren't you supposed to be an adult?"

"Enough, Nadia," I said, angry too. But she was on a roll.

"Maturity is the name of the game, right?" she asked, her words wavering with frustration. "Isn't that what you told me? Wouldn't the mature thing be facing your problems, or getting help with them? Instead of hiding away in the middle of Nowhere, Montana and refusing to talk about it?"

"That's not fair," I protested.

"You're right, it's not!" Her cheeks were red, and her dark, liquid eyes bore into mine. "You have so many people in your corner right now, why can't you see that? Do you understand how lucky you are? But you're going to run and hide because you're stupid and stubborn and then you'll, I don't know, hurt yourself and die and no one will be around to save you."

"It's fine, Nadia," I said, a bit taken aback by her forcefulness, "I'm fine."

"No you're not. And you won't talk to us about it," she replied, tears coursing now, "And we can't make you, but I wish we could." A sob caught in her throat and she took a deep breath before continuing. "I know what it's like to be scared. And alone. And I'm sorry you've been hurt by someone who was supposed to love you," she wiped her cheeks fiercely, "I know what that's like. But you have people who want to help you, and I wish you wouldn't run from that too." With an emphatic, childlike stamp of her foot, she fled the room in tears.

I looked at Hector, shaken, hoping to steady myself by sharing a derisive look over Nadia's theatrics, as we had done many times before. He didn't meet my eyes, though, just concentrated very hard on his laptop's screen for several minutes before giving up and closing the device.

"I agree with Nadia," he said, rising from his chair, "for the record."

He climbed the stairs to his room, leaving a very solemn silence in his wake. With a sigh, and a tear of my own trickling from the inner corner of my right eye, I laid back on the couch and stared at the high ceiling for a long time, regretting that the moment had come at last.

—◦—

It was that night that I announced my intentions to leave. Everyone had gathered in the dining room and conversation had flowed unceasingly since the meal began, full of news and progress on the new alpacas. All talking stopped rather abruptly after my announcement, and I saw Hector and Nadia exchange dark glances.

"No reason for that," said Matthew at last. Mrs. Ramos echoed this sentiment, surprise written in her face. I was not to be deterred.

"School starts back in a few weeks, and if I want to get home in time I'll need to get going," I explained, a bit too hearty in my rush to be reassuring.

The truth was, as Nadia had correctly presumed, I had not once checked my staff email. Going back to school and being functional seemed an insurmountable task that I had avoided thinking about entirely. It was another thing I would figure out, I resolved, somewhere down the road.

Wherever that would be.

"I thought you were committed to helping out here," said Hector, looking stressed and disapproving. "We'll need all hands on deck for the next week at least." I couldn't look at him, so I examined the swirling traces of mashed potatoes left on my plate. He thought I was a coward. Well, maybe I was.

"I've stayed as long as I can," I answered with finality, making my tone cool and professional, as I would explaining my grading rubric to an angry parent. "Nadia has shown that she doesn't need supervision, and you'll be going back to school soon, too." I sighed, wishing I could just slip into the night undetected. "This has been so lovely, and I thank you for having me, but it's time."

Mrs. Ramos and Matthew tried to argue with me for a while, joined in occasionally by Hector. Nadia, for once, was silent, apparently too angry to speak. Plates and then seats emptied around us and the ranch staff shuffled off with awkward goodbyes and goodnights.

When we finally retired, I anchored the comforter over my head and pretended to descend into an apparently deep sleep. Nadia made quite a bit of noise going to bed, no doubt hoping to rouse me for a round of late-night questioning, but I lay still as a rock. When she finally settled with the now-familiar squelching sounds of a protesting air mattress, she gave it one last shot.

"I know you don't want to talk, so just listen," she said, her voice loud and out of place in the still, dark room. "It sucks that we can't help you, but I understand that you have some things you need to settle. I just don't think you need to let him hurt you to settle it, okay?" She sighed and turned over on her mattress, growing still for a time before speaking again. "Or maybe it's not about him. Maybe this is all some sort of quarter life crisis or something? Like, you're trying to find yourself? Figure your life out? I don't know." I almost laughed as she grew quiet again, pondering the same lines of thinking I had been tangled in for weeks. Nadia was a far cry from the hurting, self-absorbed little monster I had first met. I envied her progress. "Whatever it is you're looking for," she said finally, "I hope you find it." What found me were tears, and I answered.

"Thank you," I said, just loud enough that she could hear.

There was a rustle of blankets as she sat up and stared at the blanketed lump that concealed me. I reluctantly uncovered myself and propped up on my elbows.

"Can you come back and visit again?" she asked, sounding much younger than she had ever been allowed to be. I smiled through the dark and answered with the kind of reassurance an older sister was well practiced in.

"Of course I will."

"Good." With that, she sank back down into her pillow and wriggled a little to get comfortable. "But you're taking the air mattress next time."

—◄○►—

Nadia lapsed into deep, even breaths a little after midnight and did not stir when I rose scarcely an hour later, gathering my things as quietly as I was able. I left a note for Mrs. Ramos and Hector on the nightstand, a gesture of thanks that was entirely inadequate, and hoped they would understand.

The moon was high and clear and huge in the sky as I stole down the stairs, through the silent kitchen, beneath the now-familiar gaze of the beheaded moose and elk, and out the heavy door. There, on the steps leading down the wide porch, waited Matthew, his tall dark figure striking such fear and surprise into my unsuspecting heart that I physically jumped an inch into the air.

"Boo," he said, a wry smile twisting his rugged jaw at my reaction.

"I thought you were a wendigo," I joked weakly, readjusting the strap of my duffle across my shoulder.

"Why, you hungry?" He tossed a package my way that I had no available hands to catch. It landed with a soft fwump at my feet, a large package of homemade jerky. "Sofia wanted to send you with a mess of sloppy joes, but I told her that didn't travel well," he said.

"Thanks for that," I laughed, sounding lighter than I was.

He stood and unburdened me of my bag, waiting for me to scoop up the jerky before walking with me to my slumbering vehicle.

"You sure you're ready?"

I paused with my hand on the door and looked at him. In the moonlight, the eyes that glinted in the wise, handsome face held no judgement, and I felt suddenly certain that Matthew understood what kind of journey I was on. He did, after all, seem to understand everything better than the rest of us.

I didn't answer, and it was quiet except for the hum of crickets as I climbed in and adjusted my seat and mirrors, fishing my keys from their place beside my phone in my back pocket.

The truck purred to life, and, hands on the wheel, I felt a buzz of nerves work its way up my fingers and tighten between my shoulder blades. I rolled down the window to say goodbye to Matthew. He was leaning against the frame in his cowboy posture and had lit a cigarette. It glowed tangerine in the dark.

"It was great meeting you," I said, a stunningly awkward phrase to say to someone I'd come to feel so close to. He graciously let it go without comment.

"You're never too far down that road that you can't come back, all right?" he said. "I think you know that by now."

I swallowed around the lump in my throat and rolled off into the night. The lit end of Matthew's cigarette burned brightly in my rearview until I turned the corner and was gone.

Chapter 24

A s was becoming familiar, tension fell off of me in waves the further I drove. So I went along for a while without stopping or looking at my phone, only reaching over to grab some of the jerky for a quick snack. It was well-salted and chewy and seemed to stave off both hunger and hysteria as I gnawed and journeyed further.

When I did stop, it was to feed my truck at an ancient little two pump gas station. On a whim, partially for an excuse to go inside, and because I had never done it before, I bought a scratch-off lottery ticket from the man behind the counter. If I had been hoping for a friendly face or sudden fortune, I was disappointed on both counts. The attendant held an expression of stone and the ticket, nothing of value. If I were looking for a new adventure, I would need to find one elsewhere. And with that, my shoes pointed themselves back towards the truck and I was driving again, south, as if I had a plan.

When I saw Tetons, bursting jaggedly over the horizon like teeth, I felt, suddenly, the rarest conviction that I was on the right path. Those mountains guided me steadily onward as this feeling strengthened and matured in my ribcage, a confidence that I was where I should be, and a sureness that nothing would stop me until I got where I was going. And, indeed, the premonition became fact as I, with deft purpose, navigated easily through the unfamiliar park and found the appropriate office without so much as a glance at the map.

The only problem, of course, was my phone. Smothered in my back pocket, it buzzed with a new call as I put the truck in park. My hand twitched to retrieve the thing, and stopped short. As I had decided yesterday, I would leave it. It could be a text from North Carolina, perhaps Arkansas or Montana, even. I would not have minded if that were the case. But I feared it was from Austin, and so I left it, my own pocket-sized

Schrodinger's cat. It would ring itself out and I would be too busy to check for hours yet.

Indeed, I would be more than busy.

In fact, I would be unreachable until I decided otherwise.

"I need a permit," I snapped to the bemused clerk behind the window at the backcountry office. I shoved payment in a crumpled wad through the opening and stood, vibrating with steadily increasing impatience, as she counted the bills.

"Which trail are you requesting today?" she asked, with an easy, placid smile. The look pricked irritation in me and I chose one at random from the map on the wall. Hector would have been decidedly disappointed in my lack of preparation, but I pushed that notion aside. I cared little about elevation gain or the sights along the way, I just needed to get out there.

"That's a good one," she nodded pleasantly, still smiling as she typed away at her computer. She wore a kerchief around her neck and the iconic ranger hat despite being entirely shaded and stationary at her current assignment.

"Mhm," I replied, drumming my fingers and hating her without reason. She stopped her typing to look up at me, eyes focusing on my face in what seemed to me to be slow motion.

"You should know that there is a potential for a storm in this part of the park in the coming days," she said, blinking. "We recommend that you waterproof your gear, if you haven't already." I barely registered what she was saying.

"That's fine," I said. "Can I check out a bear box also?"

It was an aggravating process, but was done nonetheless, and in time to permit a hike to the trail's first campsite, provided I was rigorous about it. Parking at the trailhead I felt, if nothing else, ready to be rigorous. My pack was heavy enough to demand exertion and the panic that still buzzed in my limbs from the calls to my phone provided enough adrenaline to supply it.

I slapped some moleskin on my heels and laced my boots carefully before strapping on my pack and leaving the truck behind. Entering the heavily forested area, I welcomed the chattering of the birds and the clearly marked path before me. Over and over, I placed one boot firmly in front of the other in defiance of the shadows that lengthened, losing my conscious mind in the repetition and physical exertion, to find the campsite a few hours later that may as well have been minutes.

Two tents were already up and occupied, an older woman the only visible camper as she tucked her boots outside the polyester glow of her temporary quarters. We waved to one another, but then she was gone with a vicious zipping sound that signaled her tent sealed tight even as it ripped open the quiet air. I was relieved, admittedly. Fatigue had manifested in the warm weight of my limbs, and holding a conversation was something I would not hold up to.

I set up my tent quickly and packed my bear box to the brim, not hungry enough to consider depleting my food supply. On impulse, I added my phone to the container and screwed it tightly closed. I had yet to see who had called me earlier, but now was not the time. After walking the appropriate distance from camp—taking care to include the other tents in my estimation—I wedged the box into the fork of a tree and walked back, a few loose lightning bugs punctuating the almost full darkness with their gleam. I stumbled a bit coming back into camp, my first clue that my few hours of luck were running out, but fell into my tent with glorious unconcern. I did not remove my boots, nor did I crawl into my sleeping bag before exhaustion found me and bore me away.

Sometime in the night I awoke to the sound of my phone vibrating, and my heart moved squelchily to the back of my throat at the very impossibility of it. I lay still, cognizant now of the cold seeping through the thin material of my tent, but did not hear it again. It was, perhaps, the buzz of an insect, or the remnants of a dream I must have been having. I kicked off my boots and sought refuge in the sleeping bag. I waited for warmth, and morning, and for frightened adrenaline to stop twanging its frenzied melody off the tendons in my legs like stressed guitar strings.

．＊．

I must have fallen back to sleep at some point, because the light streaming through the screen windows was all at once the burnished gold of an advanced morning. It was discouragingly chilly, despite the sun, but I gritted my teeth to it and climbed out into the day anyway.

My neighbors were gone already, confirming that I had slept deeply for at least a few hours, and I packed with uninterrupted speed, groaning a little at the weight of my pack before staggering back onto the trail. I retrieved the bear box, grabbing a power bar from its depths before adding the hulking thing to the burden already on my back. Chewing arduously on the hardened lump of dubiously flavored protein, I went on.

I ached heartily from the day before and the trail seemed to lead only upwards without leveling off, but my feet soon adjusted and found a rhythm that carried me steadily, if not easily, into new elevations. I gave myself up to the movement, and my mind went blank and wide-open, conscious only of the fall of my steps, my breathing, the soft sway of the trees, and the solid mountain beneath my tread.

Even now, I couldn't tell you if I had stopped to use the bathroom or retie my boots, so lost was I to the movement. It was like my body was being drawn magnetically along the trail, and my mind was free to float somewhere overhead, like a weird, sentient balloon. It was invigorating; it was entrancing; it was frightening. I came to miles later, in the early afternoon, and had a sickening moment of panic, thinking that I had wandered off the trail entirely. Light fell in golden streamers to my feet, Kinkade-style, making the ground hard to read, but a moment later I came upon the next campsite, and could have kissed the ground in relief.

No one else showed up that evening, and I ate dinner by myself, my first full meal since my last at Ramos Ranch. The lack of company was probably a good thing, the way I shoveled down my rehydrated chili mac would have looked doubtlessly alarming, but after my meal was packed away and bear box secured, I did find the loneliness a bit disconcerting.

You see, I was, after quite some time, alone. There were no tasks to draw my attention, nor animals needing care. There was no one tapping at my door, no one even to close a door against, and no one to worry about. And being alone means all kinds of things, some of which result in truly titillating true crime podcasts as well as thrilling campfire stories, but that did not concern me quite as much as being really, truly, incontrovertibly alone with myself. My mind and all its troubles no longer floated buoyantly above my head; it sat with me, and I could not ignore it. I would not ignore it.

There was, I realized, an actual reason for my furious flight into the woods. And it was for this.

My pack lay limp amongst the pine needles, relieved of its gear, but not, after all, empty. I pulled from it my last journal, only slightly more squashed than it had been the day before, when I had tossed it in so impetuously. Or so I had thought.

The notebook fell open with an effortless sort of magic, and the text gripped my eyes with its terrible hold. The page was almost black with scribbled ink. My hands had shaken badly, I remembered. Austin had withdrawn suddenly, two days from our wedding anniversary, and said he didn't know if he wanted to be married anymore. He announced this on the way out the door, bag in hand, saying that he needed to think and would stay at the barracks. It was December, I recalled, and I had been grading test papers when he made this announcement. I spilled my coffee all over them in surprise. The resultant mess was illegible, and everyone had gotten automatic A's that exam. My students were ecstatic at my mistake.

The entries were short and stream-of-consciousness, and I hadn't bothered to date any of them. These were not meant to fasten memories, these were desperate attempts to hold on.

> *Calling would only make it worse. I have to stand alone, a rock, and be here for him when he needs me, and when he's ready. I need to be in control of myself.*

> *And sometimes I can't stop myself and these thoughts will bubble to the surface. That he was lying about one thing or everything. Right now is one of those times.*

> *But I have to remember myself. Remember who he really is and believe him. Remember that hovering over his every movement isn't trust. Remember that my trust issues have been the problem, and to not let them degrade us anymore. It's amazing how much of an effort it takes.*

Delusion was hideous.

> *I can't really trust him unless I let him have free reign and see what he does with it. Austin will appreciate it, me giving him space to breathe. But this feeling . . .*

I had trailed off, drawn a line beneath it, convinced I had nothing more in me to say. I had wandered the house in a daze, trying to attend to simple tasks and forgetting what I was doing halfway through. The spilled coffee had stayed spilled for hours, and had worked a stain into the wood beneath it, now a coffee table in more than one sense.

Sometime between evening and morning found me back at my notebook.

> *It's good he hasn't called because I'd ruin it. I'd cry and break and—*

> *I just want Austin! I want my best friend back! I'm so confused and I don't understand what's changed, or why I feel like this!*

Of course this is me looking for validation again. We've talked about that. It's okay to be confused, but it's not okay to hurt him for it.

It feels like the person I know isn't real, and that I made up all the good memories, the promises, that he loves me—

He doesn't want me. He as good as said it. He said it.

I want to call, but I know he won't pick up. But I need him, and he's breaking my heart and the hurt is changing me. I wonder, once he does make up his mind, if anything will ever really be like it was.

I want more than just for this to stop. I want it to have never happened.

I was crying and oh, so sorry. The young woman in these pages was breaking, morphing grotesquely as if doused with acid and I could not reach her to take her hand as she lay alone in the dark. I cried deep, ugly sobs, with an extravagance of snot and tears and held the journal to my chest, even now aching to retrieve my phone from the faraway bear box.

I turned to lay on my back and the tears pooled in my eyes before running over down my temples, licking my ears, and resting finally in the darkened locks of my hair. The roof of the tent, lit weakly by my camp light, swam in and out of watery focus.

It was moving, somehow.

Puzzled into distraction, I sat up and reached out my hand. What should have been canvas was skittering exoskeleton, and with a gasp I pulled my hand back to my chest.

The roaches were back.

The tent pulsed with them, and they were winged and hissing and falling now onto my sleeping bag, into my hair, the barbed feet clinging to my skin as they scuttled over my face.

I screamed, and jolted awake to find myself in a tent that twitched with an entirely different sort of movement. Frozen with disgust and fear, I had a dizzying moment of confusion before a mighty howl from outside my tent sent a chill of clarity down my spine. The storm the park ranger had speculated on had arrived and was making itself known with a viciousness I could only compare to the hurricanes we saw back home. The thin material twisted savagely with the force of the wind as it probed and shoved to find an opening.

I felt more than heard the giant's footfall of a tree blowing over nearby and I screamed again. As if making a mockery of me, my tent opened wide itself, a terrible mouth yawning with the sound of ripping polyester. Frigid hail struck at me, bruising my skin and burrowing into my sleeping bag with icy rage and I cowered against the adjacent wall that still held. Another tree surrendered to the buffering wind and fell, so close my brain jumped in its skull, and I curled, still tightly gripping my journal with pages that were soon damp and frozen. In the guttering glow of my wildly swinging camp light, I glanced down and read what had been my last entry.

> *I'm lost, and I need help. But there is no one, and I've been praying for so long.*

And suddenly it was not just the wind howling. Seized by sudden rage and insanity, I ripped the soggy page from my notebook and tore it again and again with my teeth, spitting out the pulp, the wet paper violently red, both from old wounds spilled on the page, and from where sharp hail had struck, splitting my bottom lip and bruising my cheek. I may not survive the night, but neither would my journals. These writings were nothing more than a map leading me to my destruction, and the truth that would get the job done.

I wasn't hiding, as Pastor Andrew had implied, nor was I running, as Nadia had accused. I was abandoned, certainly by my husband, definitely by my God.

I was abandoned, and certainly ruined.

"*Where are you?*" I screamed, a drawn-out, crazy sob of a question. I ripped out of my sleeping bag and batted out of the tent, no longer caring if I were ripped to ribbons by hail, or flattened by falling trees. Every inch of exposed skin whipped raw and singing in freezing agony, I turned my face to the black sky and emptied my lungs over and over. "*Why did you leave me? What did I do to make you go? Why don't you love me anymore?*"

Every creeping, filthy suspicion, every swallowed question, every injustice and wound, every fear and shock and sadness burst from me and I didn't know any more if I was crying out to Austin or to God, or even to myself.

My tears froze to my eyelashes and flying pine cones drove at my cheeks. I yelled and cried, swaying in place as the world ended around me, and when my throat was raw, I rasped a while longer through the red pain. I prayed for everything to stop, to leave me be. I prayed to die.

Again, there was no answer but the wind.

CHAPTER 25

AN ETERNITY LATER FOUND us, me and the wind, quiet and spent. Hail crunched beneath my wet socks, but snow fell with softness from the sky. I returned to my tent, exhausted and numb, and fished the thick roll of duct tape from my pack to repair the rip in the siding, scooping as much hail out as I could with clumsy hands.

My fingers were numb. Every part of me, come to think of it, was numb.

After changing into dry clothes, I settled back into my sleeping bag and stared up at my camp light with red eyes. The night was quiet again, save for the feathery sound of snow kissing the top of my tent, but I found that I was not done. Tears still pooled in my eyes, and within the enormity of my loss I felt the almost-forgotten tug to write.

Sitting up again, I peeled apart the remaining pages of my journal to find a section that was half-dry, and procured a pen from the front pocket of my pack. It was a cheap number, swiped from the motel that first night, but the ink still flowed as I scribbled what remained of myself onto the page.

> *Austin lied. He lied, and he was never not lying, and I know it now. And now that I know it, I can never not know it.*

It poured out of my pen for minutes that turned easily into an hour, and the moment of discovery rose up before my weary eyes like an equally exhausted ghost.

> *He was careless.*
> *He had packed his laptop already when he realized he still needed to print his boarding pass for his flight out to California, and he logged onto my computer to retrieve it from his email. In*

the rush of departure, it seems he forgot to log out. So I found the emails.

There was a suggestive thread with an old high school girl-friend. There was a collection of racy pictures exchanged with a woman he worked with while repairing roads during one of his many deployments overseas. There were messages from anony-mous women from six different dating sites, and what wasn't explicit was logistical: he met up with almost every one of them.

The worst part, though, was his correspondence with a wom-an in California. He met her shortly after his Uncle James died, and had been talking to her ever since. These messages were differ-ent, intimate, lovely. He told her everything he was feeling, and she returned the favor, having lost her mother recently. What started as friendship bloomed quickly into something else. Her last few emails spoke of love. His last email spoke of starting a life together.

I read the whole two year relationship in just over four hours.

I had shoved the laptop from me like the keyboard had turned to spiders and ran to the bathroom to vomit. White spots starring my vi-sion, I returned and read some more, before repeating the process. There seemed to be no end to it, no end to the messages and pictures and plans and *I love yous*. When I finally put my fist through the screen, it was to preserve what was left of my mind.

None of it was real, our marriage. Every word or act of love or warm memory was negated threefold by what he gave those women in his inbox, and I had been walking around in a world that wasn't real.

And that's the part I struggle with most, the fact that my real-ity was an illusion and the man I love, my best friend in the world, never existed at all. The fact that my plans, the blessings I had attributed to a God that loved me, were all lies, every one of them.

It's enough to drive you crazy, isn't it?

So I had found the box on the shelf, what was then the only solid object in a house that was dissipating around me like smoke, and cracked an old notebook open to read words penned by a girl wanting to let the world know she existed.

And, Nadia and Hector were partially right. I ran away, and I'm still running, still unable to face the question I'm staring down this very moment:

What do I do now?

The final words faded to a light gray, the question mark mostly a squiggly depression on the page. My pen had died, but I was done writing anyway. It had lasted just as long as I needed it to.

First light was peering through the tape job on the side of my mangled little tent, and despite the trauma of the night, I knew I had to finish my hike. After pulling on my boots, I peeled the door open and stepped out into a world that was now coated in a thin layer of snow. Cold and clean, even the destruction from the wind was blanketed and calm. Fallen tree roots, torn and exposed, glistened and sparkled, the gashes left in the earth when they pulled free lay coated and quiet.

In contrast, my own soul lay mangled and brutalized in my chest, creating a physical weight that bowed me over as I picked my way around the campsite. I had melted down without the benefit of catharsis, and had only a long hike out to look forward to. I made short work of packing, retrieved my bear box, and began to put away the miles again.

My route formed a loop, meaning the trek back to my truck covered terrain I hadn't seen on the way in. I did my best to pay more attention to the world around me this time, and I dully called out to the potential bears as I watched the forest wake up with an eager life I didn't feel.

As I walked, I became aware of a thunderous rushing sound that hinted at water nearby, a fact confirmed a minute later when the trail brought me to a crude bridge spanning a wide river. Unlike the brown sluggishness of the Mississippi, this river was very much alive and moving. Swollen from the weather and the melting of snow further up the mountain, the fast-running water was white with foam and studded with rocks that glistened in the morning light. It was a powerful sight to behold, and, even in my depression, struck awe into my soul.

The bridge, however, struck fear.

It is, perhaps, too generous to even call a bridge what was more like a fallen log. Glancing from side to side and back the direction I came, I confirmed that I had not wandered off the trail, and this was the crossing marked on the map. Even so, I looked at it dubiously, hoping it might transform suddenly into something with handrails, or level footing, even. It remained, however, a slick log and, seeing no other alternative, I stepped up on it as gamely as I was capable.

Conscious that raccoons accomplished harder feats every day, I set off across the busy water with my head high and my eyes stuck firmly on a knotty tree growing on the other side. This helped for a time, before the shifting of the bear spray can against my hip startled me and drew my gaze downward and my footing just slightly off. The bridge, as already mentioned, was slick from the river's spray, and I slipped a little, throwing my arms wide in an effort to keep balance and biting down into my already split lip. Panic mixed with pain and the crush of remorse in my heart to produce a feeling so toxic and hopeless that I actually laughed from pure devastation, tottering there in my precarious position.

It was all so ridiculous, this moment, my entire life. Wobbling freakishly, I looked down into the icy crush and the thought, unbidden but exigent, throbbed through my mind in sharp, red letters that cut and bled.

Just fall.

My foot found proper purchase at the last moment and I steadied, breathing deeply through my nose and still laughing senselessly as I looked down into the perilous rush. It was cold and clean and certain, and those characteristics drew me. *Just fall.* How much easier would it be than everything else that had happened, that was happening, that would happen?

I wavered there, on that log, my pack heavy on my back and bowing me closer and closer to the water. If I fell now, the weight of my pack would submerge me quickly. The rapids and rocks promised that I would be knocked silly and unconscious in a matter of seconds, a small mercy I hoped I would be granted as I drowned. I likely wouldn't be found for hours, if not days. My heart rose painfully in my throat at the thought of my body, beaten and alone, careening frozenly down the mountain to traumatize whatever poor hiker crossed its path. My death, like my life, a cruel joke.

Tears dripped down my face now, painful in their emergence from sore, overused tear ducts and in their acquiescence to a truth the world was pressing on me now. There was no one to save me, and no one who even could. The damage was done.

My prayers had gone unanswered for years. That was an answer in itself.

I bowed closer to the water, lifting my right leg behind me as if to dive. The foamy roar beckoned me on. I focused on a large rock just below the surface. It was craggy, scored deep with lines and chips. I was going to be with the scarred things. A little closer now, and it would be over, an inch closer and I would be undone.

How do I explain this moment? Is there an excuse for how pitifully free of thought I was, particularly thoughts of my family, friends, students? Would you understand the seduction of those red letters, *Just fall,* or the kinship with things submerged and broken? There are times, even now, that I think of it, and it draws me. It is true that the abyss stares back.

What happened then, though, broke my gaze at the last possible moment. A smooth, feathered back flashed before my downward stare, and drew my red eyes upwards. It was a white bird, and it passed beneath the bridge and crested through the spray as if riding a wave. It soared, darting just out of reach of the violent water, up the river, towards the top of the mountain, still shrouded in mist. It was followed by others, a whole flock of white birds, diving under the bridge, playing and rolling and soaring up and up and into the pearly gray of the new morning.

Burdened as I was, I felt I had never seen anything so light and free. The beauty of the moment touched my raw, red heart with cool fingers, and I took a shaking breath deeply inward. As I stared after them, a breath of crisp wind blew back the sweaty strands of hair that had fallen in my face, and it felt like a loving hand smoothing them back into place. I nearly wept at the gentle touch.

I heard it then, a voice in the breeze that whispered like a friend, and dissipated the sharp red words in my mind to replace them with something new.

Restore.

I gasped sharply at the voice and looked around. Almost certain death raged below me, but my feet had found a certain hold on the bridge, and I thought little of it. My eyes searched for the speaker, sweeping the tree line on either side, and beholding nothing in the end. Still, I was sure of what I heard, and certain that the owner of the word was nearby, if just out of sight.

I was alone, but I wasn't. The birds had gone, but there was someone there with me as I stood on that bridge, and I felt it as definitely as the boots on my feet. The certainty came over me with a calm so tangible it was solid, and it seemed to steady my steps as I turned to cross over the bridge to drop safely, finally, on the other side.

CHAPTER 26

"SO, WHAT DOES THAT mean, do you think?"

It was the next day, and I was driving again, still covered in a peace so complete I would have freaked out if it had let me.

I had carried the feeling all the way back to my truck and out of Grand Tetons National Park. It sat beside me as I pulled back onto the highway and crossed into Utah. It was still there as I stopped to peer out across the weird wilderness of the Salt Flats, reveling in being warm and dry again. It covered me like a blanket when I slept that night, truly slept, in a Salt Lake City hotel, and was still there that next morning when I passed through the arid bustle of Las Vegas. It was welcome, but different, and had prompted me to do something I hadn't done in a long time.

I called my parents for advice.

"Y'all still there?" I had unleashed the tale of the past few days of my life leading up to this moment and now heard nothing coming from the phone. I wondered if I had driven through a dead zone and, if so, at what point the call had dropped. I had been talking for the better part of thirty minutes. There was a rustle from the phone's speaker, the sound of someone rising from a kitchen chair.

"Sorry, sweetie," said my mom, "it's just . . . it's a lot to process all at once."

"You could have died!" boomed my father, words pelting me like the hail I had just described to him. "Didn't we talk about being careful on this trip?"

"We did . . . " I said, wincing at his anger.

I had left out the bigger details, like my marital problems and resultant almost-plunge into the river, reasoning that those were topics best discussed face-to-face. It would appear that decision was wise, the way my dad was getting hung up on what, to me, was a minor detail.

I let him storm on for a long time, hoping we could circle back to the topic I was most wanting their opinions on. My story had apparently fueled enough concern that he was several minutes into a lengthy lecture on responsibility when I finally drove over the state line between Nevada and California. My phone pinged with a welcome text announcing my entry into the new territory and I saw that traffic had slowed down immediately ahead. I sighed. Crawling traffic mixed with parental disapproval was far from my favorite combination.

After several minutes, I came to what appeared to be a border control checkpoint, complete with a wide concrete inspection station and uniformed guards. For a wild moment, I wondered if I had grossly misread the road signs and crossed into Mexico instead and scoured my brain to determine how I got so far off track. Idling in line behind a red Mini Cooper, I was able to read the words "California Department of Agriculture," which put my initial concern to rest, but managed to raise several more questions in its stead. The line moved quickly, and the Mini Cooper was able to pull through the checkpoint without hardly slowing down. I was not to be so lucky, and I was signaled to come to a stop by one of the officers.

"Hold on, Daddy," I said into my phone, halting him as he drew breath for what promised to be several more minutes of growling, "I'm at a checkpoint."

"What?" My mother's confusion sounded through the speaker and I sighed as I rolled down my window.

"Where are you coming from?" asked the man in uniform. It was a question more complicated than he knew, but for the sake of time and in consideration of his no-nonsense sort of demeanor, I simplified.

"Utah, most recently."

"Do you have any produce?" he asked. There was a German shepherd with a tactical vest eying me from a side station.

"What?" I asked, certain I had misheard.

"Fruits? Vegetables? Vegetation of any kind?" His teeth were very white in his bronzed face, and his sunglasses were of the mirrored variety. I almost had to squint to look at him.

"Only in California," my dad grumbled through the phone.

"Oh," I said, embarrassed. "No, I don't have any produce."

"I'll need to see your firewood." He spoke without a touch of irony, which was helpful, as I would have assumed otherwise that he was making some euphemism I didn't understand.

"I don't have any firewood," I assured him and, for no reason, tacked on an apology. "Sorry?" To my surprise, he snorted.

"I'm checking to make sure you don't have anything that might carry disease or insects," he explained, with kind patience.

"Insects?" I asked, stupidly. He nodded.

"It's to prevent invasive species from harming our vegetation."

"Oh," I said again. "Well, I'm all clear on that front." He nodded, still chuckling a bit, and waved me through.

"He seemed nice," said my mom diplomatically, to remind me they were still there. I rolled my eyes; as if I could forget.

"I'll say this and then we need to move on," I said in my best teacher voice. "I'm sorry for being so erratic. I know my behavior has concerned you both and I don't want to worry you, which is why I haven't told you a lot. Suffice it to say my life is messy right now, but I'm trying to get it together." I took a quick breath and continued, not giving either of them room to comment. "That's why I've called, because I need your advice on this. What is it you always say about getting advice?"

"'Without counsel plans go wrong, but with many advisers they succeed,'" quoted my dad without hesitation.

"It's from Proverbs," Mom chimed in.

"Right," I said, never not impressed by my parent's recall of scripture, "Many advisors. That's what I'm trying to get right now."

"Okay," my dad said gruffly, after several moments, "we're here to help."

"But I think we're missing some pertinent information," added my mom, not unfairly. I flipped the sunshade down to shield my eyes and winced as I reflexively chewed on my split lower lip. I decided to give them the gist.

"Okay," I said, thinking hard, "I've been doing a lot of reflection on the past few years and I've realized that my life is a lot different than I would have expected when I was young."

"That's normal," my mom interjected, and I shook my head, forgetting she couldn't see me.

"No," I protested, "it's not in a good way. A lot of difficult things have happened—y'all haven't been privy to the details—and I haven't handled it well. I've just felt really alone and damaged and unloved." I sniffed and reached into the glovebox for a napkin to serve as a tissue.

"Sweetie, you're *so* loved," exclaimed my mother, surprised and sounding almost insulted.

"No—I know—but that's the thing," I replied, blinking away tears, "It ran deeper than that." How could I explain it, the isolation? How the failure of my relationship, and my estrangement from God, had prevented me from creating—or even really maintaining—any other relationships in my life? "I had this idea when I was younger that God would take care of me; but He didn't, and I've been so angry and bitter about it. It's hard to describe, but it's ruined me." My voice shook and I cleared my throat, getting back on topic. "So I have this terrifying moment in the woods, and I'm angry and devastated about everything. But then I hear this voice, and it says 'Restore,' and suddenly I'm calm again."

My parents were quiet on the other end, and I imagined them exchanging looks over the phone, having full conversations with only their eyes the way they sometimes did. Outside the truck, planted fields gave way to the low scrub brush and tired orange earth of the high desert. The world was mostly sky, and it was populated with monstrously swollen clouds that never seemed to move no matter how long I drove and drove and drove.

"Have you thought that it might be a reaction to stress?" Mom suggested, logical as ever. "You just needed to get it all out?"

"I thought about it," I replied, "but I think it's more than that. It's not like I just needed a good cry to feel better. Nothing in my life has resolved itself. It's all really messed up, actually," I chuckled darkly. "There's no reason I should be feeling peaceful about anything right now."

"Have you prayed about it?" The question came from my dad, and I realized now where my brother had gotten his candid spirituality. Funnily enough, I didn't mind it this time.

"God and I haven't really been on speaking terms, Daddy," I said. He laughed.

"That might be what you think," he replied, a smile in his voice. "It sounds to me like he's definitely been talking to you."

"One word is hardly a conversation," I countered, "and I'm not sure how to take it. Is it some heavenly order to clean up my life?"

"Maybe," he answered, thoughtfully, "But it sounds like you had come to that conclusion already. You should ask him."

I sighed. This was going nowhere.

"We'll pray on it," said my mom. "You pray on it, too."

"Okay," I rolled my eyes again, grateful they couldn't see me.

"And Vera?" my father said, "Whatever's happened, you aren't ruined, or alone. Your great Uncle Waylon used to preach that sometimes our paths get crooked, but God can always straighten them out in the end."

"It's a good message to preach in prison," I said dryly.

"It's a good message anywhere," he replied. "Drive safe."

We hung up and I drove on.

—◦—

Scrub brush smoothed into reddish dirt and the sun seemed closer to the earth somehow. Buildings were few and far between, and even they were sun-bleached until they seemed to melt into the landscape, a mirage. I tried my radio and found nothing but static. Picking up my phone, I opened a music app before switching it back off and throwing it to the seat beside me. Silence was better.

Perhaps an hour short of eternity later, I came to a small corner of civilization. I stopped at the Walmart and picked up a few supplies and, after circling the store a few more times for the simple luxury of stretching my legs, drove the final distance out to Joshua Tree National Park, where I purchased a camping permit and finally found a place for my beleaguered truck to rest.

In terms of forests, Joshua Tree isn't what you would expect, because joshua trees themselves are not trees. They are, as I learned at the ranger's station, yucca plants, in the asparagus family and related closely to agave, which explains quite a bit about their spiny, knobby appearance. As alien as they are, however, they did not look out of place here.

Then again, here looked almost undeniably like Mars.

I set up camp at the base of a large rock formation so temptingly foot-holed that I climbed to the top without stopping to think about it. The gritty rock rasped against me and skinned my knees, and the blaring sun drew most of the moisture from my body, but it was the view from the top that took my breath.

My muscles ached and burned but would be stronger for it, and my feet, clad securely as they were in their trail shoes, stood firm and sure. A raven swooped in bold circles across the sky and I laughed, feeling just as free and unafraid.

And I was, truly, unafraid.

As if to prove it, my hand found the cellphone in my left pocket and opened my call log. His missed calls sat there still, evidence of his attempts at contact the past few days. Service somehow finding me even up here, I pressed on the call symbol beside Austin's name and put the phone to my ear.

CHAPTER 27

"T HE HELL IS THIS, Vera?"

He had arrived and now stood next to my tent, yelling at it, clearly thinking he was yelling at me. I peered at him from my high perch and whistled. He looked up, looking foolish in his surprise and his old Panama Beach tank top. I was glad to find him foolish. Oddly, I was glad to see him.

"I'm up here!" I waved, unnecessarily.

"You want to come down here?" he called.

I didn't want to. The real question was, did I want to risk making him angry by being ornery about it? The calming presence, God, or whatever it was, nudged me companionably. I was still strong and had nothing to fear.

"Not really," I called back.

I was too far up to hear the angry huff that inevitably followed my answer, but I felt it nonetheless. I sat down and focused my eyes on the raven, still swooping around in the distance, letting the sun warm me from above as the stone did the same from below.

"You're really going to make me come up there?" He sounded aggravated, but thoughtful. I imagined him down below, eying the footholds of the rock and sizing up a clear path to me. It was a challenge, and he dearly loved those.

"I came all this way," I tossed back over the side, "you can manage a quick climb."

Up he came, with slow but deliberate progress and only a few muttered profanities. When he hauled himself beside me, shining slightly with sweat, he was no worse for the wear, and greeted me with a hug. Pressed tightly to his chest, I inhaled and imagined I could smell the dishonesty that had woven itself into his being. Lies smelled of salt and lemon: a sharp tang that made your mouth water and ache to swallow the deception and forget what truth tastes like. I broke the embrace and sat down. He joined me in taking in the view for a few minutes in silence.

The sun was aging quickly, painting the world in rusty hues and elongating shadows. The joshua trees stood, arms outstretched, stark and weird on the landscape below. It was striking and it was sad: the end of another day.

I took a water bottle out of my backpack and sipped it once before offering it to him. He accepted it gratefully and took several long swallows before reaching into his own pack. From it, he produced a single green apple, which he passed to me with a word. Lies may have smelled of salt and lemon, but regret, for me, would always smell of apples. I took a bite.

It was surreal, sitting beside him, with the comfortable familiarity even now in this alien place, and I summoned the courage I had to remain separate. His knee knocked mine, as close and easy as if we had been beneath our magnolia again, and I closed my eyes, focusing hard on the grip of my shoes, the grit of the stone under my calves, the tickle of sweat between my shoulder blades. I remembered the white bird soaring up the swollen river and opened my eyes again. Austin was looking at me, curious and cautious.

"Your hair looks nice," he said politely, eyeing the new color.

It was a lie, I was pretty sure. My hair was lank and tangled, the shower I took in Utah insufficient against the dirt and sweat I had accumulated in the mountains. The rest of me was comparably unkempt. Shamelessly clad in a tank top and shorts again, my exposed arms and legs bore layers of scratches and bruises over my scarring. My eyes, I knew, were bloodshot, and there was additional bruising on my face from the hail, now starting to turn green and yellow at the edges. I looked rough. I felt great, though, which was what I chose to focus on.

"Thanks," I smiled at him. His breath caught in his throat and he reached up to tenderly cup my jaw, running the pad of his thumb over the gash in my bottom lip, the bruises on my cheekbone.

"What happened?" he asked. His green eyes, so alarmingly clear, searched mine.

The intimate gesture had thrown me, and I physically shook my head to clear it before answering.

"It's a long story, but I'm okay," I smiled again. "No harm done." He sat silent, waiting, perhaps, for me to elaborate. I didn't.

"I've been trying to get a hold of you," he said finally. He had his phone out and showed me our text chain. His messages, dating back several weeks, were unanswered and unread.

"I haven't really been keeping track of my phone," I said, semi-truthfully.

"I was getting really worried," he said.

And he sounded it; he truly did. His tone summoned memories that I hadn't recorded in my journal, the times where the shameful behavior was mine. True, I had been desperate and deranged, dogged forever with the feeling that I was being lied to and unsure what to do with it. I had been pushed to my limits, but I could not deny that it must have been difficult. If he cared about me, even a little, much of our marriage would have been hard on him. The fault was his, but neither of us ended up being good for the other.

The apology was in my mouth when his phone vibrated, and an unlabeled number flashed across the screen. I caught the words on the tip of my tongue and swallowed them back down. He silenced and pocketed the device quickly enough for the usual conclusions to be drawn and he looked at me with a familiar question in his eyes. *How will she respond?* The soaring raven drew my eyes upward. It was time.

"You've been unfaithful," I said.

The words dropped from my lips like bricks and rolled to the edge of our perch. We stared at them as they sat there.

"What?" Austin said, dumbly. I took another breath.

"I know you've been unfaithful."

The words tipped over the edge and fell to the ground far below, so heavy we both heard and felt their impact. Austin flinched, then let out a sigh, heavy with dramatized frustration.

"This again? Haven't we settled this already? You have to learn to trust me." When I remained silent, he probed further, growing annoyed as he spoke. "What is this Vera? You ghost me for a month and then turn up out of nowhere to accuse me of cheating on you? Where have you even been?" He was growing louder. "This is crazy, you know that, right? This is how a crazy person acts. I'm so tired of having to talk sense back into you."

I felt my cheeks flush a bit as that final sentence took root someplace insecure and weak, but, undaunted, reached into my backpack to produce my notebook. It had long since dried but bore the marks and pits of our foray into the wild and weather, and was now warped and streaky, but still legible. I worked hard to keep my hands steady as I flipped to my most recent entry and held it out to him. He took a glance and swore.

"Vera, look, you've misunder—"

"Read it, Austin."

"Vera, calm down. Hear me out."

He tried to push the journal away but I wasn't having it. I shoved it into his hands and folded my arms, my eyes narrowed in a way that left no room for arguments. It was a classic teacher face, and one I usually tried not to bring home, though I could think of no better time as I watched Austin's eyes dart wildly, a little boy caught in a lie.

"No, Austin," I said quietly. "You're going to hear me."

For a moment, I thought he would refuse, and wished I had come up with a plan for that possibility. After a few seconds, though, his shoulders drew back and he focused on the words, blazing darkly across the mottled surface of the paper.

He began to read.

It's always an odd moment when you invite someone to read a piece of writing as intimate as that one. Their hands hold paper that you clenched, sodden with feeling, not long before, and their eyes skim over words that cost you something, that, perhaps, still take pieces of you. It's never as satisfying as you would think because, as living and breathing as those words are to me, whose soul is made up with a fabric of them, I know that they might lie still for the person reading them. Austin may not understand what I wrote at all, or the impact of what he did. And he just had to understand; I needed him to understand.

When he finished reading, his eyes met mine and I realized I had been staring, jaw and fists clenched in anticipation. I made an effort to relax them both and flexed my fingers a few times before settling my hands in my lap. We were quiet for a long time.

"Please don't do this to us," he said finally, quietly.

"I haven't done anything," I said, with a different sort of finality.

"No, Vera, please," he came to life suddenly, an alarm bell in every word. "Listen for a minute, okay? Things have been bad and I've been struggling. I never talked with you about it because you had such a hard time handling conflict and I didn't want to hurt you. You understand that, don't you?" He was crying, suddenly kneeling in front of me, and his hands found mine.

"Austin," I began weakly, but he cut me off.

"I love you," he said, wet eyes blazing into mine. "You're my best friend. I went crazy and tried to act out a fantasy, but I was wrong. Those women are nothing."

I found, somehow, inside myself the strength to step back from every emotion his words invoked and look at them one at a time. Grief, disgust, anger, insecurity, and, yes, even a little affection stood in a row like in a police lineup and I, safe behind the glass, stared them down. Insecurity rocked back and forth on its toes like an eager little girl, wanting to believe him. Disgust stared me down and would not release me; I understood too much now.

"No," I responded, my eyes wide, "Those women are not nothing. *She's* not nothing." I spoke her name for the first time and was surprised when pity slipped into the lineup. Just another woman that gave everything—too much, perhaps—to someone she loved, someone who now kneeled before me and denied her. Austin was still crying, but managed to register he had something wrong.

"I've been so stupid," he said quickly, "but you know I love you. Take my phone—," he fumbled for his device and tried to push it into my hand, "Take all my passwords, everything! We'll go see a counselor when I get home. We'll make this work again."

I had not thought about the future. I had no plans beyond confronting Austin with the truth. Whether to leave him or try again was a dilemma I hadn't even let myself think about, as the betrayal itself had overwhelmed me so completely as to eclipse any further considerations.

I would have expected a great internal struggle about it all; that seemed, after all, to be my defining pattern. In the end, though, Austin and his pleading sprouted a certainty in me that I wouldn't have thought myself capable of. He was saying everything he thought I wanted to hear. His words had power but, as I knew now, that didn't mean they were true.

I took my hands from his grasp.

I let him go on for a time. He went through cycles of anger and regret, but always landed on declarations of love and promises for the future. I listened quietly and worked to keep calm until he wore himself out with a final plea.

"We've built a whole life together! Vera, think about our life together!"

He was breathing hard, exhausted. He was always one to hide vulnerability behind anger, and I knew this show of emotion was new and taxing to him. On some level, even a very small one, Austin did care for me. He was so burdened by grief, this man, and no amount of my love had lessened the load. I hated that I would be adding to it now.

I reached out a hand and wiped the tears where they streamed from his eyes. Those clear, green eyes I loved so well.

"I am," I said. And that was that.

He left not long after, buoyed by a wave of anger that he caught gratefully and let it bear him back down the rock and away. My last journal was clenched tightly in his hand as his feet hit the ground and he walked back to his vehicle. He probably didn't realize he had taken it with him, and I hoped he wouldn't pitch it out into the desert when the realization struck. It hadn't escaped me that Austin had only addressed his actions, and that the impact—beyond my leaving him—had not really sunk in. One day, maybe he would try to understand and would read the last entry again.

And, anyway, I didn't need it anymore.

I fell asleep up there and woke to stars as big as my fist not four feet from my face. Had it not been for the still-warm stone at my back, I might have been floating through space. I stared up into the heavens and thought I could see Venus, or perhaps Jupiter. Austin would know. He was endlessly fascinated with space and, in the early days, we were forever stretching out on the beach at night to watch the sky. The stars blurred as a fresh batch of tears sprang to my eyes, to be whisked away promptly by the desert air. We would never lay on the beach together again.

Grief struck then, and I turned away from the sky on my side, hand clutched to my chest as the physical pain of heartbreak broke over me. I sobbed dryly, uselessly, and wondered where my certainty had gone, and if I had made a mistake.

My phone, laying on the rock beside me, illuminated suddenly in front of my face and chimed cheerfully into the silence. Grabbing it up, I opened the text without hesitation; I was done with being afraid.

It was my dad, and I squinted with throbbing eyes to make out what he had written. Daddy was nothing if not succinct, so I was unsurprised to see that he had sent me a document without anything by way of explanation. I opened it curiously, and, once again, my eighth-grade self spoke to me from the page.

It was my ancestry project, the one that had hung for years on my parent's refrigerator, corners still crinkled from where the magnets held it in place. My final grade (a 98 percent) had faded to a pinkish color, further emphasizing the parts my father had made to circle the final paragraph in bold, black pen. I pinched at the screen to enlarge the text and leaned close to read.

"If I were to choose a family artifact that best represented my Uncle Waylon, it would be his skin. That might sound odd, but, when you consider the tattoos inked into almost every inch of him, you get a bigger story than any old document or heirloom could ever tell. Waylon McCabe was abused brutally by his father, and he bore those scars from six years old onward. During his first incarceration, he was fortunate enough to have a cellmate that spoke to him of God, a heavenly father, who loved and wanted him. Over time he was born again, and devoured the Bible page by page, tattooing the verses he felt were for him on his skin. His favorite, judging from the contents of most of the sermons he left behind, was Joel 2:25, which he put on his left hand. This verse, according to Waylon, gave him hope and changed his life. If you wanted a good account of my Uncle Waylon's journey, you just had to look at his skin."

My phone dinged, and the message it signaled hovered over the page as I finished reading the paragraph.

"Got up for a midnight snack and spotted this on the fridge," my dad texted. "You should look it up."

I sat up and stretched weary arms over my head until my joints creaked. Sufficiently distracted much of the day by mental and emotional musings, I had neglected to care for all things physical and I felt both sore and hungry. I fished around in my backpack until I struck gold: a crushed granola bar wedged into the very bottom lining. I tore the wrapper and sprinkled the sustaining crumbs into my mouth as I picked up my phone again and pulled open the web browser.

I was well-educated when it came to scripture, a testament to my parents, certainly, as well as the review that teaching vacation bible school had provided, but I knew little of Joel. He was Old Testament, I was sure, and, I supposed, one of the lesser prophets. Finding an online bible that was reasonably easy to navigate, I clicked on Joel and found that the entire book was only three chapters. Not wanting to take Waylon's verse out of context, I started at the beginning and read it all the way through. A cold desert breeze lifted the hair from the back of my neck. I suddenly found it hard to believe in coincidences, as the words, vividly backlit in the surrounding darkness, leapt from my hand to crowd my eyes with images.

Judah was crawling with insects.

CHAPTER 28

I N THAT FIRST CHAPTER, Joel described the army of locusts that had descended on Judah. They had, with spiny legs and shrilly buzzing wings, enveloped the land and crawled, and chewed, and eaten, eaten, eaten. I shuddered at the thought of the swarm, the land devastated by plague, the destruction and starvation that followed. Further reading revealed that drought followed this attack, and even the animals had cried out for relief.

Whatever Judah had done, God had punished them quickly and well.

I shivered again and looked away from the text for a time. Gazing out from my perch, I was surprised and gratified to notice a slight pinkening of the horizon. I had assumed that darkness had barely fallen, when in reality I had spent the night up here. It was a wonder I hadn't frozen, or fallen prey to the snakes and scorpions that had likely stirred from the deep crevices around me. I returned to the text.

Joel meditated hard on the devastation. So certain was he that God had punished Judah, that he urged the people to repent, and deeply. What God inflicted, God could heal, and he called Judah with increasing desperation to return to the only one who could save them. And, starting in the second chapter, God does.

My eyes lit finally on Waylon's verse, 2:25 and, as he had seen fit to ink it on his body, the words swiftly tattooed themselves over one of the deepest scars in my heart.

> "And I will restore to you the years which the swarming locust has eaten,
>> The hopper, the destroyer, and the cutter,
>> My great army, which I sent among you."

Restore.

My hands began to tremble until the words blurred before my eyes. I put my phone down and stared out into Joshua Tree the exact moment the sun burst like an overripe peach over the horizon. The light glazed the land, the trees, the shrubs, and their shadows were dragged thin behind them, before dissipating like ghosts. The scorpions and crawling things scuttled back into their dark corners. The past few years of my life—those haggard, wasted, brutal years—went with them. They were over now, and better days were ahead. My eyes took in the light like medicine, and I breathed deeply of air already smelling of warmed earth.

I couldn't believe I was here. I couldn't believe that my marriage was over.

There were some things, though, that I was beginning to believe again.

I rose, reaching my arms high over my head to stretch out the cramps and aches. The light kissed my face and forearms, and I smiled as I climbed back down the rock.

More people had arrived at the campground during the evening exhaustion, and my truck was now sandwiched cozily between a station wagon and a VW Bus. Both vehicles were topped with surfboards and plastered with enough stickers to hold the ancient machines together. There was a fire ring not far from my tent, and evidence remained of a marshmallow roast. Some embers still burned and I stamped them out like a good camper.

Then, for what felt like the thousandth time, I packed up camp quickly and climbed back into the driver's seat of my truck.

I pointed my wheels vaguely east and drove. When my gas gauge signaled peril, I stopped for fuel and snacks. The world was wide and wonderful, and a certainty grew in me that I had not been abandoned, and there was good to come. I may have started my drive broken, but I knew now that I would be restored.

On impulse, I grabbed a small notebook and a new pen brimming with ink on my way to the register and, having paid, launched back out into the world to continue my adventure. As usual, I didn't know where I was going.

Whatever was to come, though, I knew I would need to write it down.

.

www.ingramcontent.com/pod-product-compliance
Lightning Source LLC
Chambersburg PA
CBHW061501030726
47503CB00005B/1772